"Great story. Shannon Stacey always has a compelling journey to happiness by writing the kind of characters you want to be best friends with and the types of places you want to call home. With humor, emotion, and captivating characters, *Under the Lights* will make you believe in love, second chances, and happily ever after. Take the journey to love with Shannon Stacey and enjoy the ride—you won't be disappointed."

—Jaci Burton, *New York Times* Bestselling Author

Praise for the novels of Shannon Stacey

"A sexy, comical, feel-good read that left me impatient for the next installment." —*USA Today*

"Deeply satisfying." —*Publishers Weekly*

"Books like this are why I read romance." —Smart Bitches, Trashy Books

"Funny, sexy, and loving." —Dear Author

"[A] perfect contemporary romance!" —*RT Book Reviews*

continued . . .

"Stacey is an author who knows how to write fun, relevant dialogue within the world of romance."

—Harlequin Junkie

"Stacey writes such fun, warm characters with the backdrop of a great small town, that I was totally engrossed."

—Smexy Books

"One of the best contemporary romance series . . . Very realistic."

—Fiction Vixen

"If you're a fan of big families, cute romances, and friends-to-lovers stories, then this book is definitely for you."

—Under the Covers Book Blog

Defending Hearts

SHANNON STACEY

JOVE BOOKS, NEW YORK

JOVE

An imprint of Penguin Random House LLC
375 Hudson Street, New York, New York 10014

DEFENDING HEARTS

A Jove Book / published by arrangement with the author

JOVE® is a registered trademark of Penguin Random House LLC.
The "J" design is a trademark of Penguin Random House LLC.
For more information, visit penguin.com.

ISBN: 978-0-515-15585-3

PUBLISHING HISTORY
Jove mass-market edition / November 2015

PRINTED IN THE UNITED STATES OF AMERICA

10   9   8   7   6   5   4   3   2

Cover illustration by Danny O'Leary.
Cover design by Judith Lagerman.
Cover photograph of football and field © David Lee / Shutterstock.
Text design by Laura K. Corless.

Penguin
Random
House

For Aja. Sometimes you're the most like me and sometimes you're the least like me, but we are undeniably sisters, for which I'm grateful every day. Your love of being outside and your quiet, steady work ethic inspired me while writing Gretchen's character, though she can't rock an amazing pair of heels like you can. I was fifteen when you came into the world, and I've loved you every single day since then.

01

Dodging bullets had a way of making a man realize he wasn't young anymore. Dodging them for no good reason made the realization a lot harder to shove to the back of his mind.

Alex Murphy sat on the thin mattress in his shitty motel room and looked at the photo on his phone's screen again. It wasn't one of the many he'd taken during his week in the volatile region, using instincts and years of experience to capture on film a population on the brink of revolution. It was one some random passerby had taken with his cell phone and it had gone viral. It was the photo the world would remember.

Alex would still sell his pictures. They told the story in a way one viral camera shot couldn't. But times and technology were constantly changing, and sometimes he felt like a dinosaur. *Photojournalismasaurus.*

Burnout. As much as he didn't want to admit it, even to himself, a decade of freelancing and travel—only to be scooped by a teenager with a cell phone and an Instagram account—had taken its toll, and it might be time to take a break. The idea of going back to Rhode Island didn't appeal to him, though. The apartment in Providence was a place to keep his stuff, but it had never felt like a home.

Using his thumb, Alex navigated to a recent photo album he'd set up on his phone, titled *Stewart Mills, NH*. After almost a decade and a half away, he'd recently spent about ten days there and, when it was time to leave, he'd found himself wishing he could stay a little longer.

He flicked through the photos, pausing over each one. Not with a technical eye, but to gauge his emotional response. Old friends laughing. People he'd known most of his life, but who were practically strangers. A town that had once been his entire world. And Coach McDonnell, who had taken the ragtag group of boys making up the Stewart Mills Eagles football team and made them men.

Alex had been on the first Stewart Mills Eagles football team to win the championship back in the day and, when the town cut the football team's funding, he'd been one of the alumni players who returned to help out with a fund-raising drive to save it. He'd gone out of love for Coach McDonnell, but rediscovering his hometown had also reminded him of how nice it could be to have roots. He hadn't felt grounded to any one place in a very long time.

He wanted to go back.

The plan was taking shape in his mind even as he closed out the photo app and pulled up his contacts. Calculating time zones was second nature to him at this point, so he knew it was safe to call Kelly McDonnell, the coach's daughter and a police officer for the town. She'd given him her cell number when he was in town, and he tapped it.

She answered on the third ring. "Hey, Alex."

"Are you busy right now?"

"Nope. I'm actually sitting in my cruiser, making sure everybody slows down and doesn't hit the power company guys replacing a transformer. What's up? Did you forget something?"

He laughed. "Nope. How are things in Stewart Mills?"

"Pretty good. Everybody's still on a bit of a high from Eagles Fest, for which I can never thank you enough."

"The Eagles are why I'm calling, actually," he said. "I was looking through the photographs I took while I was there, and the story's unfinished. I'm thinking about coming back for a while and following at least the opening of the team's season."

"Following them professionally, you mean? Like for a story?"

"If I can get releases from everybody, I'd like to do a story, yes. Or maybe even a book. There are a lot of towns going through what Stewart Mills has faced, and what you all did is pretty inspirational. And I'd like to broaden the angle, too. Make it about the entire town and not just the team, though that's the core story, of course."

"Wow." There were a few seconds of silence while she digested what he'd said. "That sounds really great, as long as you respect privacy where it's requested and recognize there are some things people wouldn't want shared."

He chuckled. "Don't worry, Officer McDonnell. I won't hurt anybody and I won't share anything people don't want shared."

"Shouldn't be a problem, then."

"Perfect. I called you because I'm hoping, since you know the community in and out, that you could recommend a place to stay. I know the motel's closed up, but maybe somebody is willing to rent an apartment or even a house on a month-to-month, short-term basis?"

"With so many people losing their homes, the rental market's incredibly tight right now." She sighed and he gave her a moment to think. "You know, Gretchen was talking to me about renting a room at the farm. She hasn't because she's nervous about having a stranger living with her grandmother, but renting to a friend can end badly when there's money involved."

"I'm not a stranger, but I'm not exactly a friend, either." He remembered Gretchen Walker from school and he'd had a chance to talk to her a few times during Eagles Fest. She was an attractive woman, but she was definitely a closed book. "All I need is a place to sleep and it wouldn't be long-term, so maybe I'm a good opportunity for a trial run."

"That's what I was thinking. The room has its own bathroom and you'd have access to the kitchen, not that her grandmother would let you go hungry. I'll talk to Gretchen and have her get back to you. She'll have to talk it over with Gram, too. Can she call you at this number?"

"The time zones will be a horror show for the next few days, so email's the best bet." When she said she was ready, he gave her his email address. "It sounds perfect on my end, so I'll look forward to hearing from her."

Once he hung up with Kelly, Alex flopped back on the mattress and stared up at the peeling ceiling. Maybe it was the professional version of a midlife crisis, but he needed a break, and Stewart Mills seemed like the perfect place to regroup and make a plan for his future.

Chronicling the current state of his hometown and the Eagles while rediscovering his roots would simply be a bonus.

"You have to stop trying to sit on Gram's lap," Gretchen Walker told the sixty-pound chocolate Lab looking up at her with adoring eyes. "You're not good for the circulation in her legs."

Cocoa tilted her head sideways and blinked before raising her paw for a high five. Gretchen sighed and gave her one. It seemed to be the only trick the newest member of the Walker family knew, so it was her answer to everything.

It had been the nurse at her grandmother's doctor's office who suggested a dog might be good company for Gram, since Gretchen had her hands full trying to work the farm, and Gram had immediately agreed. Gretchen had driven her to the shelter in the city, anticipating a fluffy little lapdog who would be content to curl up with Gram and watch her knit the days away.

Instead, Gram had fallen in love with a big Lab the color of rich hot chocolate, and Gretchen had to admit she felt an immediate connection with the dog, too. The entire household budget had to be recalculated to accommodate the beast's food costs, but it was nice to get a high five every once in a while. And Cocoa seemed to love the sound of Gram's voice, so everybody was happy.

"My rocking chair isn't big enough for both of us," Gram pointed out. "Maybe we should trade it for one of those leather love seats with the double recliner ends and the built-in cup holders."

Sure they should. What furniture store wouldn't want to trade a fancy leather love seat for a decades-old glider rocker with a cushion perfectly molded to Gram's skinny behind? "We'll see."

"You sound just like your grandfather when you say that. *We'll see* means we can't afford it and you don't want to flat out tell me no."

Gretchen didn't bother denying it. "For now, you need to train her to curl up next to your feet on the floor. She's too heavy to be on your lap. It's not good for you."

"Go wash up," Gram said without making any promises. "Breakfast is ready."

With a sigh, Gretchen went to the sink and washed her hands. She'd already gathered eggs from the chickens and fed the three horses they boarded for a family that lived in the southern part of the state. She'd have to clean their stalls and work in the gardens later, but at the moment she was starving.

"Maybe we can afford a new love seat, since the Murphy boy's going to be living here," Gram said while Gretchen took a seat at the table and took a scalding swallow of the coffee waiting for her.

"I'm still not sure this is a good idea." It had seemed like a great idea when Kelly brought it to her and through multiple emails with Alex over the last two weeks but, now that it was actually going to happen, she couldn't help but have second thoughts.

Gram set a plate of biscuits and sausage gravy in front of her. "Wouldn't be fair to change your mind at this point. He'll be here in a few hours."

"I know. It'll be strange having a man in the house again, though." It had been nine years since her grandfather passed away, and it had been only her and Gram since.

"At least he'll have his own bathroom so we won't have to worry about falling in the toilet in the middle of the night if he leaves the seat up."

Yeah, Gretchen thought. He'd have his own bathroom. He'd have *her* bathroom, the one her grandfather had built into her room years before when he realized he was going to have a teenage girl hogging the only upstairs bathroom. And Alex would also have the bedroom she'd had since she was a little girl. But giving him his own space, except for the kitchen, made more sense than sharing a bathroom with him. Gretchen had never shared a bathroom with any man, and it seemed very intimate. Intimacy was definitely not what she was going for.

"I was thinking about making a ham tonight," Gram continued. "And maybe my scalloped potatoes and creamed corn."

Gretchen never turned down her grandmother's creamed corn, but she didn't like the way this was going, and the man hadn't even arrived yet. "Alex isn't going to be a guest. It's a business arrangement."

Gram sat across the table from her with her own bowl of biscuits and gravy. "He's paying extra to eat meals with us. That's what you said."

"Normal meals. You don't have to cook anything special for him."

"I'll worry about what I'm cooking. Did you finish getting his room ready?"

Gretchen nodded, shoving a forkful of gravy-soaked biscuit into her mouth. She'd moved all of her belongings into the room next to Gram's, and everything from her bathroom into the one they'd be sharing. For Alex, they'd put on fresh bedding and placed brand-new towels and washcloths in the bathroom.

Between Cocoa and Alex Murphy, they'd shelled out a lot of cash recently. Gretchen rubbed at the back of her neck. The room and board he'd be paying would help, but things were still a little tighter than she'd like.

"You're going to come in early, right?" Gram asked. "You should clean up before Alex gets here. Maybe take a shower. Put on a little lipstick.".

Gretchen stared across the table. "What are you talking about? I don't even own lipstick, Gram."

"You can borrow some of mine. Oh, Cherry Hot Pants would be a great shade on you with that dark hair of yours."

"I am not putting *Cherry Hot Pants* on my lips." Gretchen didn't even know what else to say about that. "I'll probably say hi and point him in the direction of his room, and then I'm going back to work."

"You're never going to find a husband."

Gretchen pushed her chair back and carried her dishes to the sink. This wasn't good. Not good at all. "I'm not putting on red lipstick. I'm not looking for a husband. Alex Murphy is going to be our tenant and nothing more. I mean it, Gram."

The older woman smiled. "My great-grandmother ran a boardinghouse in London, and she took in an Irish boarder

8

who fell head over heels for my grandmother. It was very romantic."

"I don't have time for romance," Gretchen said, shoving her feet into the barn boots she'd taken off at the back door. "I've got horseshit to shovel."

Alex hit the brake pedal hard, and the used Jeep Cherokee he'd owned for three days skidded to a stop. The Jeep's nose was about three feet past the stop sign.

Now that he wasn't an honored fund-raiser guest and therefore exempt from minor traffic mistakes, he glanced around to make sure he wasn't about to be busted by any of Stewart Mills' finest.

Several stop signs had been added between the time Alex and the others had graduated and gone off to college and their return for Eagles Fest, and those weren't the only changes. The recession had hit hard, the mills had closed, and things had gotten really hard for the people of Stewart Mills. As he drove through town, he noticed again the number of empty storefronts and real estate signs. There seemed to be fewer foreclosure auction signs, though, which was hopefully a sign the worst was behind them.

He found the turnoff to the Walker farm by memory and drove slowly up the long and bumpy dirt driveway. The big white farmhouse needed a little TLC, but it was a long way from being run-down. He knew from his last visit to town that Gretchen had been running the place alone since her grandfather died, and that her grandmother had had some health issues. Nothing serious, but basically it was a one-woman show, so he'd been expecting it to be a little more rough.

He got out of the Jeep and was greeted by a chocolate Lab who immediately made it clear they were going to be the very best of friends. Behind the dog was Gretchen Walker, though her greeting was a little more reserved.

"Welcome back," she said, giving him a tight smile.

"Thanks. I'm looking forward to spending some time here."

She nodded, folding her arms across her chest. Gretchen was tall and lean, with long dark hair in a thick braid down her back. Old jeans tucked into even older barn boots hugged her legs, and she'd thrown a faded flannel shirt over a T-shirt.

Strong. As the dog sat at her feet, Alex composed a mental snapshot of her, and that was the word that popped into his head. Not only did she have physical strength, but she also had an air of resolve and determination about her. He had no doubt when something—*anything*—needed doing, Gretchen would quietly step up and get it done.

"Pretty dog," he said, remembering she wasn't the chatty type and it might be up to him to carry conversations.

"Thanks. Her name's Cocoa."

Alex smiled. "I can't imagine why."

"Yeah, it's not the most original name for a chocolate Lab, but she came with it and she seems to like it. Right, Cocoa?" The dog put up her paw and he watched Gretchen give her a high five. "She also likes high fives. A lot. She knows the basics, like *sit* or *down*. *Stay* is a little iffy. She has no idea what *get off the couch* or *no dogs on the bed* means, but if you're looking for somebody to celebrate with a high five, Cocoa's your girl."

"Who doesn't love a high five, right?" he asked the dog, who trotted back to him so they could slap palm to paw.

"Do you need help carrying things in?"

He shook his head. "I don't have much. I figured I'd say hello first and meet your grandmother. I'm sure we've met before, but it's been a long time."

"She's waiting inside."

Alex followed her around the house to the back door, which opened into the kitchen. He hadn't been away from New England so long that he'd forgotten that front doors were for company and political door knockers. After she'd kicked off her boots, she led him into the living room, where her grandmother was sitting in an old glider rocker. She set her knitting aside just in time for the big Lab to hop up in her lap. It took Cocoa a few seconds to wedge herself into a comfortable position, and he heard Gretchen sigh before she reintroduced them to each other.

"Sit for a few minutes," her grandmother said. "Let's chat."

He perched on the edge of the sofa. "Thank you for letting me rent a room in your home, Mrs. Walker."

"Call me Ida. Or Gram. Do you like scalloped potatoes?"

"Um." He tried to keep up. "Yes, ma'am. Ida. Gram. Yes, I like scalloped potatoes."

"I'm going back to work," Gretchen said. "Let me know if you need anything."

"You'll need to write the Internet password down for him," Ida told her before looking back to him. "Speaking of the Internet, you don't have any weird proclivities, do you?"

"Gram!" Gretchen stopped walking and turned back, holding her hands up in a *what are you doing?* gesture.

"If he's going to live under the same roof as my grand-daughter, I have a right to know."

"No, you don't," Gretchen said in a low voice.

"I guess I'd wonder what your definition of weird is," Alex said at the same time.

"Don't answer that, Gram."

Because they were technically his new landlords, the question could be totally illegal as far as he knew. But he wasn't particularly outraged by the turn in the conversation. "I've never received any complaints about weirdness with regard to my proclivities."

"Good." Ida gave him an approving look. "You can never be too careful."

"That's so true." He turned his gaze back to her grand-daughter. "So tell me, Gretchen, do *you* have any weird proclivities?"

"I am not discussing my proclivities with you."

"If I'm going to live under the same roof with you, don't I have a right to know?"

She shook her head, but he could see her struggling not to smile. "You have a right to know the dishwasher hasn't worked for almost a year and a half and where the extra toilet paper's kept. My proclivities, weird or not, are off-limits."

If not for the fact that her grandmother was watching them, Alex might have been tempted to poke at her a little more and try to get a reaction. He'd seen her during Eagles Fest, mostly from a distance, and he knew she had an infectious, musical laugh that seemed at odds with her stern exterior. When she was with Kelly McDonnell and their friend Jen Cooper, the high school guidance counselor, Gretchen had no problem letting her sense of humor show through. He could see glimpses of it now, and he wanted to draw it out.

But she escaped into the kitchen before he could say more, and a minute later he heard the kitchen door close with a thump. Alex turned his attention back to Ida, who was rubbing between a sleeping Cocoa's ears.

He would be in Stewart Mills for a while, so he had plenty of time to get under Gretchen Walker's skin and make her laugh.

02

Gretchen went to the detached garage because it was the closest thing she had to whatever the female equivalent of a man cave was. It had actually served as a man cave when her grandfather was alive, though it grew to be a lot more when his eleven-year-old granddaughter had become his constant shadow.

She usually raised the overhead door to let a little of the outside come in, but the rollers needed some maintenance and it was starting to stick three-quarters of the way up. Rather than wrestle with it, she went through the side door and flipped on the overhead light.

Breathing in the scent of old wood and grease, she perched on the tall wooden stool in front of the workbench. The carburetor from the old pain-in-the-ass lawn mower sat on an oil-soaked bed of cardboard, waiting to be rebuilt, but she didn't pick it up. She just looked around at the tools hanging from pegboard lining the walls, and the boxes and bins of garage debris her grandfather had accumulated over his lifetime on the Walker farm.

This was where she'd learned everything that mattered in her life. She'd learned the concepts of family and home. Stability and routine. Gramps had taught her to face problems head-on and that the only way to get things done was to suck it up and do them. And he'd taught her that, with determination and a little elbow grease, anything that was broken could be fixed.

He hadn't been the kind of man who showed emotion. Love and kissing boo-boos and wiping her very rare tears had come from Gram, but Gretchen had felt how much Gramps loved her. It showed in the hours he'd spent teaching her how to use a grinding wheel and tend to a cow with mastitis and prepare Gram's gardens for planting. With a steady hand and pride in his eyes, he'd quietly raised Gretchen to love the farm and be as capable a caretaker of it as he was.

And that's why she'd do whatever she had to for the Walker farm, including letting a man she barely knew live in the house. An insanely attractive man with short dark hair, who smelled good and looked at her with light brown eyes warm with intelligence and humor.

Gretchen pulled her cell phone out of her pocket. She thought about texting Kelly or Jen, but she had an old flip-style phone and having to push the number keys multiple times just to make one word was frustrating. Instead she flipped it open and hit Jen's assigned speed-dial number.

Jen Cooper was the guidance counselor at the high school and, though school wouldn't start for a few more weeks, Gretchen knew she'd be in her office. Kelly, being on the police force, had a more erratic schedule and was less likely to be available this time of day.

Jen answered on the third ring. "Hey, Gretchen. What's up?"

"You busy?"

"Nope. I'm eating a yogurt, wondering how the pile of crap on my desk is so tall when the kids aren't even here yet."

"Did Kelly tell you Alex Murphy was coming today?"

"Oh, that's right! How's that going?"

"Right off the bat, Gram asked him if he has any weird proclivities."

There were a few seconds when it sounded like Jen might be choking on her yogurt. "That sounds like Gram. It probably would have been better to ask him that *before* he moved in, though."

"It didn't come up in our emails."

"Well?"

"Well what?"

Jen's annoyed sigh made her sigh. "Does he have any weird proclivities?"

"Do you really think he would have told Gram if he did?"

"That's disappointing."

Gretchen laughed. "He didn't say he didn't have any, actually. Just that he hasn't received any complaints."

"*Really?* And it's only the first day. This could be interesting."

"I didn't call you to talk about Alex's proclivities, weird or not."

"Then you shouldn't have opened with them."

"I was opening with Gram's outrageousness. You're not going to believe what she suggested I do before he got here."

"Let me guess," Jen said. "You should do up your hair and maybe put on a little lip gloss."

"Lip gloss? She wanted me to slap on her Cherry Hot Pants lipstick."

"That's . . . disturbing. The name of that shade, I mean."

"That's more disturbing than her trying to hook me up with our new . . . I guess *tenant* isn't the right word. Boarder? That sounds old-fashioned."

Jen chuckled. "Right now picturing Gram in Cherry Hot Pants red is more disturbing than almost anything."

She should have called Kelly instead. "I can't even remember the last time I saw her in makeup. If the stuff has an expiration date, it was probably in the nineties."

"Okay, in all seriousness, you need to shut Gram down right away," Jen said. "It'll be hard enough having a man you barely know living in your house. Your grandmother trying to play matchmaker will make things awkward for everybody. Especially if she's opening with fetish questions. How the hell did that come up in conversation, anyway?"

"She reminded me to give him the Wi-Fi password," Gretchen told her. "Which apparently reminded *her* that she was concerned about what he might look at on the Internet."

"Hopefully taking pictures and working on his story—or book or whatever it is—will keep him out of the house for most of the hours Gram's awake. Since she doesn't have Facebook, her ability to do damage is limited to face-to-face time." Jen paused. "She doesn't have Facebook, right?"

"Not as far as I know. None of her friends do, so I've managed to convince her it's nothing she'd want, but a friend of a friend got an account to see pictures of her grandkid, so it's probably only a matter of time."

"Luckily you're her only shot for grandkids, and you live in the same house, so she doesn't need social media for that."

"Yeah." *Luckily* was one word for it. *Challenging* was perhaps a better one. Finding a guy who loved her enough to want to move into an old farmhouse with her and her grandmother wasn't easy. Especially since she rarely strayed far from the farm.

"We should get together soon," Jen said. "I don't think the three of us have had a chance to sit down and relax since Eagles Fest."

That sounded like a great idea to Gretchen. And she'd probably be ready to get out of the house—and away from the weirdness of a man living with them—before too long. "If you see Kelly, try to set up a day for lunch or something."

"I'll let you know. In the meantime, try to peek over Alex's shoulder now and then when he's on the Internet. We need better gossip in this town."

"Funny."

After she ended the call, Gretchen got off the stool and grabbed the key to the ancient ATV off the hook over the bench. It was time to head out and check the field she'd given over to pumpkins a few years back, and the four-wheeler would be faster than the tractor.

As the number of businesses who wanted to buy Walker pumpkins to resell to their customers had grown, so had the amount of land Gretchen allotted to the planting, and now it was substantial. Checking for powdery mildew and pests would keep her busy until it was time for afternoon chores and dinner.

Busy was good. The busier she was, the less time she had to think about Alex Murphy.

Alex set the last of his bags on the worn hardwood floor and used his foot to close the door behind him. So this bedroom would be his world for the near future. He'd stayed in worse. Much worse.

The furnishings were definitely more about function than décor, which he didn't mind at all. The full-sized mattress was firm and framed by a brass rail headboard and footboard, and there was a nightstand with a lamp next to it. A solid maple dresser stood next to the open closet, and there was a comfortable-looking armchair next to the window.

During their email exchanges prior to his arrival, Gretchen had asked if he needed a desk or anything else for working, but he'd told her not to bother. He didn't want to put her out, plus he'd trained himself years before not to tie his process to any particular work conditions. Sometimes he was in a hotel room with a desk and sometimes he was in a nylon tent with a laptop balanced on his knees. He could work under almost any conditions and this bedroom, plain and old-fashioned as it may be, was certainly no hardship.

Unpacking took him about twenty minutes, and he plugged his laptop in to charge. Later he'd start closely reviewing the photos he'd taken during Eagles Fest and decide which he'd like to include in his new work. Then he'd have to see about obtaining permission from the subjects to use them in a commercial project.

He also needed to get in touch with Coach McDonnell about Saturday. Tryouts for the football team would start at nine and he wanted to be there to capture the emotion of the morning. When the citizens reluctantly voted to cut the budget for the team at the town meeting in the spring, it was a hard blow to the boys. Playing football kept some out of trouble and gave others a reason to keep their grades up, especially when things were hard at home due to the economic downturn.

Things had looked bleak until Kelly McDonnell, Jen Cooper and Gretchen Walker got together and made the Eagles Fest fund-raiser happen. With the help of some grants and donations, they'd announced in July that Eagles football had been saved, and Alex knew their return to the field on Saturday would be even more exciting than usual. He intended to be there with his camera, with Coach's permission.

Alex walked to the window to check out the view. His room was at the back of the house and looked out toward the barn. He could barely make out a garage to the left and a rutted dirt road that passed between the two buildings and disappeared through a break in a line of trees. He assumed it led to fields, though he wasn't sure.

The view was considerably improved when Gretchen stepped out of the garage's side door and headed for the barn. She had a long stride and he admired the way she looked so natural and confident in her environment.

His hand itched for his camera, but he didn't give in to

the urge to pull it out of his bag. It was bad enough he was watching her from the window. Taking photographs would cross a personal line of ethics that was sometimes blurry and a moving target, but was always there.

He allowed himself to watch her for a few more seconds, admiring the way the sun lit up the highlights in her hair. In normal lighting, it was solidly dark, though not black. But when the sun hit the thick braid just right, subtle red undertones shone through and drew his eye. He wanted to unravel her braid and run his fingers through the strands just to watch the light play with the colors.

Gretchen disappeared on the far side of the barn and then, a few moments later, emerged again on a four-wheeler that had seen better days. Sitting on the machine, with her long legs drawn up so her feet rested on the running boards, pulled the worn denim of her jeans across her thighs in a way that drew his eye in a way that was far more personal than professional.

Before he stared long enough to tip over into creeper territory, Alex turned away from the window and went downstairs. With all the travel he'd done—which included staying in bed-and-breakfasts or sometimes with host families—he didn't have a lot of trouble making himself feel at home wherever he was. But for people like Ida and Gretchen, who weren't accustomed to having a boarder, it could feel awkward. The less time he spent holed up in his room, the faster they'd come to feel comfortable around him.

Gretchen's grandmother was at the computer when he walked into the living room. It was an older model perched on a big corner desk, and Ida was writing in a notebook in front of the monitor.

When he stepped on a floorboard that squeaked under his weight, she turned and gave him a smile. "How's your room?"

"It's perfect. And that's a beautiful quilt on the bed. Did you make it?"

"As tempting as it is to lie and take the credit, I never had the patience for quilting. All those tiny stitches. I enjoy knitting, though. Did you get on the Internet okay?"

"Yes, ma'am."

"Good. Every month when she pays the bill, Gretchen makes that same growly frustrated noise my husband made when he thought something was frivolous, but I need good Internet for my business."

Alex moved a couple of magazines out of the armchair near the desk so he could sit in it. If he sat on the couch, she wouldn't be able to resume what she was doing while still continuing their conversation unless she turned her back to him. "Do you mind if I ask what your business is?"

"I knit matching sweaters, hats and mittens for little girls and those fancy dolls from the different time periods in history. Jen—you know Jen Cooper, right? She helped set me up a little shop on a website that lets you sell handmade stuff. People tell me what size the child wears and her favorite color, and I knit a set for her and a matching one for the doll. I don't make a lot of money, but I'd be knitting anyway and this way I feel useful in my own little way."

Alex smiled, making a mental note to photograph Ida knitting and posing with her creations. Her business would fit right into a story about weathering rough times. "I'm sure Gretchen would say you're useful in countless ways."

"She's a good girl. I don't know what I'd do without her."

He suspected, in this case, it wasn't simply a common

platitude. While he hadn't seen a lot of the farm, he'd seen enough to know it would be a lot for Ida to have taken care of on her own after her husband passed away. Even without an expectation of the property providing a sustainable income for her, it would have been too much.

"I happened to glance out the window on my way down and saw her on a four-wheeler," he said. "She works all day out there?"

Ida nodded. "She's probably on her way to check on the pumpkins."

"Pumpkins?"

"If you go shopping this fall and the stores are selling pumpkins, there's a good chance Gretchen grew them. She's always looking for ways to make the land earn money, and the pumpkins were even more successful than she'd hoped."

Alex couldn't miss the pride in her voice. "I can't wait to see them."

He'd been looking forward to delving into the emotional story of a town overcoming financial adversity, so it looked like he'd picked the right place to stay. Gretchen and her grandmother were perfect examples of Yankee resilience and ingenuity. The fact that he wouldn't mind getting to know Gretchen a little better was just icing on the cake.

Gretchen wasn't surprised to see ham, scalloped potatoes and creamed corn on the table when she walked into the kitchen. Once Gram set her mind on a meal, she was rarely swayed. Earlier in the day Gretchen had been concerned her grandmother would get carried away making "company" meals for Alex, but right now she was starving and it smelled delicious and she didn't care.

Their new housemate came in from the living room as Gretchen was toeing off her boots, and he gave her a friendly smile. She returned it, feeling slightly awkward. She wasn't emotionally demonstrative to begin with and had what Jen and Kelly called resting bitch face, so randomly smiling at people wasn't really her thing.

"Sit down and dig in, Alex," Gram said from the stove. "We don't stand on ceremony around here."

Gretchen watched as he gave her grandmother what the older woman would call a cheeky smile and shook his head. "I can wait for the ladies to sit."

"I knew you were raised right." Gram gave him an approving nod. "I knew your parents, of course, before they moved away. Well, your stepfather, though I knew your dad, too."

Gretchen rolled up her sleeves and turned the faucet on to wash her hands. "You know everybody, Gram."

"Most everybody, I guess."

Once they were seated and served, Alex scooped some scalloped potato and ham onto his fork and took a bite. His eyes widened in appreciation, but he swallowed and wiped his lips before speaking. "This is delicious, Ida."

Gram beamed. "Thank you. It's one of my specialties."

"I hope you didn't go to any extra trouble for me."

"Not at all. You'll find farmer's wives—or grandmothers, as the case may be—like putting hearty meals on the table."

Gretchen was tempted to point out Gram hadn't made scalloped potatoes in months, even though it was one of her favorite dishes, but she shoved food in her mouth and chewed instead. She took after her grandfather in most ways, and that included treating meals as times to eat, not chitchat. But she didn't mind listening to Gram and Alex make small talk about the cuisine in various places where he'd traveled.

Gretchen had never heard of half the places, but it sounded like he led a pretty exciting life. She wasn't sure why he'd want to take pictures of the Eagles practicing when he'd documented protests outside the Sudanese embassy for a big magazine, but it wasn't really her business as long as he paid his rent.

"What made you come back to Stewart Mills?" Gram asked, clearly not too worried about what was and what wasn't their business.

"I was a little burned out from the travel," Alex said. Gretchen looked up from her plate in time to see him give a casual shrug, despite the fact that his expression was slightly more introspective. "When I was here for Eagles Fest, I really felt like I was connecting again. With . . . I don't know. With people. With my hometown. I have an apartment in Providence, but it's mostly a place to keep my stuff and sleep once in a while. I was on an assignment and I was tired, and it seemed like a great idea to come back and try to recapture how I felt during the fund-raiser."

"And you think doing a story about the town will make you some money while you're here?" Gram asked.

"I hope so. It's not just about the money, though. I was looking through the Eagles Fest photos before I made the decision to come back, and the emotion in them spoke to me. The story seemed unfinished, so I'm here to finish it."

Gretchen stopped herself from snorting at *It's not just*

about the money and scraped up the last of the scalloped potatoes on her plate. In her experience, people who said that had money to burn, and disposable income certainly wasn't something she'd ever experienced.

She really hoped her grandmother wouldn't take that as an opening to ask nosy questions about his finances. Not directly, of course, but in that friendly and curious way small-town folks had when it came to interrogating people.

But Gram was distracted by Alex's almost empty plate. "There's plenty enough for seconds, Alex. Just help yourself."

He made a show of patting his very flat stomach. "One's plenty, Ida. I don't want to have to buy new pants while I'm here."

Gretchen didn't think he was in any danger of an expanding waistline anytime soon. He was tall and a big guy in general, but very fit. Of course, she wasn't the one currently running her palm over his abdomen, but from where she was sitting, it all looked good. Really, *really* good.

Gram made a clucking sound with her tongue. "You need a wife to fix you good home-cooked meals."

Alex froze just as his lips closed over his fork, and Gretchen might have laughed at his expression if she wasn't expending all of her energy to keep herself from kicking her grandmother under the table. As soon as she got a minute alone with Gram, they were going to have to have a talk about boundaries.

After taking his time chewing and swallowing his food, Alex just plastered a polite smile on his face. "Maybe someday I'll try marriage again, but not anytime soon."

Gretchen almost groaned aloud. If he didn't want to

share his whole life story over meals, he'd have to learn not to open the door like that.

"You've been married before?" Gram asked, and this time Gretchen did kick her under the table, though gently. It was more of a nudge, really.

"I was, but my traveling turned out to be more of an issue than we thought it would, and eventually we just went our separate ways."

"Ah." Gram nodded. "Sounds very amicable."

Alex nodded, but there was something about the set of his jaw that made Gretchen think it hadn't been as amicable at the time as he made it sound.

He set his fork across his empty plate and wiped his mouth on his napkin. "If you don't mind, I'd love to take some pictures of the farm. Maybe follow you both around a little bit."

Gretchen frowned. "I thought you wanted to photograph the high school team."

"The football team is at the heart of this project, but I'd like to broaden the scope to include all of Stewart Mills. It was a town effort, saving the team."

"There's plenty of Stewart Mills out there without including our farm." Out of the corner of her eye, she saw Gram scowling in her direction and avoided full eye contact. Maybe she'd get lucky and, just this once, her grandmother would keep her opinions to herself.

"It would be good publicity," Gram said, and Gretchen sighed.

"Gram, the people who buy our pumpkins live locally, and we can't take in any more horses. What good would more publicity do for us?"

"Maybe more people will order sweaters from my online store."

"Then he can take pictures of you knitting. There's not much sense in him following me around while I'm trying to work."

Alex cleared his throat and Gretchen realized with a guilty start that she was being rude. Not only was she talking about their guest as though he wasn't in the room, but she was making him out to be a nuisance. And she didn't see any way out of it without giving in. "Sorry. You can take pictures around the farm if you want."

"I didn't mean tomorrow. Once you get used to having me underfoot, we can see if you're comfortable with it. Some people aren't, and that's okay."

He really did have a great smile, and Gretchen forced her gaze back to her plate rather than risk losing herself in it and saying something stupid. Something like *You can follow me around as much as you want, and did you know the barn has a hayloft?*

Conversation died away as they stood and set about clearing the table, much to Gretchen's relief. It wouldn't take long for Gram to find out anything she wanted to know about Alex, which would hopefully put an end to the awkward questions.

She had to admit a part of her was glad Gram wasn't shy, though. Gretchen could satisfy her curiosity about their handsome houseguest while still maintaining a polite distance.

When Alex's arm brushed against hers at the sink, it took every ounce of self-control she had not to jerk away. Standing so close to him made her feel not exactly dainty or delicate, but soft and feminine, maybe. It wasn't a feeling she was used to. He looked good, he smelled good and he was absolutely no good for her.

While she was at it, she should probably add "physical" to the list of distances she was keeping.

03

Once the kitchen had been cleaned up, Alex walked into the living room and laughed when Cocoa bounded up from a huge, flannel-covered cushion on the floor in the corner. She jogged across the room and nuzzled his hands, as though looking for something. When she didn't find it, she started jabbing at his pants pockets with her nose.

"Cocoa!" Alex and the dog both whirled at the sound of Gretchen's voice behind them. She was holding a dog biscuit in one hand and pointing at the Lab with the other. "Stop that."

"She's not bothering me," Alex said, even as the dog dumped him like a bad date for the lady with the treat.

"We're trying to teach her some manners." After another stern look, Gretchen handed over the biscuit, which Cocoa took back to her bed to enjoy. "We finally taught her she can't be in the kitchen while we eat, but basic manners are still a struggle."

"Being goofy and friendly and enthusiastic are a Lab's best qualities."

"I agree, but that doesn't mean she can be nosing around in your . . . uh, pockets." She took a deep breath. "I feel like I should apologize for Gram, too."

"Pretty sure she hadn't nosed around in my pockets."

That got a quick smile out of her. "No, but she's managed to nose around in almost every part of your life and it hasn't even been a full day yet."

Alex tried to look over her shoulder to make sure Ida wasn't listening, but Gretchen was a tall woman and he couldn't see much of the kitchen.

"She went out to work in the vegetable garden for a while."

"Oh. Does she need any help?"

"No, she doesn't. If she did, I'd be out there helping her."

The words would have come off as defensive from most people, but Gretchen said them in such a matter-of-fact tone that Alex knew it was just the way she was wired. If something needed doing, she wouldn't be standing around talking to him. She'd be doing it.

"Okay. And Ida's questions don't bother me. There's nothing about my life I need to hide from anybody, and it's just conversation." Not that talking about his weight or his ex-wife would ever be his first choice for conversation, but Ida meant well and they were pretty standard getting-to-know-you questions, really.

Cocoa must have finished her biscuit, because she walked over to lean against his leg. Alex smiled down at her and scratched behind her ears. Tilting her head up, she gave him a look that could only be described as adoring, and he felt a pang of regret that his job didn't allow him to have a dog.

No wife. No dog. No place he couldn't go without having to make do with only what fit in his carry-on bag. It was a lot easier for a guy to travel when he didn't have any checked baggage.

"Okay." Gretchen stood there just long enough for the silence to grow awkward. "Well, I'm going to go . . . do stuff. Feel free to watch television or whatever. We don't watch it very much, so don't worry about what's on."

"Okay, thanks. And I have stuff, too." He had no idea *what* stuff, but he'd find something to do.

"Come on, Cocoa."

The Lab looked up at him before raising her paw. Alex gave her a high five and then watched her follow Gretchen through the kitchen and out the back door. Once it was closed, he let out a long breath and walked to the sofa to sit down. He should go upstairs and get some work done. Maybe start outlining what he wanted to say about Stewart Mills so he could come up with a game plan for the photography.

In this case, though, he preferred to ease into the project. He had the time to simply wander and see what caught his eye or connected with him emotionally. He was a decent writer, but photographs were how he best told a story.

He was also tired and wanted to relax. While staying in every kind of lodging imaginable over the years— including a hole hidden under floorboards when he'd pissed off a drug lord in Central America by taking his picture— had made him pretty adaptable, staying with a family in their home could be the most taxing.

There wasn't even a guy in the household he could make guy talk with to put everybody at ease. Just two women who were set in their ways and not used to having a man around anymore. And Cocoa. She seemed to like him.

A framed photo on the wall opposite him caught his eye and he smiled. It was a very young Gretchen, posing with an older man Alex assumed was her grandfather in front of a beat-up old truck. She'd been serious even then, he thought, looking at her young face. Not that she looked unhappy. She was just quiet.

He wondered if it was just in her nature, or if there was a reason she didn't smile for the camera. He would have guessed environment, since her grandfather had the same reserved expression as Gretchen in the photo, but Ida was warm and open and definitely didn't hold back on the smiling.

Looking around the room, he saw another photo of her grandfather with a truck—this one shiny and possibly new—in a small stand-up frame on the desk next to the computer. But there was no Gretchen in that picture, and the man was scowling. In the background, Alex could make out part of the barn and a couple of cows watching him over the fence. Looking back and forth between the two, he couldn't tell which photograph was newer. Her grandfather looked the same age in both pictures, though the trucks certainly didn't.

Rather than sit and ponder the mystery of Gretchen, her grandfather and his trucks, Alex slipped his phone out of his pocket and pulled up his email account. He'd already talked to his agent about the Stewart Mills project—which had received a lukewarm *we'll wait and see* reception—and about going off the grid for a short break, so there was nothing much going on in his inbox. He had a stockpile of links to articles he'd been saving to read later, but his tablet was upstairs and he didn't feel like reading on the small screen.

After a few minutes, he decided to go upstairs and open his laptop. It was tempting to head outside and see what the women were doing, but he wanted to give them some time alone. While Ida didn't seem fazed by his presence, he could tell it was strange for Gretchen, so he'd let them have a break. She'd get used to him eventually, and hopefully sooner rather than later.

He was flipping through the digital edition of a magazine that featured some of his photos in an article about the preservation of castle ruins around the United Kingdom when he heard footsteps outside in the hall. Based on which door opened and closed, and Cocoa's nails clicking on the hardwood floor, it seemed Ida liked to go to bed early.

Pulled out of his work, Alex thought about going downstairs for a snack, but he decided to lie low until he'd gotten a feel for their nightly routine. Instead, he grabbed a granola bar and a bottle of water from his stash and settled back into his reading.

When he heard Gretchen walk by about an hour and a half later, he stripped down to his boxer briefs and went into his bathroom. This was obviously a household that embraced the "early to bed and early to rise" philosophy, and he was going to do his best to fit in.

Once he was between the sheets, which felt crisp and new for him, he closed his eyes. Instantly, his mind wanted to spend some time on the way Gretchen's blue eyes had looked across the dinner table from him, but Alex had too many years of experience trying to sleep in strange places or at odd times to give in and let his imagination run free.

He imagined standing on the edge of a rocky beach, watching the rough waves roll in. Forcing himself to focus only on the sound of them breaking, he lost himself in the stormy ocean and was asleep within minutes.

Gretchen woke up the next morning feeling uncharacteristically groggy and cranky, and it was all Alex Murphy's fault.

Even when she was a little girl, she'd had chores before school, so she'd quickly learned one of the golden rules of living on a farm—go to sleep when your head hits the pillow so you can get up early and be ready to work.

But last night she hadn't gone to sleep when her head hit the pillow. She hadn't gone to sleep *an hour* after her head hit the pillow. Of course there had been nights when she didn't fall asleep immediately—like when Gramps died or when she'd been racking her brain to come up with ways for the farm to earn income—but she'd never tossed and turned for hours thinking about a man.

It probably wasn't a coincidence that it was also the first time she'd ever been attracted to a man whom it would be a really bad idea to sleep with. She didn't have a lot of trouble finding male companionship when she was in the mood for it, but Alex was different. He was paying to live in her house, for one thing, so things could get messy.

But mostly he was different because he made *her* feel

different. As a rule, if she felt a sexual attraction to a man and things worked out, she acted on it. But Alex's smile made her feel jittery, as though she'd had too much coffee and not enough food. And she felt awkward around him, which was new since she wasn't in the habit of really giving a damn what people thought of her.

So she'd lain awake and tried not to think about his smile or how wide his shoulders were or how very strong and capable looking his hands were. She didn't remember what she'd dreamed about when she finally slept, but she'd woken feeling restless and out of sorts.

What she needed was some good hard physical labor. Today she was going to work herself so long and so hard, she'd be lucky if she remembered to take her clothes off before she crawled into bed. If her body ached tonight, it would be due to the hard work, not because she desperately wanted the touch of a guy she barely knew.

With a plan in place to prevent a repeat performance of the restless insomnia, Gretchen got out of bed and stretched. Then she quickly, and not very neatly, made her bed before grabbing her clothes for the day. Sharing a bathroom was more of a nuisance than she'd anticipated, but at least she wasn't sharing the bathroom with Alex, too.

She opened her door and stepped out into the hallway, where she almost ran into Alex. Instinctively, she clutched her bundle of clothes to her chest, hoping to hide the fact that she wasn't wearing a bra. "Uh . . . hi."

"Good morning." His voice was still husky from sleep, and Gretchen tried—and failed—not to imagine him saying her name in just that tone. "Ida asked me to come and see if you were up."

Mortification made her want to step back into her room and slam the door in his face. "You can't be serious."

"She said you never sleep past six and she's worried you might be sick."

Or she might just be exhausted from staying up half the night fantasizing about the man standing in front of her. "I'm not sick. You can tell her I'll be down in a few minutes, if you don't mind."

He gave her an odd look. "Why would I mind?"

"She shouldn't be asking you to do stuff for her."

"About that." He leaned against the wall, folding his arms, and Gretchen sighed. Having a discussion in the hallway before clothes and coffee wasn't improving her morning any. "I really appreciate that you're trying to set boundaries since I'm paying rent to be here. Maybe some people would be put off by some of Ida's questions or being sent to drag a sleepyhead down to breakfast, but I truly don't mind. I like her and I feel pretty at home with her."

Gretchen guessed the underlying implication there was that if she'd just relax, he could feel at home with her, too. There were distances to be maintained, though, so she simply gave him a sharp nod. "Wonderful. Since you're so comfortable with her, I guess you can tell her if she gets too nosy."

He looked slightly amused, though she couldn't imagine what she'd said that was funny. Unless he was trying not to laugh at her hair. Or the cows on her flannel sleep pants, which had been a gift from Kelly at least half a decade ago.

"Yeah," he said, standing up straight again. "I'm going to go drink my coffee now, and maybe yours, too, if you take too long."

She almost laughed, but managed to give him a stern look instead. "I've got a lot of acreage and a backhoe attachment for my tractor. You don't want to touch my coffee."

He turned and walked back toward the stairs, but she could hear him chuckling as she closed the bathroom door. And fifteen minutes later, when she'd given Cocoa some love and then walked into the kitchen, he just smiled and poured coffee into her favorite mug before setting it at her place at the table.

"Thank you," she said, pulling out her chair and sitting down.

"Please tell me she doesn't cook like this every morning," he said from across the table, which was covered with a mountain of scrambled eggs, bacon, toast and fruit.

"A body needs fuel to get through the day," Gretchen said.

She could still remember the first time her grandfather said those words to her. It had been her first morning with her grandparents, and she'd been confused by the bounty of food on the table and asked for the sugary cereal she usually ate dry out of a plastic baggie. Gram had started fussing over her, but Gramps had simply pointed at the food and told her to eat. She ate.

"A body's going to need some big plans to burn all this off," Alex said, spooning some scrambled eggs onto his plate.

Gretchen paused with her fork halfway to her mouth. "I plan to work."

Gram chuckled as she set a mason jar of homemade strawberry jam on the table and sat down. "Gretchen doesn't like to talk much over breakfast. She's usually working out in her mind what she needs to get done for the day."

"Fair enough. This looks too delicious to let get cold, anyway."

Gretchen frowned at her plate. Her grandmother was right, but hearing herself described out loud like that made Gretchen want to wince. She was damn proud of being *like* her grandfather, but she didn't actually want to *be* him. She was too young to turn into an old man, for goodness' sake.

"Do you have any plans today?" she asked Alex after taking a bracing gulp of strong, black coffee.

He looked surprised for a second, since he'd just been told she didn't like breakfast conversation, but then he nodded. "I'm heading over to see Coach in a little while. Then I'll probably wander around for a bit. I might hit the library and see if I can poke around the archives for some background history."

"I have some books that need to go back," Gram said. "And a murder mystery I requested came in. I got a call about it and then totally forgot."

"Do you want to go into town with me, or do you want me to return your books? I'm sure if you call, they'll let me pick up your murder mystery."

"You don't want to drag me around town all day, but if you don't mind stopping at the library for me, that would be wonderful."

Gretchen forced herself to keep eating and stay out of it. If Alex didn't want to help Gram out, he wouldn't have offered. And since they were so at home with each other, they could figure it out. Meanwhile, she'd just sit there and apparently channel her grandfather.

"You okay?" she heard Alex ask, and she realized he was talking to her.

"Yeah. Why?"

"You just sighed, like something was wrong."

"Just kicking myself for sleeping in," she lied. "I usually take care of the horses before breakfast, so I'm already behind."

"It's not like you to lie in bed half the day," Gram said, despite the fact that it wasn't even seven thirty. "Are you feeling okay?"

Forcing herself not to so much as glance at the reason she'd been "lying in bed half the day" lest she blush at the memory of her nocturnal thoughts, she nodded. "I'm fine, Gram. First night in a new room and all."

"Sorry about that," Alex said.

She smiled at him in case he was actually feeling guilty. "I'll be fine, and we're glad to have you here."

He smiled back at her, his dark eyes crinkling at the corners. "I'm glad to be here."

Wondering if those laugh lines were a detail her imagination would add to the fantasy version of him she'd been tormented by last night, Gretchen turned her attention back to her eggs. If she was going to work hard enough to keep fantasies of Alex at bay, her body was going to need a lot of fuel.

Alex drove down Eagles Lane—so renamed after Alex and his teammates brought home the first football championship—and did a slow roll up to Coach's house.

He'd been a sullen fifteen-year-old the first time he'd walked up the front steps of the old New Englander the McDonnells called home, and sitting on the porch with Coach that night had changed his life forever.

It had been Alex's seventh or eighth trip to the police station for fighting, and Coach happened to stop in on other business just in time to see Alex's mom break down in tears. With a husband who was out of patience with his stepson and two young daughters who didn't need his bad behavior setting an example, she didn't know what to do with Alex anymore.

Coach had comforted Joanne and then offered to take Alex home with him for the night. Overwhelmed and exhausted, Alex's mom had quickly agreed it would be for the best. After giving her son a hug that left his T-shirt damp from her tears, she'd turned around and walked out.

Sitting on Coach McDonnell's front porch, Alex had rolled his eyes as the lecture began. But by the time Coach stopped talking, Alex was too busy swiping at the tears in his eyes to roll them. They'd talked mostly about Alex's dad and how losing him couldn't derail his life. And Coach understood how he'd kept himself on the outside as his mother remarried and had more children because he'd felt like the only one who remembered his dad. And now he felt like an outsider and didn't know how to fix it.

Alex listened to the older man's advice and tried out for the football team, and from that day until he graduated, playing defensive tackle for the Stewart Mills Eagles drove him. With a strong mentor, a way to channel his restless energy, and a few teammates who became like brothers to him, he stopped lashing out. He strengthened his relationship with his mother and stepfather, and honored his father's memory by trying to be a man he'd be proud of.

It was Mrs. McDonnell who'd first noticed Alex's favorite

thing was taking pictures with the ancient camera that had been his dad's. Alex had fuzzy memories of posing for that camera before the logging accident that made him fatherless, and he had shoeboxes full of the photos his dad had saved.

It had taken Coach's wife to help him understand his bond with the camera and those shoeboxes. In capturing images of his wife and son and his town, Alex's dad was also telling his own story. Alex could see his love for his subjects in the composition, and the connection sparked a passion for photography in his soul. Mrs. McDonnell had helped him turn that passion into his life's path.

Alex pushed the memories to the back of his mind as he parked in the driveway and got out, not surprised when Coach met him on the front porch. They exchanged hugs, and then Coach gestured to the rocking chairs. "It's a nice day. Let's sit."

The creak of the wooden rocker under his weight, in the shade of the farmer's porch, felt like home to Alex. "It feels really good to be back here."

"I was surprised when Kelly told me you were coming back," Coach said. "I wasn't sure I'd see you boys again, and then Chase decided to live here, and now you."

Chase Sanders, former Eagles running back, had made his decision because he fell in love with the coach's daughter, and once he tied up all his business in New Jersey, he'd move to Stewart Mills for good. "For a little while, anyway. But when I do leave, I won't go another fourteen years without visiting."

"Good. I've missed you boys over the years. Thought about you all the time, wondering how you were."

Alex accepted the guilt and sense of shame because he'd earned them. "I thought about you, too, Coach. I'm sorry so many years passed."

"I did my best to help you boys become strong men who could go out and be successful. I feel nothing but pride that you all did that, son. And you were here when I needed you. Can't ask for more than that."

"You have no idea how glad I am that I came. And I'm glad it worked out for the team, too. Tryouts are Saturday, huh?"

"Yup." Coach rocked back in his chair and got straight to the point in his usual way. "I've met with all the parents and there are a few ground rules for you being around the boys."

"Okay." Alex had expected that. He'd even worked with the school and police department by email before he arrived, giving them the info they needed for their mandatory background check.

"The parents are going to worry when it comes to what's said about their kids for possibly the whole world to read, but everybody agrees it's not practical for you to get every word approved by every parent. So anything to do with football gets run by me. If the boys open up to you and start telling you personal things, I want that stuff brought to Jen Cooper. She'll decide whether or not to bring the parents into it."

It was going to be a royal pain in the ass and make the entire project longer than it needed to be, but Alex had known going in that it wouldn't be easy. While he wanted to encompass the town itself, the primary focus of the work would be an entire team of minors. "Okay."

Coach leaned forward, pinning him with a look that Alex remembered well from his youth. "I don't know much about the legal aspects of journalism or book writing as far as what your rights are. Maybe there is no such thing as off the record. But I vouched for you with every single parent so, if you agree to those terms, I personally want your word on it. Between you and me, son."

Alex and the other guys had learned early and well that giving your word to Coach McDonnell wasn't something done lightly. No matter how rough things were in life, honoring your word was something that couldn't be taken from you.

"You have my word, Coach. I won't do anything that hurts those boys, or casts anybody in a negative light." He leaned across the gap between the chairs and shook Coach's hand.

"That's settled, then. Tryouts start at nine. So how are things going for you at the Walker farm? You settling in okay there?"

Unbidden, an image of Gretchen in silly flannel sleep pants with cows on them filled Alex's mind. They were pink, and the black-and-white cows were wearing pink shoes and straw hats with pink bows. They were fun and silly, and he'd bet anything they were a gift. They didn't seem like the kind of thing Gretchen would buy for herself, but she definitely loved them. The flannel was soft and worn, and often washed, judging by how faded they were.

The cute cows had almost—though not quite—managed to distract Alex from the fact that Gretchen looked hot as hell in a tank top with sleep-tousled hair. It had been only seconds before she'd covered her chest with the bundle of clothes she was carrying, but it was long enough to leave Alex with the memory of firm, round breasts and well-toned arms.

"Hey."

Coach's voice broke into thoughts that were going nowhere good, and Alex shifted in his rocker. "Sorry. Lost my train of thought. Everything's good at the farm. Gretchen's a bit of a tough nut, but Ida's a wonderful lady."

"So she's Ida, but I'm still Mrs. McDonnell?"

Alex immediately jumped to his feet. He hadn't heard the coach's wife step outside. "Hey, Mrs. McDonnell! I was going to come in and say hi but we got to talking."

When he crossed the porch to her, she hugged him and kissed his cheek. "You do know you can call me Helen, right?"

"It just doesn't feel right," he admitted. He knew the other guys felt the same way, and although they sometimes called her Mrs. McD, calling her by her first name just felt wrong.

"I'd ask if you had breakfast, but I know Ida, so I won't bother. Would you like a coffee or juice or something?"

"No, thank you. And you're not kidding about Ida. I've eaten more in the last two meals than I had in the entire week before."

"And both of them thin as rails. Must be nice to be blessed with the Walker metabolism," Mrs. McDonnell said with good humor.

Alex didn't think Gretchen was thin as a rail at all, considering the delicious curves of her breasts and backside, but that wasn't a conversation he was going to have with *anybody*, never mind Coach and his wife.

Mrs. McDonnell touched his shoulder affectionately

before opening the screen door. "I'll leave you two to talk. Give a shout if you need anything."

Once he was back in the rocker, Alex leaned back and blew out a breath. "You guys know what a special place this porch is, right?"

Coach laughed, nodding his head. "We do. But it's not the porch, son. It's the people who come and sit on it."

Alex couldn't argue with that. Instead, they talked football for a while and watched the occasional car go by. The library research beckoned and he needed a few things at the market, but they could wait.

For now he was content to sit and rebuild a connection he hadn't realized how much he'd missed having in his life.

04

Gretchen wasn't surprised to see the Stewart Mills Police Department's SUV drive up shortly before noon. Because Kelly had helped facilitate Alex's moving into the house, she'd want to stop by and make sure everything was going okay. Or she'd talked to Jen and wanted to tease Gretchen about her new tenant's possibly weird proclivities.

As she got out of the cruiser, Kelly ended a cell phone conversation and slid the phone into her pocket. Gretchen wondered if it was a work call or Chase, but judging by the smile on Kelly's face, it was probably her fiancé.

"Hey," Kelly said, spotting Gretchen near the garage. "I thought I'd stop by and say hi."

"Hi."

"Hilarious. Tell me everything."

Gretchen laughed and then shrugged. "Okay. I gathered

eggs and then I took care of the horses. Then I checked on the pumpkins, which are doing really well this year. I had to order a part for the tractor. Now I'm going to split some wood."

"Stop! Fine. Not everything."

Gretchen knew what Kelly wanted to hear, but she had no intention of sharing with her friend how attractive she found her new housemate, or how long she'd tossed and turned trying to forget that so she could sleep.

"How are things going with Alex? I feel invested since I helped arrange it."

"It was definitely a good idea to use him as a test run for having a boarder. He's fine. I mean, I kind of know him, and your dad knows him really well. Gram knows his family. But now that Alex is staying here, I can see that there's no way I could have a stranger living with us."

"Do you want me to see about other arrangements for Alex?"

"No. He's fine, like I said." Gretchen wasn't sure how to explain it. "It's just . . . weird."

"Weird how? Is he making you uncomfortable?"

She laughed. "Relax, Officer McDonnell. *He's* not weird and he's done nothing to make me feel uncomfortable at all. It's just weird having a guy in the house."

"What does Gram think of him?"

"Gram wants to fatten him up, of course."

"Obviously I barely looked Alex's way during Eagles Fest, since I was too busy trying to hide the fact I was ogling Chase, but I seem to remember he looks pretty good just the way he is."

Gretchen was usually fairly good at hiding her thoughts,

but she could feel a touch of heat across her cheeks. "He's in pretty good shape, I guess. I didn't really notice."

"You are *so* lying to me right now."

"Of course I noticed the man's in good shape. Have you seen how he's built? When a man that tall with shoulders like that is standing next to you at the kitchen sink, trust me, you notice."

"Are you blushing?" Kelly laughed. "I don't know if I've ever seen you blush before."

"It's hot. Some of us work for a living instead of riding around in air-conditioned cruisers, you know."

"Don't try that *the best defense is a good offense* crap on me. Coach's daughter, remember?" Kelly spread her feet a little and folded her arms over her chest. Gretchen and Jen used to give her a hard time about her "cop stance," until Kelly had finally explained it was simply the most comfortable way to stand when wearing boots and a vest while weighed down by all the stuff attached to her belt. "Any awkward run-ins in the bathroom yet?"

Gretchen rolled her eyes. "He has his own bathroom. That was the whole point of me moving into the room next to Gram's, which you already know."

There had been the slightly awkward run-in in the hallway, but she was keeping that to herself. It was bad enough Gram might get it in her head that Alex and Gretchen would make a lovely couple. She didn't need her best friends in on the matchmaking, too.

The back screen door banged closed and they both looked in time to see Cocoa come barreling toward them. Laughing, Kelly crouched down to meet the exuberant greeting from the Lab.

"How long have I been here and you just caught on?"

Gretchen snorted. "She was probably napping on Gram's lap again. A watchdog, she's not."

"She's a little big to be on Gram's legs, isn't she?"

"Tell me about it. Actually, tell *Gram* about it, since she's the one not cracking down on Cocoa. The dog does learn eventually, but not if the nice old lady is enabling her."

Kelly scratched under the dog's chin. "You stay off Gram's lap."

Cocoa gave her a high five and then went to find a good spot to pee. Gretchen uncapped her water bottle and took a swig before offering it to Kelly, who shook her head.

"How's Chase?" she asked before Kelly could resume their conversation about Alex.

"He's good. Busy, which is good and bad. Good because he wants to make everything right. Bad because it's keeping him in New Jersey."

Gretchen nodded. Shortly before Eagles Fest, Chase's business partner had run off with their money, and his girlfriend had run off with another man. Both had been a blessing in disguise, since it turned out Kelly McDonnell was the love of his life, but he wasn't the kind of guy to turn his back on his obligations. He had some jobs to finish and debts to pay off before he came home for good. "It's only temporary."

Kelly smiled. "I know. And he's coming home this weekend for three days."

Before Gretchen could respond, Kelly's cell phone rang and she pulled it out of her pocket. It sounded work-related, so Gretchen watched Cocoa wrestle with a stick while Kelly talked.

"I have to run." Kelly slid the phone back into her pocket. "We have a resident who's absolutely sure she turned her kitchen light off before she did errands and came home to find it on, which means there's probably a serial killer in one of her closets."

Gretchen laughed. Kelly loved being a police officer and she was good at it, but it would drive Gretchen insane to deal with the stuff her friend did every day. Kelly never put names or identifying details to the calls out of respect for the fact that she policed a very small community, but she'd told stories that made Gretchen and Jen laugh so hard their stomachs hurt.

Once Kelly was gone, Gretchen spent a few minutes playing with Cocoa before bringing her inside. She might live on a farm, but Cocoa was meant to be a companion for Gram, and Gretchen did her best to make the Lab earn the obscene amount of dog food she went through.

Then she pulled on her thick leather gloves and went out to chop some wood. There was nothing like swinging a splitting maul to make a girl tired enough to sleep.

It was late afternoon when Alex returned to the farm and parked his Jeep next to Gretchen's old truck. He hadn't accomplished a lot, besides stopping in the library for Ida, but he didn't consider the day a waste. There were worse things than passing the time with the McDonnells, that was for sure.

He brought Ida her library book, which got him a lazy high five from Cocoa. "Is she supposed to be on your lap like that?"

Ida sighed. "Barely twenty-four hours and you're as bad as Gretchen."

But she coaxed the dog off her lap and got her to curl up on the cushion next to her feet. Cocoa heaved a sigh and gave Alex a sad, accusatory look before going back to sleep.

"How's Helen?"

"She's good. Said to give you her best, of course. What's Gretchen up to?"

"Last I knew, she was splitting wood. She was going to work on the tractor, but they sent her the wrong part. I'm glad I wasn't on the other end of *that* phone call, let me tell you. That girl gets more like her grandfather every day."

There was never any mention of Gretchen being like her mother or father, Alex noted. No mention of parents at all, and he couldn't help but wonder why. He was guessing, based on the last name, that Gretchen's father was the son of Ida and her husband, but there was no guarantee. If Gretchen's mother had been unmarried or kept her name, or if the Walkers adopted Gretchen, that could explain it, too. No matter how hard he tried, he couldn't remember anybody in town ever talking about her mom or dad when they were kids.

He wanted to ask, but he'd already noticed there were no photos of Gretchen's parents in the living room, and he could only guess the circumstances of her being raised by her grandparents was a sore or painful subject.

"I'm not in the mood to sit at the computer," he said. "I might go see if Gretchen needs any help."

Ida chuckled. "Good luck with that."

Alex grabbed a couple of water bottles out of the fridge

on his way through the kitchen and went outside. A loud crack told him she was off to the right, so he went around the house.

Behind the barn was what looked to him like an incredibly huge pile of cut logs. Off to the side was a three-sided shed to protect the split and stacked wood. In between was Gretchen, her back to him as she stood a log on the massive cutoff tree trunk serving as her chopping block.

He watched her pause, and then she lifted the splitting maul and swung it down in a fluid motion. It hit with a loud *thunk* and the log split into two chunks. She bent over and retrieved one before balancing it on its end.

He wanted his camera in his hand to catch her in midswing, but she hadn't given him permission yet.

Then she bent to pick up the other half of the original log, and his interest shifted from an artistic assessment of her form to a very male appreciation of her ass. Unfortunately, he must have made some subtle sound of approval because she whirled to face him.

"Sorry." He held up the water bottles. "I didn't mean to startle you. Just thought you might like a drink."

"Thanks." She held out her hand and he passed one over. After draining a quarter of it, she recapped it and tossed it into the grass nearby. "Back up if you don't want to get hit."

He backed up. "Looks like hard work."

"It's gotta be done." She pulled her gloves on and grabbed the splitting maul while eyeballing the log she'd set on the block. "For future reference, maybe don't sneak up on a woman holding an ax."

"I'll make a note of that. Don't they have some kind of contraption that does that for you?"

"Yeah. It's called a splitting maul." She hefted the maul and brought it down on the log, splitting it neatly down the middle.

"I'm serious." Even if things were tight financially for the farm now, a hydraulic splitter should have been something her grandfather got back when they were flush.

"So am I." She leaned the maul against the splitting block and pulled off her gloves. "Our stove's big enough to take them unsplit, so once cold weather sets in it's just a matter of feeding the fire until spring. We only keep a little split on hand to get the fire going or to get us through the occasional cold night in the fall."

Since it took only a quick glance at the woodshed to know her definition of *a little* was quite a few chunks of split wood apart from his, Alex still didn't see why they wouldn't use a splitter.

"My grandfather always said splitting wood was good for the soul," she continued, a nostalgic smile playing on her mouth. "It's good physical work that helps you get your mind right. And it's good exercise, too."

Alex groaned and rubbed his stomach. "I need some of that. Your grandmother's cooking is going to undo years of dietary discipline."

"Dietary discipline?" She tilted her head as she asked the question, clearly interested. "I remember you were pretty big in high school. Like muscular big, I mean."

He nodded. "I was. Working out and practices and games and plenty of carbs and protein kept me hitting hard on the field. I didn't play ball in college, though, and I kept on eating the same way. Without the workouts and the football, I went from badass big to just plain old big pretty quickly."

"I don't get into actual exercise, but the meals Gram cooks—especially the *good farm breakfasts*, as she calls them—would probably go straight to my butt if I didn't work around the property so much."

He liked her butt quite a bit, just the way it was. Her body was lean and strong, but still had a sweet curve filling out the seat of her jeans. Not that he'd mind if it *were* filling out a larger size of jeans, either. He might admire the hell out of her figure, but it wasn't what attracted him to her in the first place. That would be her appealing mix of quiet strength and warm humor.

"It was hard work getting myself back in shape again," he said, which was a gross understatement. The few years it took to lose the weight he'd put on in college, post-football, had been some of the hardest he'd ever had.

"Well, feel free to get as much exercise as you want while you're here," she said, gesturing to the splitting maul.

If her face wasn't usually so still and reserved, he might not have noticed the hint of challenge in her expression. She didn't think he could do it.

"I'll take a turn," he said, not about to back down. "I don't have any gloves, though."

"My grandfather's are on the shelf over the radio in the garage. They'll fit you."

Of course she still had her grandfather's gloves. The only way he'd get out of splitting wood would be to admit he couldn't do it, and there was no chance of that happening. "I'll be right back."

He found the gloves—thick suede softened by age and

use—and pulled them on. They were slightly snug over the knuckles, but they'd work. For a while, anyway. He wasn't sure how many swings of that maul he had in him, so ill-fitting gloves could help him save face if he had to quit.

When he got back to the chopping block, she walked over to the woodpile. After rolling a good-sized log free, she tipped it up on its end to serve as a seat and then took her gloves off. She set her water bottle next to the gloves, but then she looked back at him, frowning. "You do know how to do this, right?"

He wondered if he played dumb whether she'd stand behind him—chest pressed to his back and arms around him—to correct his form as though it were his golf swing. But there was a limit to how much pride he was willing to sacrifice for her touch.

"I've got this." When he winked, she rolled her eyes and sat down on her log to watch.

"You have your phone, though, right?" he called to her. "Just in case you have to call 911?"

When her eyes widened and she looked like she was going to get up, he laughed. "I'm kidding."

He hoped. Once she was comfortable on the log, she crossed her arms and looked at him expectantly. The amusement behind her masked expression—her certainty that he was about to fail spectacularly at splitting one piece of wood into two pieces of wood—annoyed him.

Since he was about to get sweaty, Alex grabbed the bottom of his T-shirt and pulled it up over his head. After tossing it onto the grass, he picked up the splitting maul and braced himself.

A man could give a girl a little warning. Gretchen was glad Alex didn't glance her way after tossing his shirt aside, because there was a very real possibility her mouth was hanging open.

Whatever he'd done to get in shape after his college days had been very effective, because he wasn't a man who looked in need of dietary discipline. He didn't have the ripped and rippled look of those guys on the fitness magazine covers, but that didn't really float Gretchen's boat, anyway.

Alex was just solid. He was toned and had some muscle definition, but he still looked like he'd be comfortable to cuddle on the couch with. She felt a ridiculous urge to run her hands over that broad chest, with its light sprinkle of dark hair, and then out over those shoulders.

Funny, she hadn't known she even had a thing for shoulders until Alex showed up.

While his arms were slightly darker, his skin was tanned enough so that she knew going shirtless wasn't something he was doing just to show off for her. And his jeans hugged his butt and thighs just enough to show off the fact that his bottom half was in as good a shape as his top half.

Because she didn't want to get caught staring, Gretchen picked up her water bottle and took a sip. She might want to ration it, though, unless she somehow became immune to the sight of his body and cooled off. Too much of this view and she might be pouring it over her head.

When he hefted the maul and began swinging it up and

over, she held her breath, not knowing if it was the mouth-watering effect the motion had on his muscles or the fact that she was worried about his lack of experience.

When the log split cleanly in half, she let out the breath. And because she'd watched it fall, she wasn't ogling his abs when he turned to give her a triumphant look. He looked so proud of himself, she couldn't help but smile.

"Nice," she said. "You should be able to do half a cord without breaking a sweat."

He laughed out loud while bending to pick up one of the halves. "Not a chance. But I'll split for a while if you stack."

It was better than sitting on a log mooning over him. She pulled her gloves back on, and as he split the logs, she picked up the pieces and stacked them in the shed. It definitely wasn't his first time splitting wood, but she had no doubt he was going to feel it in the morning.

He didn't seem to mind working in comfortable silence, which suited Gretchen just fine. Or maybe he couldn't spare the oxygen to talk. Either way, they worked for almost an hour before she noticed signs of fatigue in him. Tired muscles could get him hurt.

She was about to tell him it was time to wrap it up when the screen door slammed. It only took a few seconds for Cocoa to find them and, of course, she made a beeline straight for Alex. The dog had no sense of loyalty whatsoever.

Alex leaned the maul against the block and tugged the gloves off so he could ruffle the dog's fur. "Saved by man's best friend."

"Cocoa comes out and joins me when Gram starts cooking," Gretchen said, pulling off her own gloves. "Time to start picking up, anyway. If you take the maul and the gloves back to the garage, I'll make sure the chickens and the horses have water."

"Sounds like a deal." When he reached for his T-shirt, though, Cocoa grabbed it and took off toward the house.

"Cocoa!" Gretchen yelled, but the dog didn't even slow down.

"I think that's the fastest I've ever seen her move."

"She *is* lazy, but when she's in a puppy kind of mood, her energy level is exhausting."

"The chickens must love her."

Gretchen blew out a breath and shook her head. "She kept trying to get in the fence at first, but she finally caught on. Now she mostly ignores them, since they're pretty far back behind the garage."

"And you keep them fenced?"

"Yeah. We don't like the furry woodland creatures getting to them, if you know what I mean. Plus, it's kind of a secret, but Gram hates chickens. She's afraid of them, though she won't admit to that part."

Alex's eyebrow arched. "Really? Tough affliction for a farmer's wife."

"Gramps always said she was a wife worth tending to the chickens himself for." She felt the familiar bittersweet pang—sorrow at his loss, but grateful for the happy memories of him.

"I'm sorry I didn't know your grandfather. I mean, I knew who he was, but I didn't really know him."

She shrugged. "You were ahead of me in school, and I tended to stick close to the farm. We ran with different crowds. Do you want me to go after your shirt?"

"Nah." He shrugged, drawing her attention to his amazing

shoulders. As if she hadn't already memorized them. "I'll grab another before dinner and find that one at some point. She won't dig a hole and bury it, will she?"

That made her laugh. "No. It's already in her bed, tucked down between the cushion and the wall so you can't see it."

It didn't take her long to give the chickens and the horses fresh water, but Alex still beat her into the house. She stepped into the kitchen just in time to watch his broad back disappear into the living room, probably in search of his shirt.

Gram beckoned her to the stove and dropped her voice to a conspiratorial whisper. "I don't care how old I am. It does a woman good to see a body like that shirtless."

Gretchen was glad she was standing slightly behind Gram, because she might have blushed. "Because your dog ran off with his shirt."

"I should give her a treat."

"You're so bad." Gretchen leaned over the stove to peer into the pot and then kissed Gram's cheek. "It was hot today. Do I have time to grab a quick shower before supper?"

"The sauce is simmering and I haven't put the pasta in yet. I'll wait and cook that when I hear the water shut off."

"I'll be quick."

Alex had disappeared, so Gretchen assumed he'd gone to his room to clean up for dinner. She hoped he wasn't in the shower, because the hot water heater could handle only one at a time.

After a quick round of tug-of-war with Cocoa, Gretchen ran up the stairs, using her fingers to unravel her braid as she went. She paused briefly outside Alex's door but didn't hear the shower running, thank goodness. After stopping in her room to grab a change of clothes, she went into her and Gram's bathroom and locked the door.

Gram had cleaned in there during the day, and Gretchen had to rummage around for the wide-toothed comb she used on her hair. She finally found it in the second drawer, but when she lifted it out, she saw it had been sitting on top of the small basket Gram kept her makeup in.

On a silly whim, she dug through it until she found a black lipstick tube with a sticker labeled *Cherry Hot Pants* on the bottom. Pulling the cap off, she twisted the bottom a little and smiled. It was definitely red. And a very-special-occasion lipstick, based on how little it had been used.

She leaned closer to the mirror and frowned at her reflection. First she made a kissy face, but she didn't think the lipstick would go on smoothly that way. So she parted her lips and slowly painted them. Then she smacked them together, because she'd seen that on television, before standing back to look at herself.

She looked like a little girl who'd gotten into her mother's makeup basket. While she'd managed not to smear the Cherry Hot Pants around her mouth, it definitely didn't have the polished look that Jen's lipstick always had.

Gram had been right, though, about the red looking good with her coloring. With her dark hair, the color made the bow of her mouth stand out. If she knew how to put some bounce in her hair and give herself smoky eye makeup, she could look like a sexy, retro pinup girl. But, considering how she'd done with the tube of Cherry Hot Pants, she wasn't going anywhere near her eyeballs with a mascara wand.

Sighing, she plucked a tissue out of the box and wiped at her lips.

Giving herself a makeover might change her face, but it wasn't going to change who she was. And not only did she like who she was, she didn't really give a damn if Alex Murphy *didn't*.

Gretchen knew all about the differences between people who stuck and people who didn't stick, and she wasn't going to open herself up to somebody just passing through.

05

On Saturday morning, Alex was at the practice field bright and early to scope out vantage points, the sun's angle and how the shadows were falling. Coach was there even earlier, talking to his assistant coaches, who were sitting on the bleachers with travel mugs of coffee when Alex arrived.

He didn't really know any of the other guys. Often teachers willing to give the time and energy, the coaching support staff tended to come and go, and there had been some turnover at the high school. But Coach was practically an institution, and none of them even wanted to try to imagine what would happen to Eagles football when he retired.

Because he'd arrived so early, Alex was ready when the first kids showed up on the sidelines. Hunter Cass, the running back, jogged out to the center of the field with his arms up and his voice raised in some kind of triumphant yell. Alex fired off shots at will. He had plenty of memory in the camera and he could pick through the results later, on his laptop.

He recognized a couple of the other boys from Eagles Fest. PJ, the cornerback who never shut up. And Ronnie, whom Alex had spent some quality time with thanks to the kid having the sense of direction of a broken compass. And he'd probably get to know more of them in the weeks to come.

Spirits were high. For quite a few of the boys, the tryouts were merely a formality. It was a small school, and the core of the team tended to move on to the new year intact, other than freshmen coming in and seniors going out. But there was a heightened sense of celebration with the start of this season simply because it had come so close to not happening.

There was a lull in the action when Coach sat them down and gave them a pep talk before explaining how the process would go. Alex caught a few of the freshmen, their nervousness and eager anticipation coming through for the camera. And he got a few good shots of Coach doing what he did best—laying out his expectations and inspiring young men to meet them.

Over the course of the morning, he took countless shots of the players being put through their paces. Even through the lens of his camera, he could recognize some of the hallmarks of a Walt McDonnell–coached team. There was no sabotaging to protect their spots on the roster. No gloating. No throwing insults at those who weren't quite up to the varsity level yet.

Every boy on that field was dedicated to making the

entire team the best it could be, and there were a couple of times Alex almost got choked up watching them. He knew better than almost anybody what being a part of the Eagles meant, and it was so much more than simply playing a game or dating cheerleaders, though he'd done his share of that back in the day.

He was half hidden behind the bleachers, looking for action shots as the assistant coach working with the offense threw passes to potential wide receivers. Because the coach was testing them, they had to fully extend or dive for the balls, which made for good photography.

Just as he was about to fully depress the shutter button, a face appeared in front of the lens. "Photobomb!"

Even as his eyes and the camera refocused, Alex laughed. "Sanders, you asshole."

"That's a Pulitzer Prize shot right there. Don't delete it. And make sure you thank me in your speech."

Alex lowered the camera, letting it dangle from the strap around his neck so he could shake Chase's hand. "Good to see you. Not necessarily in extreme close-up, but still good to see you."

"I couldn't believe it when I heard you were coming back to Stewart Mills. I mean, I know why *I* came back. There's only one Kelly McDonnell, but there's a lot of world out there for you to photograph."

"Yeah, there is, and I've photographed a lot of it. Being back here last month just felt right somehow and I didn't feel like the story was done. It's hard to explain."

"I get it." Chase looked over the field, where the coaches were signaling for a break. "You had lunch yet? We can walk to O'Rourke's from here."

O'Rourke's wasn't the only place in town to eat, but it was one of the best, and Alex wasn't starving—thanks to Ida's breakfast—but he could eat. "That sounds like one hell of a good plan."

Cassandra Jones showed them to their booth personally, making small talk along the way. She and her husband, Don, had owned the restaurant for years, but her maiden name was slapped on the business after a town-wide debate on where the apostrophe would go made Cass forgo the Jones just for the sake of getting the sign made.

Once they'd ordered—and Chase had thoroughly mocked Alex's choice of a salad with grilled chicken—Alex stuck a straw in his tall glass of iced tea and drained a quarter of it.

"How are things going?" Chase asked. "Getting some good stuff?"

"I just started really. I took some photos of the town, but tryouts starting this morning kind of kicks everything off. And I'll have to start talking to people pretty soon, I guess."

"You guess? Your enthusiasm is overwhelming."

Alex shrugged. "The talking isn't my favorite part of the job. I prefer being behind the camera. And I underestimated how much the fact that I'm from here would change things. Even though impartiality isn't a big deal, since I'm not here in a journalistic capacity, I'm not used to having my own personal history all tangled up in my subject matter."

"Are you rethinking the project?"

"No, I'll finish the story. I'm still not sure if it'll be a book or just a long photo essay, but I knew going into it I wouldn't make that decision until later. Mostly I just wanted a break from the travel and to see how things are going here."

"How about the farm? Is it weird, staying there?"

Weird was an interesting word, but he thought he knew what Chase was getting at. "Gretchen's younger than us, plus she ran with a different crowd, so I don't remember her well. It's almost like being strangers, and I'm used to boarding with people I don't know. But it would probably be weird if we'd been friends in high school, I guess."

"So . . ." Chase let the words trail off, obviously hoping his raised eyebrow would fill in the rest for him.

"So?"

"So Gretchen's not hard on the eyes. Your eyes. Not mine. I only have eyes for Kelly, of course."

Alex chuckled. Chase wasn't lying. He'd had it bad for Coach's daughter pretty much from the moment he'd rolled into town for the Eagles Fest fund-raiser. "Yes, Gretchen is attractive. I wish she'd give me permission to photograph her."

"That's not really the direction I was going in, but okay."

"I know exactly what direction you were going in, and that's a wrong turn. She's not the kind of woman you screw around with—especially while living with her—and then tip your hat to as you ride off into the sunset."

"I don't know about that. Kelly said she rarely gets away from the farm for more than a few hours and she doesn't date much. Having you under the same roof on a temporary basis might be just the thing she needs. Is she giving you any signals?"

"I don't know." It was hard to tell with Gretchen.

Sometimes he thought she was interested, and then other times she was so closed off to him he wasn't sure she even liked him very much. "I don't want things to get messy when, as you said, I'm living under her roof."

Chase shook his head. "Your loss, man."

"You're not going to turn into one of those guys who gets married and then tries to get his friends all married off so he's not the only one, are you?"

"Maybe." Chase grinned. "I'm not married yet, but I'm close enough to know I want all my friends to get to feel the way I do right now."

Alex rolled his eyes at the cheesy words that sounded like dialogue straight out of some romantic movie, but he didn't bother to point out he'd tried the marriage thing once and it hadn't worked out. His lifestyle wasn't conducive to a long-term relationship, and changing that lifestyle would put one hell of a dent in his ability to sustain his career.

But he didn't go into that. It would be a douche-bag move to bring up his divorce when Chase was so damn happy to be talking about marriage. So he took a sip of his drink and then shrugged. "Maybe someday."

"Enough relationship crap. Let's talk football. While you were watching through that lens, did anybody really stand out this morning?"

When Cocoa turned a couple of joyful circles with her tongue hanging out before heading for the back door, Gretchen knew Alex was home. The dog recognized the sound of his Jeep and, naturally, she could hear it before her or Gram.

Not quite a week and the dog already considered Alex a part of the family, Gretchen mused as she saved the budget file she'd been working on and pushed away from the computer desk. She hated budgets and computers and being inside, but she forced herself to do it once a week anyway and used self-bribery if necessary. Tonight she was going to watch a favorite action movie for what was probably the twentieth time, but only if she got the stupid budget done.

Rubbing the back of her neck, she walked into the kitchen just in time to see Cocoa's tail disappear out of the screen door she'd pushed open. "Alex is back."

Gram slid on a mitt and opened the oven door. "I figured he must be home when Cocoa went jogging through."

Frowning, Gretchen pulled three napkins out of the rack and started setting the table. As she added the silverware and plates, she wondered what—if anything—it meant that it bugged her how Gram used the word *home* when it came to Alex. At the end of the day, Gretchen would say he was *back*, while her grandmother said he was home.

It was a subtle difference, maybe, but she preferred the separation. It was hard enough, with Gram and Cocoa acting like he was the long-lost member of the family they'd been waiting for forever, to keep a line drawn in the sand between them. Landlord. Tenant. It should be easy enough to stay on her own side of the line.

But when Alex walked through the door and his gaze sought hers immediately, she felt as if his smile was a wave washing away the line she'd so carefully drawn. "Hey, Gretchen. Ida."

"You have perfect timing," Gram said, pulling a meat

loaf out of the oven. "That just needs to sit for a few minutes and then I'll slice it up."

"It smells delicious. Just give me a few seconds and I'll make up a salad."

Once he'd gone, Cocoa on his heels, Gretchen went to the fridge and started pulling out the salad fixings. She'd start on the salad to save time. Alex had gone grocery shopping several days before and stocked the fridge with fruits and vegetables. Since then, they'd gotten in the habit of having salad with their supper.

Gretchen hadn't missed his little tricks for cutting back on Gram's food without having to say something that might hurt her feelings or make her feel as if she needed to change the way she cooked. For instance, he claimed it saved on hand-washing dishes if he just put his salad right on his dinner plate, but Gretchen saw the way he used the mound of lettuce and various veggies to minimize the amount of space for the rest of the meal. And he always ate the first helping of salad and took seconds before starting on Gram's food.

It was sweet, she thought as she sliced a cucumber. He must have recognized how important feeding her family—and her tenant—was to Gram, so he went out of his way to find a way to balance his eating habits with her cooking habits.

By the time Alex walked back into the kitchen, the salad was almost done and Gretchen had worked herself into feeling a serious case of the warm and fuzzies for him. It made her smile at him and initiate the conversation for once.

"How did tryouts go? Did you get some good pictures?" she asked, setting the big wooden salad bowl in the middle of the table.

"I did. And the tryouts were great. The energy level's ramped up because they're more excited than usual to get back to football, and the emotion really comes through in pictures. It was a really good day."

Gretchen felt the warm glow of pride and satisfaction. The whole town had pulled together to save Eagles football, but it was she and Kelly and Jen who had led the committee. Kelly had come up with the fund-raiser idea and bringing the guys from the first championship team home for alumni events, but where one of them went, they all went together. Gretchen hadn't been as much help to Kelly as Jen, who spent countless hours on the Internet looking up and applying for grants and donations, but she'd done her part.

Hearing that the team still felt good about what they'd done and appreciated it made the work all the more satisfying. It had started as Kelly trying to save the team that meant everything to her dad and giving the boys a continued reason to stay out of trouble, but in the end it had been a massive community effort that Gretchen was proud to have been a part of.

"Oh, and Chase showed up," Alex continued. He went to the fridge to get the iced tea pitcher. "We went to lunch and caught up since Kelly had to cover Dylan's shift for a few hours."

"It's a bummer she had to go in. I know she was excited for Chase to come home for the weekend."

"If she's as lovestruck as he seems, I'm not surprised."

Gretchen laughed. "She is."

They finished setting the table, dancing around each other in the kitchen in a way that already felt strangely familiar. After only a few days, they'd established something of a routine and it was quickly heading toward being comfortable.

They made small talk during dinner. As usual, Gram and Alex carried most of the conversation, but Gretchen found herself joining in more often than she usually would. They talked about the kids on the team, mostly, and Alex talked a little about how much Coach had meant to him back when he was that age.

There were things she'd always known about him, even if she couldn't remember exactly when or how she learned them. His dad had died when he was very young. His mom had remarried a guy Alex didn't get along with very well, and then she'd given him two half sisters the stepdad spoiled with affection. He'd gotten in a lot of trouble before he joined the football team, though. She remembered that much.

When they were done, they all worked together to clean up. Gretchen had stopped protesting that Alex was paying extra to have his meals provided, which meant he shouldn't have to help with the dishes. He wasn't the kind of man who'd sit around and watch others work while he did nothing, especially if the people doing the work were women.

She liked that about him. It was one of the many things she liked about him, actually ranking right up there with his smile and his sense of humor and the way he treated Cocoa. She shifted a little away from him as he slid the dish towel through its plastic loop. She also liked the way he smelled and his height and his shoulders and . . .

"I need to sit my butt down at the computer some more," she said rather abruptly, in an effort to derail her train of thought. "But first, I'm going to go check on the horses.

Cinnamon's been kicking at her stall and I need to keep an eye on the door. Make sure she's not weakening the structure. If I can't figure out why she's agitated, I'll have to call Beverly."

Beverly Jacobson owned the horses, and Gretchen never made any assumptions when it came to their care. She figured Cinnamon was probably bored or there was a particularly persistent fly bothering her, but she couldn't be sure. Gretchen gave the Jacobson family frequent updates by email, but if she thought there might be a problem, she called Beverly right away.

"Maybe she's bored," Gram suggested.

"I don't know. I follow Beverly's instructions on exercising them and stuff. Maybe she misses them and wants to go for a ride."

"Do you two ladies ride?" Alex asked.

"Not me," Gram said. "I got thrown as a kid and after I hit the ground, the damn beast kicked me in the shoulder. I'm not a fan of horses."

"I ride well enough to take them for short trips out, but Beverly prefers they not become too accustomed to anybody else's riding style." She shrugged. "She's got some hang-ups when it comes to her horses, but she pays us well to take care of them, so I just do what the lady says."

"You want some help? Checking out her stall, I mean."

No, she didn't really want to be alone in the barn with him. Feeling too comfortable with him was a bad idea, because then she might be tempted to do something really stupid, like touch him. "No thanks. It won't take me long."

He looked at her for a few seemingly endless seconds, until she had to fight to keep from squirming. It was as though he knew what she was thinking, and wanted to call her on it. "Okay. Let me know if you change your mind."

Gretchen nodded and went to shove her feet into her boots. She didn't have time to wonder what Alex Murphy was thinking about. She had to get the horses taken care of and the bookkeeping done if she was going to reward herself with watching her movie.

Alex deleted the last three sentences he'd written and then stared at the blinking cursor. He was a storyteller at heart. It just happened that telling those stories through photographs came more naturally to him than telling them with words. He could usually put together a compelling piece, though, and frustration made him tap his fingers next to the touch pad.

Rather than keep trying to force general background information on Stewart Mills into interesting and cohesive paragraphs, he saved the file and closed the laptop. He should probably take another look at the photos he'd been snapping. At the end of each day, he did a quick run-through, discarding the hundreds that weren't quite right. But then— after a cooling-off period—he'd do another pass, magnifying each photo to analyze the detail and composition. Then he'd sort them between two folders—one for possible inclusion, depending on how long the project turned out to be, and one for shots that spoke to him on an emotional level and would almost certainly be used.

Tonight, though, he was restless. Tired of being in his room—even though it had been only a couple of hours—and tired of being wrapped up in his own head, he stood and put the computer on top of the dresser. Then he stretched his arms up over his head, twisting at the waist one way and then the other to ease the kink in his back.

Since he hadn't heard the floor creak or the click of Cocoa's nails, he knew Ida hadn't gone to bed yet. He'd go downstairs and visit for a while, he decided, and maybe grab himself a snack.

Gretchen had been working at the computer when he went upstairs, and he could tell by her posture she didn't enjoy whatever she was doing. She'd been hunched over the keyboard, her shoulders tense as she stared at the screen and occasionally poked at it.

She wasn't at the desk when he came downstairs, though. Instead, she was on the couch with her feet up on the coffee table and Cocoa's head on her lap. Gretchen was idly scratching the dog's belly while Ida sat in her rocker, knitting and watching the television.

"Bourne, huh?" he asked when he reached the bottom of the stairs, and all three of them turned to look at him.

"Gretchen knows every line of this movie by heart," Ida said, shaking her head. "Heck, I think even Cocoa knows every line of this movie."

"I like a woman who likes Jason Bourne." He said it playfully, but he didn't miss the way Gretchen's cheeks flushed as she yanked her gaze back to the TV screen.

"Sit down, then, and watch it," Ida said. "I'll be going upstairs soon, so you can keep Gretchen company."

That didn't sound like a bad way to spend the evening. He sat on the open end of the couch and chuckled when

Cocoa stretched her body out so her back paws were touching his thigh. She wasn't willing to take her head off of Gretchen's lap, but she wanted to give him some love, too.

"I'm never going to get her upstairs with me," Ida said, giving the dog an affectionate glance before she resumed her knitting.

Alex leaned his head back against the sofa and looked at the television screen. He liked their couch a lot. Maybe it was because Gretchen was tall, as her grandfather had been, but it had a high back on it. Too often sofa cushions stopped just below his shoulders and he couldn't relax his neck.

He'd seen the Bourne movies often enough that he had no trouble dropping into this one despite its being almost halfway over, and he decided immediately that closing up his laptop had been the right idea.

He'd come back to Stewart Mills, in part, to fight that feeling of burning out. Relaxing with a good movie and good company was exactly what he was *supposed* to be doing, he reminded himself.

Ida made it only another fifteen minutes before she yawned and stood up. "I'm going to head up now, and maybe knit in bed for a little while. Come on, Cocoa. Time to go outside."

The dog pretended she didn't hear her, but Alex could tell by the way Cocoa pushed against him with her feet that she was awake and knew it was bedtime. When Ida said her name again, she whimpered a little and tried to burrow her head under Gretchen's thigh.

"I'll bring her up with me, Gram." Gretchen stroked her chocolate-colored fur. "I'll put her outside when the movie's over and then let her into your room when I go up to bed."

"She's turning into a spoiled brat," Ida said, but she crossed over to give Cocoa a quick belly rub. The Lab held up her paw for a good-night high five. "Good night, all."

As soon as Ida went up the stairs alone, Cocoa heaved a contented sigh and stretched out again. Alex idly stroked her side and hip while watching a particularly well-done car chase scene play out across the television screen. He could get used to this.

During a lull in the action, Gretchen managed to get herself out from under Cocoa's head and went to the kitchen. A few minutes later, she returned with a couple of peanut butter cookies for herself and a small treat for Cocoa. And she handed him a small cluster of the seedless green grapes he liked to snack on. They were hydrating, a little sweet and just satisfying enough to keep him from snacking on other things. Like peanut butter cookies.

"Thanks," he said, taking the grapes from her and popping one into his mouth.

After a minute, he glanced over just in time to see Gretchen's tongue flick out and catch a crumb from her lip. He told himself the pang of yearning that hit him was nothing but baked goods envy, but he suspected they could switch food and he'd still want to watch her mouth.

Once he'd satisfied the urge to snack—which was the only urge he had any intention of satisfying in the near future—he put the branch of empty stems on the side table and rested his head against the couch again. He was tired, but he knew the rest of the movie was action-packed enough to keep him awake, no matter how many times he'd seen it. He was afraid if he fell asleep and started snoring, Gretchen might leave him there and he'd wake up at three in the morning, stiff and barely able to move.

He also didn't want to sleep right now, because he was enjoying himself too much. Sure, he'd seen the movie before. And Gretchen wasn't one for a lot of conversation. But the silence was companionable, not awkward, and every once in a while she'd make a comment about an action sequence or chuckle at an improbable stunt. It was nice, hanging out together with the dog between them.

He rubbed Cocoa's side, loving the feel of her fur under his hand. She was snoring a little, which amused him, and every so often her foot would twitch against his thigh.

They were heading into the big action finale when his fingers and Gretchen's brushed together at the middle of Cocoa's back. She jerked her hand away, which startled Cocoa. The Lab sat up and looked around, as if searching for whatever had disturbed her, and then turned to Alex.

"Sorry, girl," he said. "Maybe just one back rub at a time."

Gretchen smiled as Cocoa sighed and resumed her former position, but Alex noticed she concentrated on scratching behind the dog's ears, and her hand didn't wander past Cocoa's neck again.

When the movie was over, Gretchen went outside with Cocoa while Alex threw away his grape stems and poured himself a glass of water. He sipped it slowly, watching the dog run around the backyard while Gretchen made exaggerated gestures he assumed translated to *Just pee already, so we can go to bed*.

When they finally came in, Gretchen looked slightly

surprised to see him, as if she'd expected him to be upstairs already. After locking the door, she kicked her shoes off. "We're going upstairs, so . . . good night."

"Good night." Cocoa trotted over to him for a high five. "See you bright and early in the morning."

"Watch it. You're starting to sound like a farm boy."

He snorted. "That's not likely."

She gave him a tight smile and then called the dog to her. Alex watched them leave and then dumped the rest of the water down the drain. He might be enjoying his time at the Walker farm, but he didn't have it in him to be a farm boy. A man could only take so many pictures of horses and a tractor.

06

On Wednesday, Gretchen slid into the booth next to Kelly and across from Jen with a happy sigh of anticipation. It wasn't often all three of them were free to meet for a nice meal, so when Kelly had texted them about lunch at O'Rourke's, she hadn't even hesitated before texting back that she'd be there.

"I've been thinking about O'Rourke's cheeseburgers since I got your text," she said before taking a sip of the soda they'd ordered for her.

"I love their burgers," Kelly agreed. "Chase had one the other day and, when he told me about it, the craving kicked in."

"Craving?" Jen raised an eyebrow.

"Not *that* kind of craving. You know we're not even thinking about a family until he's done in New Jersey. I've just desperately wanted a burger since he told me *he* had one. He said Alex had a salad, which I don't get at all. Who goes to a restaurant and has nothing but a salad?"

"I can have a salad at home," Jen agreed.

Gretchen just unrolled her silverware from her napkin and said nothing. Alex probably didn't consider his weight gain and subsequent loss some kind of deep, dark secret, but it was still his business to share or not. And she didn't really want her friends thinking they were hanging around having heart-to-heart discussions.

Jen leaned toward her, squinting a little in the subdued lighting. "Are you getting enough sleep?"

No, she wasn't, but she forced a casual laugh. "Thanks a lot."

"What's keeping you up late, huh?" Kelly actually nudged her in the ribs with her elbow.

They couldn't possibly think she was sleeping with Alex. But, judging by the way they were both looking at her so expectantly, that's exactly what they appeared to be thinking. And they wanted details.

Even if she were willing to spill, the only detail she had was the fact that their hands had accidentally touched while petting the dog, and she'd jerked away from him like he had the plague. Not one of her finer moments, and certainly not one she particularly cared to share.

Gretchen got a short reprieve from answering while they ordered their lunches, and she jumped in with a new topic as soon as their server walked away. "Alex said he's gotten some great photos of the team. Said Coach has a good crop of kids to work with."

"Alex said, huh?" Jen smiled. "Does he have anything to do with why you're not getting enough sleep?"

She forced herself to remain expressionless. "Since Alex is currently living in my house, we've had plenty of opportunity to talk about the football team during daylight hours."

"Just seems funny we were talking about you not sleeping and he was the next person you mentioned."

"*You* were talking about me not sleeping. *I* was talking about the football team. Kelly's dad is the coach. Two plus two, Miss Cooper." They both just looked at her and waited. "Fine. He's attractive. I haven't . . . dated, in a while. There might be a little insomnia and they might be connected."

"Oh, bummer." Kelly sighed. "I was hoping you weren't sleeping because you were *with* him, not because you're *not* with him."

"I'm not going to be with him, either," Gretchen said vehemently. "It would be way too awkward with him living in the house. He and Gram are already buddies and Cocoa thinks he's her human Prince Charming on two legs. If things were anything more than landlord and tenant between us, it could get messy."

"Some itches just have to be scratched," Jen said.

Gretchen wanted to ask her friend when the last time was that she'd practiced that particular bit of preaching, but she remembered just in time that Jen had had sex with Sam Leavitt while he was home for Eagles Fest, and Jen did *not* want to talk about that. They were all supposed to pretend it never happened.

The server brought their plates, and after she walked away, Gretchen dumped a huge puddle of ketchup next to her fries. "Once Alex is gone, I might make more of an effort to get out once in a while. I think the guy at the auto parts store is interested, but he's afraid to make a move."

"Because you're putting off a *stay away* signal, maybe?" Jen posed it as a question, but Gretchen knew it wasn't meant that way.

Kelly let her soda cup down with a thump. "Gretchen, you need to let a guy open your pickle jar once in a while."

Gretchen gave her a sideways look. "Is that what the kids are calling it these days? Because, trust me, I wouldn't *mind* a guy opening my pickle jar once in a while."

"There's an electric can opener joke in there somewhere," Jen said.

Kelly rolled her eyes. "I mean you need to *literally* let a guy open your pickle jar."

"I don't get it." Gretchen used her straw to stir the ice in her drink. "That actually made more sense as a really bad euphemism for sex."

"You're so strong and capable that guys probably feel useless around you."

"So I should pretend to be so weak that I can't open a jar of pickles just so he can feel strong and manly?" Gretchen snorted. "Does Chase open your pickles?"

"No." Kelly sighed. "The last time I gave him a jar of pickles to open, he couldn't do it and he didn't want to admit it, so he tried knocking the lid against the counter to break the seal. He broke the seal *and* the jar, and we were finding sticky spots on the floor for three days. And the apartment smelled like a deli."

"I never buy pickles," Jen said, stealing a fry from Kelly's plate. "Now I know what to tell my mom when she asks why I'm still single."

Gretchen laughed. "Maybe you need to wander around town with a jar of pickles until some strong, handsome man opens it for you and proves he's your true love. Like Cinderella's slipper, only with pickles."

"You guys are idiots," Kelly muttered. "Look, I'm a police officer. That can be intimidating to some men, in the same way Gretchen can be intimidating. It's not about being weak. I think it's just nice to show a softer side once in a while, and let him flex his biceps."

"First Gram tries to pawn her Cherry Hot Pants lipstick off on me and now this. It's like getting relationship advice from 1956."

"That shade of lipstick sounds like it would be great with your coloring," Kelly said.

Gretchen shoved a fry in her mouth so she had an excuse not to respond. She certainly wasn't going to tell them she'd been playing with her grandmother's makeup basket, best friends or not. They'd have her at Jen's house, hot rollers in her hair and goop on her face, before she'd even finished chewing her lunch.

"We should make a day trip to the mall for makeovers," Jen said. "Get our hair done. Let the women at the makeup counter practice on us. It would be fun."

To Gretchen, it sounded about as much fun as scraping chicken shit off the bottom of her boots, but Kelly got excited. That worked, since it meant Gretchen could sit back and relax—and not talk about Alex—while the other two talked about mascara and trying on shoes and all sorts of mall-related things.

As she tuned them out and dredged a fry through ketchup, an old memory resurfaced in Gretchen's mind. She wasn't sure how old she'd been, but she hadn't been with her grandparents very long. Sitting at the kitchen table, she'd watched their marital banter with a mixture of awe and confusion. Her parents had rarely spoken to each other with affection or teasing in their voices.

Gram had handed Gramps a jar of preserves and asked him to open it for her. Her grandfather had made a big deal out of breaking the seal, and Gram had given him a flirty smile and run her hand up his arm before taking the jar back. Then Gramps had slapped Gram on the butt and made her giggle.

Maybe there was something to the pickle jar theory, after all.

After spending several hours taking background shots of the town square and the old covered bridge, Alex was packing his gear in the back of the Jeep when he heard footsteps in the loose gravel behind him. He turned and then almost took a step backward when he saw that it was Edna Beecher.

She was a tiny scrap of a woman, but fierce. And very scary. And the worst part of it was, she'd been ancient for as long as he could remember, so being rude and getting in the Jeep to drive away wasn't an option. He tried his damnedest to respect his elders, even the Wicked Witch of Stewart Mills.

"Hi, Miss Beecher."

"I've got my eye on you, young man," she said, glaring as if he'd actually done something wrong. "And so does the FBI."

If he hadn't been raised in town, that might have set off some alarm bells. Edna had been ratting out her fellow citizens to the FBI since before he was born, though, so he was pretty sure the only people who cared were the poor agents who had to field the nuisance calls. "I'll keep that in mind should I decide to change career paths to something more criminal."

"More criminal than stalking? And taking pictures of young people?"

The sense of mild amusement with which he'd been regarding Edna evaporated instantly. "What exactly did you tell them?"

Her mouth tightened and she narrowed her eyes in a squinty way that reminded him of the old westerns his stepfather liked. Facing down the villain in the street at high noon. "I told them you're suspicious. And that you're taking photographs of the young boys."

Forcing himself to stay calm, he kept his voice level. "And did you also happen to mention to the FBI that it's my job to take photographs?"

"You were skulking."

"Miss Beecher, I *never* skulk. There are valid reasons, however, for a photographer to try to stay on the fringes and mostly out of sight. The most important reason being so that I don't distract the people I'm photographing from what they're doing."

"You can put whatever fancy spin on it you want, young man. I'm watching you. And so are they."

She turned and walked away, leaving him staring after her and feeling as though he'd just been run over by a truck. Did she have any idea of the destruction that kind of accusation could cause in his life?

After considering his options, he got into his Jeep and drove directly to the police station. Maybe they'd all been doing their community a disservice by humoring the woman for so many years, or maybe he was simply the first person with something to lose by her ridiculous accusation. Either way, he wasn't going to smile and pat her on the head.

As luck would have it, Kelly was pouring herself a coffee when he walked through the front door. Stewart Mills was in the process of planning a remodel to secure the entryway, requiring everybody who visited to be buzzed in, but for now he was free to walk right over to her.

"Hey, Alex."

"Good afternoon, Officer McDonnell." It was still hard to believe Coach's daughter had grown up to be a cop, so they had a lot of fun calling her that during Eagles Fest. Especially the night she'd caught them breaking into the high school to look at their trophy. His memory of the night was a little hazy, but he liked to think that was Chase's idea.

Kelly tilted her head, and then laughed. "That sounds very official."

"Actually, I *am* here on police business."

"Then come on over to my desk and sit down. Unless you'd rather talk to somebody else. I have a personal relationship with a friend of yours, so no hard feelings if you'd rather talk to Dylan—uh, Officer Clark. Or even the chief."

"You'll do fine." He followed her to her desk and then sat on the metal visitor's chair across from her. "Edna Beecher told the FBI I'm skulking around suspiciously, taking pictures of young boys."

Kelly tried to hide her amusement, but the corners of her mouth gave her away. "Nobody takes Edna seriously, even—or maybe *especially*—the FBI. You know that."

"I just don't want rumors I'm stalking teen boys with

my camera going around the Internet, you know? I have a professional reputation. I'm on a scholarship committee and several award panels."

"If it makes you feel any better, we did get a phone call from them almost immediately, since there are kids involved. I talked to the agent myself and that's the end of it. I promise."

"Kelly, with the way social media is nowadays, if I get tarred with that brush, I may never totally shake it."

"I understand that. Edna limits her interaction to the FBI. I know for a fact she thinks the Internet is run by the Communists trying to plant subliminal messages in our brains and won't go near it. And I personally *know* the FBI special agent I spoke to. She'll make a note in Edna's file and forget it. Because I vouched for you, she probably won't even do a Google search, never mind dig around. This is a dead end."

He still wasn't thrilled about it, but he didn't really have any choice but to trust Kelly. And there was nothing else he could do, anyway. "Thank you. And the Communists? She does know what year it is, right? Can you do some kind of mandatory psych testing on her?"

Kelly sighed. "She's a pain in the ass, but she's a pain in the ass of sound mind and body."

"How old is she, anyway?"

"I only know her birth year through official law enforcement documents, which means I can't tell you. Sorry." She grinned. "We should *all* hope to live so long, though."

"If you hear anything else about my alleged skulking, or if you get any kind of inquiry, I'd appreciate a heads-up. I know things can get messy for you, with people you know asking favors, but I'm going to ask it, anyway."

"Alex, if I think somebody might take a serious look at you, I'll tell you. But it's not going to happen."

He stood and shook her hand. It seemed a little weird, since she was Coach's daughter and engaged to a friend of his, but he'd come on official business and she was in uniform. "I appreciate it. I guess I'll head back to the farm and go through the photos I took today."

"Tell Gretchen I said hi. And Gram."

"I will."

He stopped for gas in town and had almost managed to shove the Edna Beecher incident out of his mind by the time he hit the turnoff for the farm. As he pulled up to the house, he slowed down because Cocoa was out and, though she wouldn't run in front of the Jeep, he needed to keep an eye on her. Sometimes her enthusiasm was stronger than her common sense.

Then he noticed the truck was up on jack stands, and Gretchen was in the process of shimmying out from under it. Leaving his stuff in the Jeep for the time being, Alex got out and was greeted by Cocoa, who acted as if he'd been gone for *years* and was afraid she'd never see him again. He crouched down to ruffle the fur around her neck and scratch her head. Then he gave her a high five and they walked around the Jeep to see what Gretchen was up to.

She was out from under the truck and brushing dirt off of her jeans. "Hi, Alex."

"What the hell are you up to now?" He'd swear she never just sat and relaxed, but was always doing something.

Gretchen frowned as if it was the stupidest question she'd ever heard. "I was changing the oil in the truck."

"Wouldn't it be easier to have Deck do it?"

"I don't see a lot of sense in paying somebody to do something I can do myself."

Of course she didn't. "I guess your grandfather taught you how to do pretty much everything around the farm, huh?"

"Yup."

He couldn't quite bring himself to ask outright about her parents, but he'd be lying if he said he wasn't very curious about her family. "So you probably stuck to home a lot, then. That explains why I don't have too many memories of you when we were young."

She gave him a guarded look. "What do you mean?"

"I don't remember a lot about elementary school, but I think I remember Kelly and Jen running around together. Not you, though. I do remember the three of you in high school, but I don't know if it's just that I saw Kelly more because of football and you were together a lot."

"I didn't live in Stewart Mills until halfway through fifth grade."

That surprised him. "Really? For some reason, I thought you were born here."

"I was."

He could tell he was heading into emotional territory for her by the way she made her face and voice totally emotionless. The more she felt, the less she gave away, and the more he wanted to know. "Did your parents move away after you were born?"

"Yup."

"And they moved back when you were in fifth grade?"

"That's when Stewart Mills became home, yes."

It took a few seconds for him to realize she hadn't answered the question exactly as he'd asked it. "I'd really like to hear about it. Not for my story, but totally off the record. Living with you two as I do, I can't help but be curious."

She stared at him for a few long seconds, and then she shrugged. "My dad hated the farm. He and Gramps didn't get along, so he dropped out his senior year of high school. Met my mom. They had me, and then took off. They both had some problems and drank a lot. They had trouble keeping jobs and we moved constantly. Evictions. Running from people they owed money to."

Her voice was so flat, he felt bad for pushing. "You don't have to tell me this, Gretchen. I shouldn't have asked."

Another shrug, this time just one shoulder. "It got really bad when I was about ten. They were fighting all the time and drinking and I think we were pretty much homeless. My mom used to take me to gas stations right before they were closing and it was time to throw away the nasty old steamed hot dogs and pizza slices. The people that worked there would give it to us for free. Then things got so bad, they decided to come here and hit up his parents for money."

He couldn't wrap his mind around it. The fact that there was worse than living on stale gas station food left him speechless, though he wouldn't have asked, anyway.

"I'd never met my grandparents. Gramps was quiet and just watched us, because that's how he was. But Gram cried and wrapped her arms around me." Gretchen paused, and then the wall cracked and her eyes shimmered with tears. "I think it was the first time I'd ever been hugged."

His heart ached for her. "Where are your parents now?"

"I have no idea. The farm was still doing pretty well financially back then and Gramps had just bought himself a new pickup. I remember it being bright red because it was the shiniest truck I'd ever seen, and I was afraid to touch it and leave fingerprints on the paint. Gram had six hundred dollars in cash tucked away and she gave it to them. Then Gramps signed that truck over to my dad, and my parents signed papers giving me to Gramps and Gram. When my parents left the lawyer's office, that was the last time I ever saw them."

Alex leaned back, trying to process that. She had a way of saying things so matter-of-factly it was impossible for a person to know how to respond. Should he offer sympathy for her having shitty parents? Knowing her, probably not. Then he remembered the framed photo on the desk. "Is that the truck in the picture in the living room?"

She smiled and nodded. "Yeah. When he passed away, Gram and I were going through pictures to find a few to put on display at the funeral home and we found that one. He's scowling at the camera because he hated having his picture taken and he didn't see why she was making a fuss about a truck. But it was the first new vehicle they'd ever owned—or *would* ever own—and she wanted a picture.

"Right after my parents left, I told Gramps I was sorry he had to buy a used truck with a dent in it because he'd given his pretty new one to my dad. He just smiled and said it was a bargain, and he was just glad my dad hadn't been smart enough to ask for the property. I was too young to understand what he meant then, but looking at that photo with Gram, I realized he meant he would have given everything he had— even the farm—to keep me with him and Gram."

In that instant, he felt like he really understood Gretchen for the first time. Her devotion to her grandmother and her determination to keep the farm going, even if it meant growing pumpkins and changing her own oil, made sense. "You're a lucky lady to have grandparents like that."

"Yup." She inhaled deeply, as if centering herself, and then she gave him a small smile. "Best day of my life."

He thought about asking her if he could use that story, or pieces of it, but discarded the idea almost immediately. She wouldn't want that, and the asking would just make things awkward again. "Need any help?"

"I'm done. Just have to get the truck back on the ground and clean up. We're having burgers tonight, though, so if you want to fire up the grill when Gram's ready, that would be awesome."

"Sounds good. I've got to carry my stuff in and then I'll find her."

Cocoa went with him, watching with interest as he pulled his camera bag out of the back. He decided to leave the tripod in there, and then closed the hatch. "Come on, girl. Let's go find Ida."

She thumped her tail on the ground until Alex started to move, and then she shadowed him into the house. Ida was still knitting, but she set it down when he walked in.

"Did you get some good pictures today?"

"I did. And I see blue yarn there. Did you finish the purple set for the little girl in Ohio?"

She beamed. "I did, and it came out beautiful. I did a picot edging with a white yarn with sparkles in it, and it might be the cutest set yet."

"Did you pack it up already? I could take some photos of it for your online store if you want."

"I was hoping you'd offer." She reached down to rub the dog's back. "He's a good boy, isn't he, Cocoa?"

When the Lab gazed up at him, her tongue lolling out of her mouth and her tail thumping, Alex laughed. She was a joyful dog, and he could see why Ida had taken an instant liking to her.

"I'm going to run this stuff upstairs," he said. "Gretchen said I could fire up the grill whenever you're ready since she's done changing the oil in her truck."

"That girl's always working, though she did meet the girls for lunch today." Ida shook her head and leaned over the arm of the rocker to drop her knitting into the basket. "Maybe some night you should take her to O'Rourke's for a nice dinner. She likes it there. I'll stay home with Cocoa and make myself some soup and sandwiches."

Because she wasn't looking up at him—probably by design—he couldn't tell exactly what she meant by that. Was it simply meant to be a treat for her selfless granddaughter? Or was she trying to hook them up?

"Maybe," was all he said, because Gretchen wouldn't appreciate this conversation happening without her. "I'll be back down in a few minutes."

As he carried his bag up the stairs, he mulled over her words. Taking Gretchen into town for dinner sounded nice, actually. He liked talking to her, and it wasn't easy to make her stop and relax for a while.

But he suspected if he asked Gretchen to join him for a meal at O'Rourke's, she'd come up with a reason why it was impractical or insist Ida join them. And that was assuming she didn't flat out say no, which was also a possibility.

The thought of a date night with her was intriguing, though, and Alex knew imagining the sound of the ocean wasn't going to be enough to bring instant sleep tonight.

07

Gretchen tried to time putting the salad together with the burgers being done, which meant glancing out the window every few minutes at Alex, who was manning the grill.

Looking at him was certainly no hardship. It was a hot day, and standing in front of the grill probably didn't help, because his T-shirt was molded to his body. And every so often, he'd pull up the hem and use it to wipe his face. Twice she managed to time her glance out the window with that glimpse of bared skin, and both times she stopped and gave herself the time to appreciate the view.

He kept up a conversation with Cocoa the entire time he was cooking, too, which amused Gretchen. The dog was thrilled to be out in the yard while supper was prepared, instead of in her bed, and it was obvious she credited that to Alex by the way she gazed up at him in adoration. Occasionally she'd circle the grill, hoping he'd dropped something, or she'd do a circuit around the yard to see what was up, but mostly Cocoa sat and listened to Alex talk.

Gretchen wondered what he was talking to her about, but she refused to sink so low as to try to sneak up on them to eavesdrop. Instead she left them to their conversation and pulled out the macaroni salad Gram had made earlier in the day.

Everybody loved Gram's macaroni salad, and she never made it while people were actually in the house, because she didn't want anybody else to have the recipe. She'd made a big batch this time, so Gretchen was hoping there would be enough left over to save some for Jen and Kelly. Some of her happiest memories were the times they all gathered around Gram's kitchen table with bowls of macaroni salad.

When Alex began laying cheese over the burgers, Gretchen started pulling condiments out of the fridge and setting them in the center of the table. Mayo, ketchup, mustard. She couldn't find the pickles, though, so she assumed they'd used them up and went to the pantry for a new jar.

Alex walked through the door, juggling the platter of cheeseburgers, a plate piled with toasted buns, and the spatula, while Cocoa danced around his feet. "I don't know what you put in the hamburger, but these smell amazing."

"I don't even know. Gram just grabs a few jars out of the spice cabinet and mixes it up. I've never really paid attention to which jars."

"I might have to ask her. Where did she go?"

"She had to make a phone call, but it'll only take her a few minutes."

He set the burgers and buns on the table, then walked over to the sink to set down the spatula. Gretchen watched him as she gripped the top of the pickle jar. Then, as she met the resistance of the unbroken seal, she stopped. It was ridiculous. Downright stupid, even. She could open her own damn jars.

The words came out of her mouth before she could stop them. "Can you open this for me?"

As soon as he turned, a questioning expression on his face, she wished she could take the question back. If she told him to never mind and popped the seal, he'd think she was an idiot. Instead she was forced to hold up the jar as he moved close to take it from her.

He had nice hands, she thought as he gripped the jar. They were large, with long fingers that curled over the lid. As he began to twist, she let her gaze travel up his tan forearm to the well-toned biceps below his T-shirt sleeve. As she stared, the muscles flexed and she wished she had more condiment jars in need of opening.

The loud pop of the seal made her jump, and Gretchen stifled an embarrassed chuckle.

"Thanks," she muttered, reaching for the jar. She was afraid if she said any more or raised her voice, she'd sound as breathless as she felt. He'd opened a pickle jar, for goodness' sake. There was nothing sexual about that.

But when her hand went to close around the glass and her fingers had to practically thread through his in order to take it, she felt a rush of heat through her body that couldn't be described any other way *but* sexual.

Was it her imagination or did his hand linger a few seconds longer than necessary?

Shannon Stacey

"I'm just in time," Gram said from the doorway. "Those burgers look perfectly grilled, Alex."

He winked at Gretchen before turning away, and all she could do was stand there and hope Gram hadn't seen it. Any of it.

When they sat down to eat, Gretchen kept her eyes on the food. Maybe the wink was just a way of saying the *you're welcome* to her *thank you*, without having to tell Gram she hadn't been able to open the jar of pickles. Or maybe she hadn't imagined his touch lingering, and he was flirting with her.

What the hell had she been thinking? It was one thing to want a man to open her pickle jar, so to speak, but Alex couldn't be that guy. She'd even explained that to Jen and Kelly. But somehow, when she was around him, she forgot there were logical reasons she should be opening her own damn pickle jar.

"This macaroni salad is amazing," Alex said, dragging Gretchen away from her thoughts.

"It's kind of famous around here," Gram said, not even trying for modest.

"I'm not surprised. I thought the burgers would be the star of the show because they're delicious, but this macaroni salad is, without a doubt, the best I've ever had. What do you put in it?"

"She won't even tell me," Gretchen said.

"I don't trust you not to tell Kelly or Jen. And they'll tell somebody else—maybe even Cass, who'll start making it at O'Rourke's—and then everybody will have it."

"Gram likes when people make a big deal out of it at potluck dinners." Gretchen smiled. "If we opened a café that served nothing but Cheryl Decker's meatballs with a side of Gram's macaroni salad, we'd probably be rich."

"I remember the meatballs from the Eagles Fest spaghetti dinner," Alex said. "They were extremely good, but I think I'd go with Ida's macaroni salad as the entrée, with a side of Cheryl's meatballs."

Gram beamed, which made Gretchen want to roll her eyes. But she noticed he left a little more lettuce on his plate than usual, choosing seconds on the macaroni salad instead, which meant he wasn't just blowing smoke. He must really like it a lot to go off his usual meal plan.

When they'd cleaned up the kitchen, the last thing Gretchen wanted to do was go sit in the living room, where she'd spend the entire evening trying to avoid making eye contact with Alex because of the stupid pickle jar.

"I'm going to go take a look at the pumpkins," she told them. "Because I went into town today, I didn't earlier, and I didn't get out there yesterday, either."

"I'd like to see them," Alex said.

"What?"

"The pumpkins. I'd like to see them."

She frowned. "Why?"

"I don't know. Because I've heard a lot about them, but I haven't seen them. And I've seen pumpkins at little pumpkin patches for Halloween, but I've never seen a field of them growing before."

"You could take a picture," Ida said. "I don't know if I have any good pictures of the pumpkin patch for my photo album."

"I'd be happy to."

Gretchen looked back and forth between them, trying

to come up with a single logical reason why she shouldn't take Alex out to the field with her. But there was nothing, so she had no choice but to give in.

So much for avoiding being with Alex for the rest of the evening.

By the time Alex went upstairs for his camera and met Gretchen outside, she was leaning against her truck with her arms crossed, giving off the impression she'd been waiting for him for hours.

She was being especially prickly, which amused him because it meant she was trying to hide something, or at least deflect attention away from herself. And he'd bet anything it had to do with the jar.

That moment had thrown him off, too. Something had changed in that split second, but where he was the kind of guy who wanted to explore it and see what it meant, Gretchen was trying to shut it down and pretend it never happened.

He couldn't do that. Whatever it was had definitely happened, even if he couldn't quite figure out why it had affected him so much.

So he'd opened a jar of pickles for the woman. So what? It wasn't the first time Alex had opened a jar for a lady, and it probably wouldn't be the last. But all he could think about was their fingers almost interlocked around the glass. The way that blue gaze had locked with his. The slight parting of her lips.

"Are you ready?"

She sounded as impatient as she looked, but he just

smiled at her. "Yeah. We're taking the truck? Don't you usually take the ATV?"

"I take the four-wheeler around the farm because it's better on gas. But with two of us, we'll just take the truck. Probably safer for that camera, too."

The camera had been through more hostile situations and terrain than she could possibly imagine, but he didn't bother arguing. Riding behind her on the ATV, with her between his thighs—because he didn't think for a second she'd let him drive—was probably more than he could handle at the moment.

The road was bumpy and the truck didn't exactly have a state-of-the-art suspension system, so Alex did very little talking and a lot of bracing himself as she drove out past the tree line to the field she'd turned into a pumpkin patch.

To his eye, the field looked to be at least a couple of acres, if not three, and there were a lot of pumpkins. "You take care of this by yourself?"

She put the truck in park and got out, so he followed suit. "They're more work than I thought they'd be, but it's manageable. The field's well suited for them, which helps. You can see the rain barrels set around, and it took me forever to lay out the soaker hoses. If we have a dry spell, I have to water them, so it was worth the work. I haven't really had an insect problem—knock on wood—so I've gotten the hang of it."

"When do you harvest them? You don't do it all by hand, do you?"

She laughed. "That's how you harvest a pumpkin. A sharp knife, a strong back, and a wagon hooked to the tractor. And I usually start in September, as they become ripe."

"And they keep until Halloween?"

"Mostly. The earliest ones, we don't usually save that long. Gram has a seasoning recipe that makes the best roasted pumpkin seeds you'll ever taste. And she starts the pie filling. Even though I have the field broken up in sections so I can keep up with going through and turning them so they don't get a flat surface, some of them aren't pretty enough to be Halloween pumpkins. Those Gram uses to can up her famous pumpkin pie filling, and the local stores sell the jars leading up to Thanksgiving."

Alex stopped walking, looking around him. "I'm impressed, Gretchen. Do you have any idea how amazing you are?"

She stopped, too, turning to face him with color burning on her cheeks. "If you put seeds in good ground and tend them, stuff grows. That's not amazing. It's just farming."

"A lot of people would have given up, you know. Once the milking doesn't pay enough and the cows are gone, the farms slowly slip into disrepair or get taken by the bank or the government. Or people go out and get nine-to-five jobs and it just becomes a house with more outbuildings than most."

"I'm not really qualified to do much out in the job market," Gretchen said, turning slightly so she was looking out over the pumpkins instead of at him. "By the time I found a job and commuted to it and . . . I hate being inside. My paychecks wouldn't have been big, anyway, so if I'm going to scrape out a living, I'd rather do it outside."

"It's Ida, too," he said. "With her knitting, and I guess the pumpkin pie filling, which I hadn't heard about. The way you both just find a way to keep the farm going is pretty amazing, whether you want to accept that or not."

She shrugged one shoulder. "Our needs are pretty simple. Gramps didn't leave us with a mortgage on the farm, so we mostly need to pay taxes, heat the house and put food on the table."

He was willing to bet the taxes weren't cheap and neither was heating that house, but he let it go. She wasn't going to admit she and her grandmother were special, no matter how hard he tried to convince her otherwise. "How did you decide on pumpkins?"

"We grew a few near the garden every year for pies, and they did really well. I decided to try it and I've planted a little more of the field every year. This is it, though. This is all I can manage by myself. The rest of the fields we just hay off."

"What about corn? Don't people love fresh corn?"

"We were doing corn for a while, but you can't go a mile around here without passing by somebody selling corn on the side of the road, and we're too far off the beaten path to compete with the farm stands out on the main road. And even if I hired seasonal help, I don't have the equipment to compete with the bigger outfits who supply the stores, so corn wasn't making money. We still have some, of course, but it's mainly just for us. The more food we grow, the less we have to buy."

He loved watching her as she talked. When it came to the farm, she was a fascinating blend of practicality and passion that he had to admit he found sexy as hell. Very conscious of the camera in his hand, he wanted nothing more than to capture that aspect of her personality on film, or the digital version of it, anyway.

"I wish you'd let me photograph you." She scowled, and

he tried to head the inevitable rejection off at the pass. "At least let me take a few. Not for my work, but for you. For Ida, actually. I could take a picture of you with the truck. I bet your grandmother would get a kick out of having that framed and sitting next to the photo of your grandfather."

"I hate pictures," she said, but he could tell his words had hit home. There wasn't much she wouldn't do for her grandmother.

"It would be a perfect Christmas present. In the photo of your grandfather, you can see the barn and cows behind him. I could take one of you right now, with the pumpkins behind you and the truck. It's not only side-by-side images of Ida's husband and granddaughter, but it's a history of this farm. It shows the resilience and how, even when things change, this place and the people you are remain the same."

When she looked out over the fields, pride shining in her expression, he knew he had her. "I think she'd like that."

Gretchen assumed she'd walk over to the truck, say cheese and then they'd go. After ten minutes of moving the truck a little bit this way and facing it a little bit that way, she knew it wasn't going to be so simple.

"Photography lives or dies in the lighting," he explained.

"I've already run over two pumpkins," she shot back. "It probably took my grandmother less than a minute to get that picture of Gramps and it's a perfectly fine picture."

"Natural lighting in the evening is tricky."

She would have driven off and left him there to walk back, but now that he'd sold her on the picture, she knew he was right about it being a perfect present for Gram.

She'd probably get all weepy with the happy tears and hug her, which was a good thing on Christmas morning.

"Okay, that's good," Alex called, and Gretchen turned the truck off. She'd put up with this now because it would be worth it in December.

After slamming the door for good measure, Gretchen leaned back against the cab and crossed her arms. "Cheese."

She didn't hear a shutter sound, but after a second, Alex looked at the screen on the back of the camera and frowned. "You look like you want to strangle the person you're looking at."

She smiled. A real one.

"You'd be surprised how many hours I'll invest in getting a perfect shot," he said casually, fiddling with the camera. "Hours and hours."

She rolled her eyes and uncrossed her arms, letting them dangle at her side. That felt weird, so she put her hands on her hips. That was even more weird, so she let them dangle again. "I don't know what to do with my arms."

"Most people don't." He finished whatever he was doing with the camera and looked up at her, smiling. "Let's see. Don't lean against the truck like that. It makes you slouchy, and your height and your posture are too beautiful for that."

Even though he probably meant that in a professional way and not as a personal compliment, his words melted away Gretchen's annoyance with him. She stood up straight, but she still wasn't sure what to do with her arms. She crossed them again.

"You're killing me, Gretchen."

"Not yet, but I'm thinking about it," she teased, which made him laugh.

"Okay," he said. "Pull the braid over your shoulder so we can see it, then slide your fingers into your front pockets and hook your thumb over the pockets themselves. Now lean back against the truck again, but only your butt and only enough to hold your weight. Everything from the waist up stays tall."

She followed his instructions while trying to stay relaxed. If she thought too much about what she was doing, it felt stupid, but she trusted him to know what he was doing. He'd certainly won enough awards for doing it.

"That's good. Now bend one leg a little—whichever one you want—but keep your spine off the truck." He nodded and then lifted the camera. "No, don't do that smile. Just relax your face. Good. Now I want you to think about this land. Imagine how proud your grandfather would be of what you've done and how you've taken care of things the way he raised you to do."

He *would* be proud, she knew. He was always proud of her and, though he wasn't one for offering open affection, he never let her doubt for a second how proud he was of her. And he'd be proud she was doing right by Gram, too. This farm had been her home since she married Gramps at eighteen, and there was nothing Gretchen wouldn't do to make sure she never had to leave it.

"Got it." Alex lowered the camera and smiled at her.

"How do you know? You haven't even looked at the screen yet."

"I just know. Plus, I've been taking pictures longer than cameras have had LCD screens, so I learned early to just go with my gut."

She took her hands out of her pockets as he moved toward her. He was fiddling with the camera as he walked, and when he got to the truck, he held it up so she could see the screen.

For a few seconds, she had trouble grasping that it was actually her in the picture. Leaning against her truck, with pumpkins in the background, was a beautiful woman. She was relaxed, but pride in her surroundings still came through in the way she held herself. Her face was strong, but softened by a nostalgic glow and a warm smile.

"Wow." It was all she could say.

"That's what I see when I look at you," he said, and she realized just how close he was to her.

She looked up at him, meeting his gaze. "I don't understand how you do that. I don't think most people see that when they look at me. But you can get a camera to see . . . It's like the soul of me in that picture. How do you do that?"

His dark eyes crinkled when he grinned. "I'd tell you, but then everybody would be a photographer. It's kind of like your grandmother's macaroni salad, I guess. If everybody knows how it's done, it's not really special."

"That's not really a comparison. What you do is a gift."

"So is Ida's macaroni salad."

She started to laugh, but then he reached up and tucked a strand of her hair behind her ear. "You're incredibly beautiful, Gretchen, and being able to capture what you feel about this place so you can see it, too, is definitely a gift."

He was going to kiss her. She *wanted* him to kiss her. And right here and now, in the warm summer evening with the light fading, she couldn't think of a single reason it would be a bad idea.

Alex ran his fingertip over her lips and down her chin, making her shiver. "If I kiss you, are you going to be all prickly about it later?"

"Probably."

"Should I let that stop me?"

Gretchen rested her hand at his waist and shook her head. "I'll probably be prickly about something later, whether you kiss me or not, so we might as well enjoy this moment while it lasts."

He stepped across her legs with his left foot, so she was between the pickup and his body, and ran his hand down the length of her braid. Then he cupped her cheek and lowered his mouth to hers.

Her eyelids slid closed as their lips met, and she sighed as their breath mingled. His thumb pressed against her cheekbone as he kissed her, and she let go of his waist to run her hand up his arm, from the camera he held and over his strong biceps to his shoulder. She'd wanted to touch those shoulders for a long time, and she dug her fingertips into the muscle as his tongue dipped between her lips.

Kissing Alex was everything she'd imagined it to be during those restless nights when sleep didn't come right away. She cradled his neck between her hands, her fingernails brushing his hairline, and nipped at his bottom lip.

He made a low growling sound and moved closer, so his body pressed hers up against the truck. The kiss grew more urgent and she felt breathless as his tongue danced over hers. She ran her hands down his chest to his waist, wanting to pull his T-shirt up and feel his bare skin.

Then she heard the barking. Through the haze of want and need, Gretchen heard Cocoa's excited greeting, and

Alex must have, too. One more heated, frustrated kiss against her mouth and then he lifted his head.

"She found us."

Gretchen didn't have the ability to make coherent words yet, so she just nodded as Alex pushed back from the truck and untangled their legs. Once he moved, she could see Cocoa barreling joyfully toward them, her tongue hanging out as she ran.

She went to Gretchen first, jumping up on her so Gretchen could give her a neck rub. Then she went to Alex and sat at his feet. As the frustration eased from Alex's face to be replaced by affection for the dog with the poor timing, Cocoa barked once and lifted her paw for a high five.

08

Alex stared at the ceiling, and only the fact that the light had changed let him know he must have slept at some point. He'd been staring at the ceiling in the dark, thinking about the feel of Gretchen's mouth, and now he was staring at the ceiling in the dim light of dawn.

That kiss had rocked his world. There was no other way to say it. He'd wanted her before, but he'd wanted other women in his past. But then he'd kissed her and it had been different. From the minute Cocoa barked and interrupted the kiss, he'd thought of nothing else. And he had no doubt if not for the canine interruption, he would have been more than happy to make love to her right there on the ground, in the middle of her pumpkin patch.

And she'd been thinking about it, too, he knew when they all sat down to breakfast forty minutes later. Gretchen was quieter than usual, and was doing everything but turning her chair around to avoid meeting his eyes. But a few times, when she thought he wasn't looking, he caught her staring at his mouth.

The tension was so thick between them, he was almost relieved when she practically ran out of the kitchen to do her morning chores. Ida was either oblivious or was pretending to be, keeping up a constant stream of chatter.

He made his own escape at the first opportunity. Before a midmorning meeting with Dylan Clark, the youngest member of the Stewart Mills Police Department, Alex needed to do a few errands. Maybe not enough to fill the time, but it beat engaging in a game of evasion with Gretchen.

First up was the gas station, where he filled up the Jeep before pulling it into a parking spot. It was going to take a lot more coffee to get through this day after the night he'd had, so he went inside to get a cup.

"Hey, Janie," he said when he saw the woman behind the counter, before making a beeline to the industrial coffeemaker on the back counter. He didn't even care how long it had been sitting there. The stronger, the better, as far as he was concerned.

Chase had dated Janie Vestal in high school, so she and Alex knew each other well. She'd been a cheerleader in addition to being one of his best friends' girlfriends, but they'd lost touch when they went off to college, as Alex had with everybody from Stewart Mills. She was married with a couple of kids now.

"How's your project going?" She took his money for the coffee and handed him his change.

Even though he hadn't talked to her about it yet, Alex

wasn't surprised she knew about it. There was no doubt in his mind *everybody* knew about it. "Okay, so far. Mostly I've been concentrating on the football team, though I've done a little digging into the town's history."

"It's been rough for everybody since the mills closed. I keep hearing rumors of a buyer, but so far nothing's been in the news. I figure if it's not in the news, it's not worth getting excited about."

"I really hope the rumors turn out to be true," he said, and he meant it. The mills reopening, no matter what the production was, would be a huge boost for the town.

"People are starting to get their feet back under them a little, I guess. You can kind of tell how the town's doing by how much cheap beer we sell and how bad the shoplifting is."

"Got pretty bad for a while, huh?"

Janie nodded. "We even had a girl shoplifting, uh . . . feminine products here recently. Almost broke my heart. And, no, I'm not going to tell you who it was."

Alex frowned at her. "The last thing I'd ever do is humiliate a child. You know me better than that. Even if I didn't hold myself to a higher ethical and moral standard than that, Coach would hand me my ass if I tried that."

That made her laugh. "Wouldn't be the first time he had to keep you in line."

"And thank God for that." He chatted with her for a few more minutes, and then went back to his Jeep. Rather than sit in the parking lot and drink the coffee, he found a place to park on the street and walked through the town square to the picnic table.

With autumn breathing down their necks, the mornings and evenings were markedly chilly, but Alex didn't mind.

He actually enjoyed experiencing the transition of seasons, especially in New England, which he rarely got to enjoy because of his travel schedule. Cold started the day, until the sun warmed the air and everybody started removing layers of clothes. Then the temperature would drop again as the sun went down.

He was just finishing his coffee when he heard voices. Swiveling on the bench seat, he saw a couple of guys walking in his direction. He didn't think they'd even noticed him yet, and they were laughing and tossing a football back and forth between them. PJ, the cornerback who never seemed to shut up, was telling Paul Decker a story as they walked.

Deck had been on the defensive side of the ball, same as Alex, back during their glory days, and he hadn't worked quite as hard keeping the post-football weight off. He was happy, though, and married with a couple of sons. And it looked like he'd been spending more time with boys on the current team, too, since Eagles Fest. He should probably set up a time to talk to Deck and maybe to his wife, to get some quotes. Unlike many of them, Deck had never moved away from Stewart Mills.

"Think fast, Murphy."

Alex dropped the cardboard cup just in time to catch the football Deck threw and keep it from bouncing off the side of his head. "What the hell?"

"Nice reflexes," PJ said, grinning.

"It's a good thing that cup was empty or I'd kick both your asses right now."

PJ snorted. "Maybe Deck's, but I played against you in the exhibition game, remember? I'm pretty sure you can't catch me."

"Maybe not," Alex muttered. "But you have to show up for practice at some point and then I'll know where you are."

The kid knew he was just yanking his chain, so he laughed and grabbed the football away from Alex. "I have to get to my job and make some money before school starts. Thanks for the talk, Deck."

"Anytime, PJ."

Once the kid had walked off, Deck sat on the bench opposite Alex and scrubbed at his face with his hands. "Not too many nice days left before it's cold."

"Nope. What were you and the kid up to?"

"I was changing a tire when he walked by, and we got to talking. We were in the middle of the conversation but he has to work, so I walked with him a ways. He's doing pretty good. They're *all* doing better."

"Coach told me you've been spending some time with them since Eagles Fest."

"When I can, which isn't as much as I'd like. I've got a business to run and boys of my own, but they all know they can stop by the garage anytime. Sometimes they sit on a tire and talk to me while I work."

Deck owned Decker's Wreckers, a name that made Alex chuckle every time he saw the sign. "I'd like to talk to you and Cheryl sometime. Maybe invite myself over for meatballs and get a few stories out of you."

He laughed. "The meatballs we can do. The stories? We'll see. Cheryl and I were talking about your book project and, it's like she said. There aren't any secrets in this town, but we keep things *in* this town. I've known you my whole life, but in a lot of ways you're not really from here anymore. No offense."

"None taken." He couldn't really take offense at the truth. "Stories or no stories, I still want the meatballs."

"I'll let Cheryl know and get in touch. Although we know you're not suffering a lack of food out there on the Walker farm. Ida's cooking is no joke."

"No shit. I'm kind of glad they don't seem to own a bathroom scale. But even Ida concedes nobody makes meatballs like Cheryl. I remember them from the fundraiser dinner, and I have to agree."

"Gretchen got you tending pumpkins yet?"

Alex felt a jolt at hearing her name after he'd done such a good job of not thinking about her for at least a half hour. Picking up the empty cup he'd dropped just to have something to do with his hands and to look at, he shook his head. "She's pretty stubborn and doesn't accept a lot of help. And she's got this hair across her ass about me paying rent, so I have to be treated differently."

"She can be stubborn, that's for damn sure."

Not wanting to go any further down any conversational path leading to Gretchen, Alex pulled out his phone to look at the time. "I should run. I'm meeting Dylan Clark to dig a little deeper into how a guy who's not from around here feels about the community and what they did for Eagles Fest."

"He's a good guy. Good cop." Deck sighed and pushed himself to his feet. "I need to get back to the garage, anyway."

They shook hands and then Alex tossed his cup in the garbage barrel before heading back to the Jeep. He'd do his interview with the police officer and then stop at the post office to ship some sweater sets Ida had packaged up.

He'd manage to burn the rest of the day off in town

somehow—maybe take some more pictures—but eventually he'd have to make his way back to the farm. Then he'd see Gretchen and that would lead to thinking about kissing her again.

At least in the Walker house, taking cold showers was never a problem.

Gretchen was hiding in the hayloft. She knew it was stupid and that she'd have to go into the house eventually, but she couldn't stop her damn face from feeling hot and flushed every time she thought about that kiss in the pumpkin patch.

And she couldn't stop thinking about that damn kiss.

She didn't know how to do this. Kisses were supposed to be just kisses. They were like the foreplay to foreplay. But not Alex's kiss. Just the memory of his mouth on hers made her want to dance around the hayloft with a broom, with bluebirds flying around her head, whistling a happy tune.

She didn't dance, of course. Other than the awkward middle school shuffle at the one school dance she'd ever gone to, Gretchen hadn't danced in her life. But his kiss hadn't been like any other she'd ever had. If not for the dog, she might have shoved Alex up against the side of the truck and had her way with him.

And *that* thought certainly didn't help her hot, flushed cheeks problem.

Pulling out her phone, she decided to ask for advice, but whom to ask? Kelly would have been her first choice, because she'd recently gone through the whole first-kiss thing with Chase, but she was rather disgustingly in love and wanted everybody else to be in love, too. Jen would be more practical about the whole thing, because *she* certainly wasn't in love with anybody at the moment.

That's what Gretchen needed. Advice on what to do about kisses that made you feel like a cartoon princess if you were trying not to fall in love.

Jen answered on the third ring. "Hey, what's up?"

"Not much." Just hiding in the hayloft from the man who lived in her house. "You busy?"

"Not any more than usual. You okay?"

"Alex kissed me last night."

"Okay." There was a long moment of silence. "I swear, it's hard enough to guess your mood in person, but by your voice? Forget it. Is this a *yay, Alex kissed me* call or an *oh crap, Alex kissed me* call?"

Gretchen laughed at the way her friend exaggerated the cheerfulness of the former and the dread in the latter. "I don't know. What I do know is that every time I think about the kiss, I blush, so I'm hiding in the barn."

"So . . . you need me to bring you supplies?"

"Smart-ass. I need you to tell me how I'm supposed to live with a man who kissed me, but I'm not supposed to have sex with."

Jen sighed. "There's no supposed to or not supposed to. Did you like the kiss? I mean, do you *want* to have sex with the guy?"

"I let him open a jar of pickles for me," Gretchen admitted, feeling even more like an idiot than she had before she called Jen.

"Wow. Okay, so you want him. He wants you, or he wouldn't have kissed you in a way that has you hiding in your barn. Tell me what the problem is, and don't give me any crap about him being a boarder."

"That might be all I have." Or it might be all she was willing to admit to. She didn't want to poke too much at the mass of conflicted feelings she was having about Alex. The fact that there were feelings at all *was* the problem.

"I don't even know what to say. I don't remember you ever being like this, even when we were teenagers and you're *supposed* to be a hot mess of hormones."

"I should have called Kelly."

"She would have given you a dreamy sigh and asked if you want to have a double wedding."

Gretchen laughed. "She's not quite that bad."

"You have to go in the house. The food and coffee is in there."

"Good point. I was willing to fast if necessary, but coffee's a deal breaker." Gretchen heard Cocoa bark out in the yard and knew her solitude was about to come to an end. "How do I not think about the kiss?"

"If you start to think about the kiss, think about something else instead. Like . . . I don't know. Taxes or something. Something that doesn't make you want to have sex."

"Taxes aren't sexy."

"There you go."

"I think Gram's calling me, so I have to come out of hiding now. Thanks for the talk."

"Call me tomorrow and let me know how it goes."

Gretchen said she would, though she wasn't about to get in the habit of calling her friends with daily status updates. Then she climbed out of the hayloft and tried to brace herself for the deluge of tax-related thoughts she was probably going to have to suffer through before she could reasonably escape to her room. Even if she claimed a headache, which she never did, she had to at least eat supper first. She was hungry.

As soon as she stepped out of the barn, Cocoa spotted her. With a joyous bark, she ran to her, which of course alerted Gram to her location.

"There you are," she said. "I was looking all over for you."

"Sorry. I was up in the hayloft." Great. She had no excuse for being up there that didn't involve hiding.

"It's time to eat," Gram said, not digging any further.

Alex was just setting the salad bowl on the table when they walked in, and Gretchen did a quick calculation of how many weeks she had left before the tax bill came. Then she looked directly at him and smiled. "Hi, Alex."

"How was your day?"

Confusing and restless and, now, slightly awkward. "It was fine, thanks."

How was it possible to regret kissing a man and yet want the man to kiss you at the same damn time? Gretchen yanked out her chair and sat, wishing she were more savvy when it came to men. Usually, savvy wasn't required. If she liked a guy, she dated him. If she didn't, she didn't accept any offered invitation. Why was Alex any different?

It had to be the fact that he was living—temporarily, of course—under the same roof she was. Because of Gram, Gretchen had never been in the habit of bringing men home with her. Once she'd been out with a guy enough times that she was comfortable with the idea, they went to his place. She could leave when she wanted and her home was a drama-free space.

That couldn't happen with the man sitting across from her, filling half his plate with salad.

"I heard you on the phone earlier, Alex," Gram said. "I couldn't hear the conversation, of course, but you sounded angry. Is everything okay?"

Gretchen looked up, concerned and curious at the same time. She knew Alex had a temper problem when they were kids, until Coach McDonnell straightened him out, but he seemed so even tempered now, it was hard to imagine him yelling on the phone.

But all he did was laugh and shake his head. "I wasn't angry. That was my agent and we were having a disagreement about me heading to New York City for some meetings. I was just trying to talk over him because his superpower seems to be talking forever without having to take a breath."

"He wants you to go to the city?"

Alex nodded. "He thinks once I'm there and we've gone over some work opportunities, I'll forget I wanted a hiatus."

Gretchen wondered if his agent was right. Once Alex was back in the big city, there probably wouldn't be a lot of incentive to come back to Stewart Mills. Yet another reason not to kiss him.

But that kiss, though . . .

She wondered how much their taxes would go up if she built a shed at the edge of the pumpkin field. She'd been thinking about it for a while, because there were supplies and tools she didn't use anywhere else on the farm, and it was dumb to haul them back and forth. But another outbuilding meant another tax hike.

Jen was a genius, Gretchen thought, shoving a bite of

ham into her mouth. Not only was she not blushing at the dinner table, but she was also going to drive herself so nuts thinking about taxes, she'd finally get around to visiting the town hall and getting information on the shed.

"Oh, I meant to ask you last night, but I forgot," Gram said. "What did you think of the pumpkins, Alex? Did you get any pictures for me?"

Damn. Gretchen kept her eyes on her plate, trying to ignore the conversation.

"I did, actually," Alex said. "I can show them to you later."

"You guys were out there a long time."

"I was showing him the soaker hoses," Gretchen said, not wanting to risk Alex even hinting about what they'd really been up to.

"Fascinating stuff," he said, and she looked up to scowl at him. His gaze met hers, sparkling with humor, and she rolled her eyes. "It seems like a lot of work."

Work she could handle talking about, Gretchen thought. Talk about work, think about taxes and spend as much time as possible anywhere but in the house.

Her gaze drifted to his mouth. She just couldn't think about that kiss.

09

Alex sat in the shade of the covered bridge, eating from an ice cream cup he'd bought at the convenience store. Ice cream was a rare treat for him, but he figured he'd earned one. It had been almost a week since he kissed Gretchen out in the field of pumpkins, and he'd managed not to explode from the sexual frustration that had been bad even *before* the kiss. Since that night, it had been building and building with no hope of release anytime soon.

He wouldn't say Gretchen was avoiding him, but he couldn't think of a single time they'd been alone since then. Maybe technically they'd been alone in a room for a few minutes, but Ida was still in the house. And she was Gretchen's grandmother. Call him old-fashioned, but he couldn't quite bring himself to make out with a woman while her grandmother was in the other room.

"Hey, Mr. Murphy."

Alex almost dropped his ice cream cup, but he recovered before it hit the ground. He hadn't heard anybody approaching, but now he saw Hunter Cass walking toward him. He was one of the kids whose family had been hit pretty hard when the mills closed and who had started unraveling both academically and behaviorally when the team's funding was cut.

"How are things going, kid?"

He was expecting a shrug, since that had been the kid's primary form of communication when the alumni team members first returned to Stewart Mills for Eagles Fest. But Hunter smiled and hopped up onto the picnic table, sitting on the top with his feet resting on the bench.

"Things are good. Pretty sure I'll make the team, and Molly and I are back together. And my dad found a good job. He has to travel a bit, but the money's not bad and he and my mom aren't fighting now. Or drinking."

"I'm glad to hear it. I know things were rough there for a while."

"Having you guys around really helped, too. All of us. When they cut the team, we thought it was over. Like *everything* was over, you know? But you guys all got out and did okay and none of you played pro football."

Alex leaned back against a support beam and considered the kid. While this was what he'd come back for—the emotional impact of Eagles Fest and how the town had rallied—this was an open and unguarded moment for the boy. While he might revisit some of the conversation later in a more formal interview, Alex was willing to relax for now and just be an ear for the kid to bend.

"I know you were discouraged when the football program was cut. And, to be honest, I'm not sure how we all would have done without going to college and, for some of us, it was the championship that gave us the boost we needed to get accepted. But I can see how it would help to see that football didn't *define* our lives. There's life without football, I promise."

"I had focused so much on a football scholarship getting me out of here that I didn't know how I'd have a life without it." Hunter shrugged. "I mean, I know none of the top football programs look at a school our size, but there are colleges that would take me. But now I know the only thing I can depend on for sure is my grades, because those are the only things I can control."

Alex felt a swell of pride that he'd been a part of helping this kid get back on track. Not only back on track, but on a better track. He knew most of it was Coach, but having a town full of people fighting to support them had made a difference for every kid on the football team.

"Sounds like you've got your head on straight," he said. "And you know you've got plenty of people to talk to if you ever need advice or a shoulder. Including me. You've got my email address."

Hunter nodded and hopped off the table. "I'm supposed to be grabbing sodas for me and Molly, so I'm going to head out. See you around."

Feeling less frustrated thanks to the ice cream and the good feelings his conversation with Hunter left him with, Alex walked back to the school. Even though practice was over, he wanted to shoot some more pictures, and the light was good today.

When he stepped out to the sidelines, though, he was surprised to see Gretchen and Cocoa out on the field. She was playing with the dog, who was running in circles around her and clearly having the time of her life.

He was able to get a few good shots of them playing before the dog saw him and ran to greet him. Gretchen followed more slowly, her face pink from the exertion in the heat. "Hey. I didn't expect to see you two here."

"I dropped Gram off at the doctor's office, so Cocoa and I thought we'd come over and see if anything was going on. I guess we missed it."

"It was hot today and the kids have been working hard, so Coach let them cut out early. I figured I'd take advantage of the time to take some stock shots. The signs and the logos on the field and stuff. I talked to Jen yesterday and she mentioned it would be nice to have some generic but high-quality photos for newsletters and the yearbook and stuff. Photos with no kids in them so they're not dated."

"You talked to Jen yesterday?"

She looked surprised and for a second he wondered if she was jealous, but then he realized she might be worried he'd told her friend about what they'd almost gotten up to in the pumpkin patch.

"Yeah, we talked about my work," he said. "I wanted to interview her about her part in Eagles Fest's success, plus to talk to her about some of the things the kids have said. It was a deal I made with Coach. Anything personal needs to be approved. So is Ida okay? You said you left her at the doctor's office."

"Oh, she's fine. Just a regularly scheduled thing to check on her blood pressure and see if she needs her medication adjusted. It runs a bit high, so we keep an eye on it." Gretchen rubbed the top of Cocoa's head. "That's one of the reasons we got this girl. The nurses said having a pet companion can be good for the blood pressure."

Cocoa panted and offered her paw. Gretchen sighed and gave her a high five, which made Alex laugh. "She needs to learn a few new tricks."

"I bought her a Frisbee, but she ran off with it and I still haven't found it."

"I remember seeing a pile of tennis balls by the barn, but I haven't seen a Frisbee anywhere."

Gretchen laughed and shook her head. "I hope she didn't eat it. Anyway, I guess we'll head back now. Gram should be about done and I have a bowl in the truck so I can give Cocoa some water."

"I mentioned it to Ida, but I don't know if she told you. I'm meeting a couple at the pizza place for supper. They were able to keep their house because of a program the governor helped connect them with, so I want to get their story. I don't know how late I'll be, but I'll miss dinner for sure."

"Okay."

He felt his body prepare to move, as if to step forward and kiss her good-bye, but she bent over to clip the leash back on Cocoa's collar. When she stood, she was facing the exit and she gave him a little wave.

"I'll see you either later tonight or in the morning, then."

He nodded, but she was already walking away with Cocoa. The dog looked back at him, as if wondering why they were leaving him behind, but then she felt the tug of the leash and turned to face forward again.

Alex watched them go, feeling the frustration rise again.

It was too hot to walk back to the store for another ice cream cup, so he took his camera out of its bag and got to work.

Gretchen came fully awake in the dark, throwing the sheet back to get up before she even fully registered *why* she was awake.

Cocoa was barking. Not the *want to be best friends?* bark for animals that wandered into the yard, or the half-hearted stranger-danger bark for the rare occasion the UPS truck bounced up the driveway. If a dog could panic, Cocoa was panicking.

With bare feet, Gretchen ran to her door and threw it open. Cocoa was in Gram's room, so she opened the door and stepped inside. The sight of her grandmother on the floor made Gretchen's chest and throat tighten with fear. "Gram!"

"Oh, hush, you silly dog." Gram pushed herself to hands and knees, and Gretchen rushed to help her. "I tripped."

"Maybe you should sit for a minute." There was a knock behind her, and Gretchen turned around to find an empty doorway.

"Everybody decent?" Alex called from around the corner.

"Yes."

"I'm fine." Gram slapped at Gretchen's hand.

Gretchen really wanted her to sit on the floor for a minute, in case she was hurt, but Alex stepped in front of her and extended his hand to Gram. She took it and he hauled her to her feet.

"Thank you."

"Did you bruise anything?" Gretchen couldn't shake

the horrible image of Gram on the floor, and the fear was slow in receding. "Did you—"

"If you're about to ask me if I broke a hip, Gretchen Marie Walker, you can shut it right now. I'm only sixty-eight years old, young lady."

Gretchen shut her mouth and stood up. Gram was right, of course. Ida Walker wasn't fragile, by any means. But keeping her mouth shut didn't mean she wasn't still afraid.

Gram had been cooking the day Gramps passed away. She was making biscuits to go with the beef stew simmering on the stove, and Gretchen went out to the barn to help Gramps finish up whatever he'd been doing before supper. He was lying on the floor when she walked in, and it was already too late. His heart, the doctors told them later.

Gretchen could still remember the smell of the burned black tar the forgotten beef stew had turned into, and to this day, she still had a hard time keeping the memories at bay when Gram made it.

"I'm sorry," she said, trying to shake off the painful memories. Gram had tripped. That was all. "It just scared me."

"You guys can hang out in here and chat if you want, but I'm going to finish what I started. I'll be right back."

"You should take some ibuprofen while you're in there," Gretchen said. "For your knee. You know, just in case."

Gram waved a hand at her impatiently as she left the room. A few seconds later, the bathroom door closed and Gretchen let out a shaky breath. "Sorry we woke you up."

Alex frowned at her. "You're kidding, right?"

"Okay. God, I think I lost five years off my life. Is my hair gray? I feel like my hair is gray now."

He chuckled and smoothed her hair away from her face. "It's not. It's as dark and beautiful as ever."

She slapped at his hand. "Don't do that."

"You sure are prickly when you have the crap scared out of you in the middle of the night."

That got a chuckle out of her, and she felt the last of the fear fading away. So maybe she'd overreacted a little. "I don't know if I'll be able to go back to sleep. I feel like I just drank an entire pot of coffee."

"You will, once the adrenaline rush is over."

When Gram came back and saw them both still standing there, she waved a hand toward the door. "I'm fine. And I'm going back to bed, so unless you guys want to stand there and watch me sleep, I suggest you go back to bed, too."

Cocoa made a whining sound and stared up at Gretchen with so much intensity, she thought the dog was trying to send her a psychic message. "I think the excitement was too much for Cocoa. Since she's up and expects to go out, I'm going to take her outside. Then I'll let her back in and maybe she'll settle down."

"I'll take her," Alex said. "Come on, Cocoa."

"Did you take some ibuprofen?" Gretchen asked after they were gone.

"I did. I think I'll have a bruise in the morning, but not a bad one." She sat on the edge of the bed and lifted the hem of her nightgown to her thigh. "Since I know you'll worry, you can see for yourself."

It wasn't bad, which did make Gretchen feel better. "I wasn't going to ask you if you broke a hip, by the way. I was worried about your wrists and your kneecap, which has nothing to do with age."

Gram cupped her face in her hands and kissed her forehead. "You're a blessing, Gretchen. Even when you're fussing over me."

"Almost as much as you fuss over me." Gretchen pulled Gram's nightgown down and stood up straight. "We've got to take care of each other. We're all we have."

"And Cocoa," Gram said.

"And Cocoa."

A few minutes later, they heard the telltale clicking of dog nails in the hall and Cocoa walked in. After sniffing at Gram, she plopped down on her bed and looked at Gretchen as if she had no idea why she was in their room in the middle of the night.

After blowing Gram a kiss, Gretchen turned off the light and closed the door softly behind her.

Her nerves hadn't settled yet, though, and she knew if she went and put her head on the pillow, she was going to relive the moment she'd seen Gram on the floor over and over. That would almost certainly lead her down the dark path to reliving the moment she'd found Gramps on the barn floor.

Instead she went down the stairs, treading lightly in hopes that Cocoa would already be asleep. Maybe if she had a cookie and some milk, it would calm her down. Or a handful of cookies.

Alex had just popped a grape into his mouth when Gretchen walked into the kitchen. Since he couldn't say anything, he lifted his hand to wave. When she slapped her palm against his in a high five, he almost choked on the grape.

"Cocoa's doing a good job of training you," she said, walking past him to get to the cookie jar tucked away behind the coffeemaker.

The massive grape finally chewed, he swallowed it so he could talk. "You're funny at one thirty in the morning."

"And you're not wearing a shirt."

He looked down at his naked chest and bare feet. "Sometimes I skip the sweatpants, so tonight could have been a lot more embarrassing."

She paused with a chocolate chip cookie halfway to her mouth. "That would have been interesting. Although you probably would have stopped to put them on."

"I don't know. I was getting out of bed when Cocoa started barking, but once you yelled *Gram*, there was nothing in my head but getting there. Luckily, I could hear her talking and knew she was conscious, so I pulled up short in case she wasn't decent. But, honestly, I might have a couple of gray hairs lurking now, too."

"It was scary." She took a bite of the cookie and then walked to the fridge to pour herself a cup of milk. "But I don't want to talk about it anymore, because I came down here to shake it off so I can get some sleep."

"Then we'll talk about something else."

She considered that, tilting her head. "Like what?"

"Anything. Pumpkins. Football. Cookies. Wait. Not cookies. We can talk about what incredible willpower I must have to stand here and eat grapes while you stuff your face with homemade baked goods."

"I'm not stuffing my face," she said right before she stuffed the rest of the cookie into her mouth.

There were a lot of words Alex would use to describe

Gretchen. Strong. Beautiful. Striking. Dedicated. Loyal. Hardworking. But standing there in the kitchen in her silly cow pajama pants and a tank top, with cookie crumbs at the corners of her mouth, she was just plain cute as hell.

She gulped down some milk and then frowned at him. "You're staring at me."

"Because you're cute."

"Cute?"

"And you have cookie crumbs on your mouth." He popped the last grape into his mouth while she grabbed a napkin. "Grapes don't have that problem."

"They also don't have chocolate chips."

"Now you're just being mean."

She tossed the napkin in the trash and rinsed her cup before setting it in the bottom of the sink. "Better mean than cute."

"What's the matter with cute?"

She shrugged, tapping her fingers on the counter. "I don't know. I don't think anybody's ever called me cute before. Jen's the cute one."

"You're all attractive women, but I definitely think you're the cute one." He put his hand over hers to stop the tapping, curling his fingers around hers. "I love your hands."

"Got a thing for calluses and stubby fingernails, do you?"

He ran his thumb over her knuckles. "You have strong, capable hands, but with long and slender fingers."

"They're just hands."

"Do I have to go get the camera again?"

"I'm not hand modeling for you in the middle of the night." When he lifted her hand and kissed the back of it, she sighed. "I mean it."

Then he tugged her closer, until their bodies were almost touching. "I like your mouth, too."

"Is it cute?"

He smiled and let go of her hand to run his thumb over it. "It's definitely something."

When he lowered his head to kiss her, she closed her eyes and leaned into him. Her hands started at his waist, but as he deepened the kiss, her palms ran over his naked back. He hadn't been lying when he told her he loved her hands, and he loved the feel of them on his skin even more.

He skimmed his hands over her rib cage until the curves between his thumbs and fingers were cupped under her breasts. She wasn't wearing a bra under the tank top and she moaned when he brushed his thumbs lightly over her nipples.

But when he slid one hand under the hem of the shirt and ran his fingers over the warm flesh of her stomach, he felt her tense up.

Then she put her hands against his shoulders and gently pushed, so he lifted his head. Her expression was soft and her cheeks were flushed, but her mouth was set in a determined line.

"We can't do this," she said.

"Why?"

"Well, for one thing, Gram's upstairs."

"She's sleeping. What's the other thing?"

"You rent a room from us, so there have to be boundaries. Technically, I'm your landlord."

"First of all, I don't remember any laws about sex with your landlord as long as it's not sex in lieu of rent. Secondly—and technically—Ida's my landlord, not you. And third,

I'll throw my shit in the Jeep and go rent a motel room and then come back."

She laughed, and her breath was warm against his chest. "The only motel in Stewart Mills has been boarded up for a while now."

"Then I'll live in my Jeep." He wanted her that much. She sighed and took a step backward, so he took her hand.

"I'm going to go to bed now," she said, and he could tell she was telling herself that as much as telling him. "Turn the lights off when you go up?"

"Yeah, I'll turn the lights off." She started to walk away, but he kept hold of her hand. "When you change your mind, you let me know. Immediately. No matter what I'm doing."

"I think you mean *if* I change my mind."

He grinned, running his fingertips over her palm as she pulled her hand free. "Whatever you say."

10

_____

"Dana and Patty are going to a big craft expo in Boston tomorrow."

Gretchen looked at her grandmother over the back of the horse she was brushing. Gram didn't venture into the barn very often, so there was a reason for the visit. "That sounds like fun."

"It does. They invited me to go with them, actually."

And she must want to go, since she'd come outside to tell her now instead of waiting until dinner to bring it up. "Do you want to go?"

Gram hesitated, and knowing why broke Gretchen's heart. "They're planning to stay over one night, because it's a long drive. They're going to stay with Dana's cousin and take the train in, but that's still several meals and the train cost, plus the admission."

"Dana's cousin doesn't mind taking all three of you in?" Not needing a motel room would give her some breathing room.

"Not at all. She has a big house, but her kids are all grown now. She has it listed because they want to downsize to a condo, but until they do, she has extra room."

"You should go, then. It'll be fun and you guys haven't done anything together for a long time."

"I have enough money from my sweaters, but I was planning to keep that aside in case we needed it."

Gretchen stroked Cinnamon's mane and walked around the front of her to the stall door. "We're doing okay, Gram. I promise. Later on, we'll figure out how much you'll need and make sure you have enough. Plus some spending money because I know you'll come home with yarn."

"Maybe just a little."

Gretchen laughed. "Yarn is how you make the sweaters. It's like your tool. So of course you need to buy some. And the pumpkins look great. I've already started getting some bulk preorders from the local stores by email, so we'll be in good shape when the tax bill comes. And we have wood. You know as long as we have heat and can pay the taxes, we'll be just fine."

Gran's face lit up. "I'm going to go call Dana back, then. And figure out what I want to wear. I'll need comfortable shoes, but it *is* Boston, so I want to look nice."

She wandered away, still talking, and Gretchen sighed. It was good to see Gram excited about the trip, and she'd do what she had to do to make sure her grandmother had enough money to have a good time. Luckily her friends were pretty down-to-earth, so there wouldn't be any extravagant splurges on the agenda.

Gretchen left the stall and fastened the door behind her. She'd already brushed the other two horses and cleaned the stalls, so she was done in the barn for now. After giving Cinnamon—who had calmed down since the humidity broke a little—an extra pat, she put the brush away.

She was still waiting for a final date from Beverly, but the Jacobsons would be sending a truck and horse trailer for the horses soon. They moved south for the cold months and did most of their riding then. But every year they brought Cinnamon and her barn mates back with them just because they couldn't bear to be so far away from them.

Beverly had made a few comments over the summer that made Gretchen wonder if they were considering moving to their winter home on a year-round basis, which would mean the Walkers wouldn't be boarding the Jacobson horses anymore. That would mean a serious financial crunch, but she didn't panic. If and when that source of income dried up, she'd find another. That was life on the farm.

When she left the barn, blinking against the bright sun, Gretchen realized it would be Cocoa's first night without Gram, and wondered how the Lab would take it. She'd have to drag the dog's bed into her room and try to settle her there, but if Cocoa got upset, it could be a long night. If she didn't settle at all, maybe they'd go down and sleep on the couch, since they'd napped together before and at least that would be a little familiar to Cocoa.

Or maybe she'd sneak her into Alex's room and close the door, she thought with a grin. A whining Cocoa would be good payback for all the sleep Gretchen had lost after that second kiss.

Halfway across the yard, Gretchen stopped walking. She'd been so focused on how Cocoa would handle Gram being away that she'd totally missed a more obvious potential pitfall of her grandmother spending the night in Boston.

Gretchen wasn't going to be alone in the house. She was going to be alone in the house *with Alex*. And, as cute as she was, Gretchen didn't think Cocoa was going to be the most effective of chaperones should Alex decide to try for another kiss.

But the next day, about two hours before Dana was supposed to pick her up, Gram decided to take Cocoa to Boston with her. Gretchen was pretty sure her grandmother had lost her mind.

"Are you sure this is a good idea?" Gretchen asked her for the umpteenth time. "She has no social skills at all."

"You keep telling me Cocoa's companionship is good for me," Ida told her. "And I told you Dana's cousin has three golden retrievers and doesn't mind at all if she comes. It'll do Cocoa good to hang out with some furry friends. She can teach them all how to high-five."

"What about the car ride? She'll get dog hair all over Dana's car, and what about bathroom breaks?"

Ida laughed. "If you think my friends and I are going to get from here to Massachusetts without pit stops, you're crazy."

"I think she'd be happier staying here."

"She needs to learn to ride in the car," Ida insisted. "And, like you just pointed out yourself, she needs some socialization. If we want to take her into town for parades or just to do some errands, she needs to know how to behave."

"What if she gets away from you?"

"I'm not taking her around the city with me. She's going to stay with the other dogs in a huge fenced yard while we're at the craft show. And Dana's cousin will be with her."

Gretchen slowly shook her head, knowing this argument was as good as lost. "Make sure her collar and tags are on her all the time. And you need to use the leash when you make bathroom stops. She might stay close to you here, but she could get spooked or distracted and run off."

"I'm not going to let her run off." Ida looked down at Cocoa, who was thumping her tail on the ground. "You want to go on a road trip?"

"By the time you pack her food, you won't have any room left for yarn," Gretchen said.

"We'll be fine. Come on, Cocoa. Let's go pack you a bag."

Gretchen watched them go into the kitchen and then dropped onto the sofa with a sigh. She'd had some reservations about Cocoa being enough of a chaperone to keep Gretchen from doing something she might regret, but now she had no chaperone at all. All she had was her own willpower, and she was afraid that tank was about empty, with her self-control running on fumes.

Alex wasn't surprised when Gretchen was more quiet than usual over supper. Ida had called to tell her they'd arrived and that Cocoa was having fun with her new golden retriever friends, but he knew Gretchen would worry about them both until they were safely back on the farm.

He also wondered if she was feeling awkward about being alone in the house with him. Alex was fairly sure that was deliberate, though he wasn't sure if Gretchen had figured out Cocoa's social skills weren't Ida's sole motivation in taking the dog with her. Her good-bye to Alex had been *Enjoy having the house to yourselves*, followed by a wink. It didn't take a genius to figure out she was giving him a green light. Which was weird, but she was a pretty up-front kind of woman.

To distract Gretchen from worrying about Ida, he'd tried to get her into town for a meal, but she'd told him she needed to fix some loose wire in the chicken fencing and it was easier to get it done while Cocoa wasn't around.

When she'd come in from her evening chores, he'd offered to make them sandwiches and salads while she showered, which was an offer she *did* take him up on. So now she was sitting across the table from him, idly pushing a chunk of tomato around on her plate.

She was too quiet, and he decided it was time to lighten the mood. "I feel like we should do something fun and naughty while your grandmother's away."

She gave him a stern look, though the slight bow of her lips gave away her amusement. "You do realize *I'm* the strict one in the household, right?"

"Which will make doing something naughty that much more unexpected and fun."

She got up and scraped her plate before setting it beside the sink. Then she leaned against the stove, crossed her arms and shrugged. "I'd suggest tipping cows, but we sold them off years ago. I don't recommend trying to tip horses."

He stared at her, 99 percent sure she was messing with

him, but she only stared back with an arched brow. "You're kidding . . . right?"

After a few more seconds, her expression relaxed and that rare grin that turned him inside out lit up her face. "Yes, I'm kidding. Well, I'm kidding about suggesting we tip cows. I'm serious about not trying to tip horses. That's always a bad idea."

"I'll make a note of that for the future." He slid back his chair and stood to carry his plate to the sink, which put him within arm's reach of her. "But that crosses one possibility for tonight off the list."

She turned toward him, her body language open and inviting. "I'm sure we can think of something."

The slight huskiness to her voice was the subtle invitation he was looking for. "I was thinking we could play a game of strip cribbage."

"I don't think strip cribbage is a thing."

He shrugged. "Neither was strip poker until some poor bastard ran out of money and bet his boxers."

She laughed and he let the sound wash over him. He loved when she laughed, and he also loved that she did it more often now. "We could watch a movie."

"I fail to see how that involves stripping in any way." He held up his hand. "*You* stripping, to be more exact, since you're a smart-ass and were probably going to suggest a movie with stripping in it."

She crossed her arms, which made him sigh. It was like a sign—*extreme stubbornness ahead*. "You seem very determined to get my clothes off of me. I know these cow pajama pants are awesome, but if you go on the Internet, you can probably buy your own pair."

"We could race. Whoever gets *on* my bed first gets to watch the loser strip."

"What if it's a tie?"

Leave it to Gretchen to want to establish rules for getting naked in a hurry. "The stairs and the doorways are too narrow, so it's not possible for it to end in a tie."

"You're an athlete. You'd have to give me a head start."

That made him laugh. "I played football in high school. You chasing that chicken that got loose while you were fixing the fence was more running than I've done in years, so I should be the one who gets a head start."

"But I'm tired from chasing the chicken."

"I have this mental image of us still standing here at five o'clock tomorrow morning, arguing about the rules of this race."

"Go!"

Before his mind could even process what was happening, Gretchen was halfway to the kitchen door. He took off after her, but she had long legs, and he didn't even get close enough to try to pass her until she was almost to the stairs.

She took the corner better than he did and gained some ground, but he took the steps two at a time and was right on her heels when she reached the top. He passed her, but the burst of speed also gave him momentum, and he realized too late that he was wearing socks and she wasn't.

As they reached his doorway, he tried to turn, but his feet didn't have traction. She cut to his inside and gave him a little shove, which put him just off balance enough to get her through the doorway first.

But before she could leap onto the bed, he was behind her. Because of the brass footboard, she had to go around the bed, and he made his move. As she jumped, he wrapped his arms around her waist and twisted, so he fell onto his back with her on top of him.

"Football skills," he growled into her hair. "I played defense, so if you run, I take you down."

Breathless and laughing, Gretchen jabbed her elbow into him and, when he realized his hold, rolled off onto the mattress. "That was a tie."

"No way. My butt hit the mattress first."

"Because you cheated."

"I cheated? Maybe if you'd stayed in the kitchen and made more rules instead of yelling out *go* with no *ready* or *set*, I would have known what those rules were."

"I think we can compromise." She propped herself on her elbow and looked down at him. "You have to strip because cheating disqualifies you, so clearly you lost. But I'll admit the start of the race maybe wasn't *totally* fair. So you have to strip, but as a penalty I should have to help you."

He pretended to think about that for all of about two seconds. "I can live with that."

Once she caught her breath, Gretchen got to her feet and put out her hand to help Alex up.

She'd spent most of the evening, including dinner, trying to figure out what she'd do if Alex made a move tonight. Waffling back and forth had almost given her a headache, so eventually she'd told herself she'd make up her mind if and when the situation arose.

And when it did arise, she knew it was stupid to continue denying herself something she wanted so badly. So what if he was going to leave and she'd probably never hear from him again? She was going to end up missing him one way or the other, so she may as well enjoy him now.

So when he'd turned the flirting up a notch, she hadn't really tried to shut him down. This moment had been more or less inevitable since Gram announced her intention to take the dog with her. Not that Cocoa cared what the humans got up to, but she was a good excuse to hide behind. When there was a chocolate Lab sprawled in your bed, there wasn't a lot of room left for a man of Alex's size.

Now she pulled on Alex's hands so he sat up, but he didn't let her pull him to his feet. Instead, he hauled her in until she was standing between his legs, looking down at him. Letting go of her hands, he cupped her ass and tilted his head back so he could see her face.

"You move pretty fast once you make up your mind," he said. "Let's not rush this part, though."

She didn't intend to. She'd been denying herself the highly anticipated pleasure of Alex's touch for too long to let it be over too soon. "I'll try to take my time getting your clothes off, but it won't be easy."

"Any chance of you getting naked first?"

She grinned, slowly shaking her head. "I don't want you distracted."

"You don't have to be naked to distract me." He squeezed her ass, pulling her even closer, so she had to brace her hands on his shoulders to keep from falling on top of him. While he might have enjoyed that, she had other plans.

Reaching back, she took his hands and made another attempt at pulling him to his feet. This time when he resisted, she tugged harder and won the battle.

Once he was standing, she hooked her arms around his neck and stood on her tiptoes to kiss him because she wanted his lips on hers before she did anything else.

This kiss was even better, his mouth hot and demanding, because she wasn't torn between wanting him and knowing they should stop. There was no ongoing argument in her mind or trying to ignore the intense need that his touch inflamed in her.

There would be no stopping this time.

She bunched the fabric of his T-shirt in her hands, slowly gathering the fabric as they kissed. When she got to his chest, she stepped back and made him pull his arms out before working it over his head. T-shirt tossed away, she ran her hands over his naked chest and smiled.

"What's that look for?" he asked.

"I've spent a lot of time imagining running my hands over your body, so now that I have the chance, I intend to enjoy it."

"You won't hear any complaints from me."

"Before we go any further—" He groaned and she scowled at him. "You said I wouldn't hear any complaints from you."

"I didn't say a word."

"That was a complaint sound."

He looped one finger through a lock of her hair. "I was simply acknowledging that now's a perfect time to stop and have a conversation."

"I just want to know if you have protection or if I have to make a trip to my room, because I'd rather do it now than later." She'd ordered a box of condoms on the Internet, making sure a few other things they needed were packed with it, because when Chase bought condoms in the hope of getting lucky with Kelly, it was handled with the usual Stewart Mills discretion. Even Gram had known about the purchase.

"My nightstand drawer," he said, tugging on the strands of hair wrapped around his finger.

"Good." She reached down and unbuttoned his jeans, laughing when his stomach muscles tightened in reaction to the touch of her knuckles. They didn't relax any when she very slowly worked the zipper down, either.

"You're killing me."

"The race was your idea."

He sucked in a breath when she tucked her fingers under his waistband. "I assumed I would win."

She might have laughed if she wasn't so aware of the erection pressing against the open fly of his jeans. It was probably getting painful for him, so she worked the denim down over his hips. He exhaled slowly, as if in relief, and obediently stepped out of the jeans and let her pull off his socks as she tapped each knee.

As she stood, she ran her hands up his thighs, letting her fingertips slide under the legs of his boxer briefs. Scratching lightly with her fingernails, she tilted her head back to see his face. He had his eyes closed and looked like a man whose self-control was hanging by a thread.

Deciding to leave the boxer briefs for the time being, Gretchen stood straight and ran her fingertip down his chin and over his Adam's apple. He opened his eyes and gave her a hopeful smile. "Is it time for you to get naked now?"

"I'm not done stripping you yet."

"You were just down there and I'm not naked, so I thought maybe you lost your nerve."

"You're pretty mouthy for a guy who's almost naked."

"It's *your* mouth I'm more interested in." He cupped the back of her head in one of those big hands, pulling her close. "I love your mouth."

He kissed her deeply until she moaned against his lips and her fingernails bit into his shoulders. His other hand yanked up on the hem of her T-shirt so he could get under it and feel her bare skin.

"I think we can start stripping me now," she said against his mouth.

He didn't waste any time getting her out of her clothes. And as he slid her cow pajama pants down her legs, managing to take her underwear with them, he made an appreciative moaning sound. Seconds later, he kicked his boxer briefs into the pile and pulled her up against him.

His skin was hot, and the length of his erection pressed against her lower belly. She moved her hips a little, rubbing across his sensitive flesh, and his hand fisted in her hair. With a growl, his mouth took hers again. The kiss was hard and fast, and then he turned, lifting her onto the bed.

The look he gave her was almost enough to send her over the edge, and she grabbed his hand to yank him down beside her. He grinned and pushed her hair back from her face. "I love your eyes."

"You don't have to say pretty words to get in my pants, you know. My pants are already on the floor."

He kissed the center of her throat before shaking his head. Stretching out beside her, he slid his hand down her stomach to the aching juncture of her thighs. "I told you I love your eyes because I love your eyes."

"Gaze into them all you want," she told him, her body

practically quivering in anticipation, "but just move those fingers a little bit lower."

Her hips bucked against his hand when he hit the sweet spot and she whimpered, but he just smiled as he slipped one finger inside her. "I guess I don't have to wonder if you really want me."

She didn't answer him for a few seconds, savoring the friction of his hand against her sensitive flesh. "I've wanted you since the day you got here."

"Really?" He worked another finger inside her. She sucked in a breath, grinding against his hand. "You're very good at hiding your thoughts."

"I think it was the shoulders." She trailed her nails over his shoulder, making him shiver. "And your smile."

He stroked her and kissed her until her hips bucked against his hand and she was practically ready to beg him for more. When he bent his head to run his tongue around her nipple before sucking it into his mouth, she couldn't take it anymore.

Reaching down between them, she wrapped her fingers around the hard length of his erection and stroked, squeezing just slightly. He inhaled sharply, then muttered a curse against her skin.

"You can't keep doing that," he warned in a husky voice.

"I think it's only fair, don't you?" She brushed her thumb over the tip, and then laughed when he reached down and jerked her hand away.

"You won't be laughing if I come and you haven't yet," he warned.

He had a point, she thought as he got off the bed to grab a condom from the nightstand drawer. He also had a very fine ass, and once he was covered and between her thighs, she filled her hands with it.

When he pushed into her, Gretchen closed her eyes and dug her fingers into his flesh to urge him on. He rocked his hips, filling her more completely with every stroke, until he was totally inside her.

Alex stilled, bending his head to close his mouth around her nipple. He sucked, gently at first, and then harder. When she made an impatient sound, deep in her throat, he lifted his head to grin at her. Then he lowered his lips to her other breast.

When she couldn't take it anymore, she cupped his jaw in her hands and hauled his face to hers. She kissed him, dipping her tongue against his, as she lifted her hips to force him to move.

Slowly at first, Alex obeyed her unspoken command. With slow, even thrusts, he moved within her. She slid her fingers into his hair, then ran her hands down his neck and over his shoulders. The muscles in his back flexed with each thrust, and she trailed her nails over them.

His pace quickened and he nipped at her mouth, then at her throat. "God, you're beautiful. Don't close your eyes. Look at me."

She opened her eyes, looking into his intense gaze. "I need more. Please. I can't . . ."

He lifted her knees, opening her even more to his body. The thrusts were deeper and harder, and Gretchen felt her breath catch in her chest. Then she felt his hand—his thumb brushing over the sensitive nub where their bodies met. "Yes."

The orgasm rocked her, and she curled her fingers around the brass rails of the headboard, her back arching off the bed. Alex's breath came in ragged, hot bursts against her skin as he found his own release.

When he collapsed on top of her, Gretchen let go of the headboard and wrapped her arms around his waist to hold him close. He kissed her neck and her throat, then kissed the top of her breast, his breath still coming in quick, shallow pants.

"I needed that so much," he said, his words slightly muffled as he spoke against her neck. "Needed *you* so much."

"I needed that, too." She kissed his hair. "It was worth the wait, though. Maybe even better because the anticipation built up, you know."

"Interesting theory. Give me a few minutes and we'll test it out." He brushed a few strands of her hair away from his face. "We'll see if it's just as good without the wait and the buildup of anticipation."

Gretchen smiled and ran her fingers through his hair. She had absolutely no doubt it would be.

11

Gretchen woke slowly to the sun streaming over her face and did something she almost never did—she rolled over, pulled the light blanket over her head and closed her eyes again.

Today, she didn't care about the chickens or the horses or those stupid pumpkins. She wanted to stay in bed and savor the feeling of contentment and slightly sore muscles. Maybe she'd take a long, hot bath. Then she'd spend the rest of the day in her cow pajama pants, curled up on the couch with a book.

Or with Alex.

She wasn't sure where he'd gone, but she was surprised he'd awakened before her. Not that he was lazy in the mornings, but she was an up-before-the-dawn kind of girl by nature. And she also hoped wherever he'd gone involved the kitchen and the coffeemaker.

Coffee. She was willing to get out of bed for coffee. And since she was up, she may as well go out and gather any eggs the chickens saw fit to gift them. While she was out there, she may as well take care of the horses.

So much for spending the day in her robe, she thought with a disgusted sigh. After a quick shower to help kick her into gear, she got dressed and went in search of Alex. When she was halfway down the stairs, she caught the scent of coffee, but she didn't smell breakfast.

"Good morning," he said when she walked into the kitchen.

He was leaning against the counter, sipping from a mug. Shirtless and barefoot, he was only wearing unbuttoned jeans, and Gretchen had to admit Alex Murphy wasn't a bad sight to wake up to.

Especially when he reached over and picked up another coffee mug, which he held out to her. She took a long sip and then smiled at him. "Good morning."

"I was thinking," he said. "After you take care of whatever you need to outside, we should go to O'Rourke's and have breakfast."

"We have breakfast stuff." While Gram would know better than she did what was in the fridge and the pantry, they always had food. "Don't we?"

"Yeah, but wouldn't it be nice to relax and let somebody else do all the work? We can take our time and have coffee refills and then stick somebody else with the dirty dishes."

That did sound nice. *Really* nice. It wasn't quite a flannel robe all day, but it would still feel a little decadent and lazy. "I like that idea."

"Good." He gave her a look that practically sizzled over the rim of his mug. "I like having you to myself."

She rushed through her morning chores as quickly as possible, which made her laugh. She'd gone from wanting to skip chores to doing them like they were an Olympic event just because Alex wanted to take her out to breakfast. And the promise of unlimited coffee refills didn't hurt, either.

O'Rourke's was busier than she'd expected, though, and she belatedly realized it was Saturday morning. Living her entire life around the farm, there were times she knew what day it was only because there was a calendar hanging on the pantry door where Gram kept track of things.

And, of course, everybody looked up as they were led to an open table, and she knew there would be a lot of whispering. Not that it bothered her what they thought, but it always annoyed her when people gossiped in a way that was obvious to the person being talked about. She'd seen it when Kelly started dating Chase, and it had gotten on her nerves then, too.

"You can tell people we were here because I was interviewing you, if it makes you feel better," Alex said when they'd been seated and served coffee.

"What?"

"You've been wound as tight as an eight-day watch since we walked in." He shrugged. "I've bought a few people lunch here while talking to them for my story, so it's something I'm known to do. Of course, some people might think it odd I brought you here when I'm staying in your house, but you can tell them it was my way of saying thank you."

She realized he thought she was uncomfortable because people might think she was on a date with him. A breakfast date, no less. "Why would I need to tell anybody anything? Everybody in the place is here for the same reason we are. Food."

"It doesn't bother you that they might think we're sleeping together?"

"Doesn't faze me in the least." She took a sip of her coffee, considering that. "I guess I care what Gram thinks."

"I could be wrong, but I suspect Ida wouldn't really have a problem with us having a morning-after breakfast, if you know what I mean."

She did know, but she didn't think they were on the same page as far as her grandmother. No, Gram wouldn't get bent out of shape about Gretchen sleeping with a man. But considering how Gram considered Alex practically part of the family already, it wasn't her judgment Gretchen feared. It was Gram's expectations.

"I also don't want Gram to think morning-after breakfasts might become a usual thing for us, if you know what *I* mean."

"Ah. She's a smart lady. I think she'll figure out what's up without too much drama."

"Probably." Gretchen opened her menu and looked over the breakfast choices. Maybe it was the workout she'd gotten last night, or maybe it was because she'd usually eaten by now, but she was starving. "Do you know what you're having? They have a fruit cup."

He gave her a look over the top of his menu. "I don't think

a fruit cup is going to cut it today. I'm in a French toast kind of mood, and I think I earned myself some bacon, don't you?"

She felt warmth on her cheeks as she nodded. "Definitely."

When their server returned, they ordered their breakfasts, including a side of bacon for Alex.

"Tell me about your favorite photograph you've ever taken," she said, propping her chin on her hands.

"Well, there's this hot woman and a truck and some pumpkins."

"I'm serious," she said, though she was kind of laughing as she said it.

"Actually, I *am* very proud of that photo. But of the other ones I've taken . . . there have been so many."

He talked about some of them, and Gretchen was content to sit and listen to the pride in his voice. Sometimes he used technical words she didn't understand, but he had a way of talking about his work that was very sexy. He was confident, knew what he was doing and did it well.

When their breakfasts arrived, they did less talking and more eating. Gram was a good cook—at least as good as anybody who cooked for Cass and Don at O'Rourke's—but Alex had been right. Sometimes it just tasted better when you could sit back and let somebody else do all the work.

Once their plates were cleared, they each had a third cup of coffee, which they took their time drinking. The crowd had thinned, and empty tables meant they didn't feel rushed at all.

"How come you don't get more chickens?" he asked out of the blue.

"The chickens we have are enough of a pain in the ass. Why would I want more?"

"Couldn't you sell the eggs? With everybody jumping on the organic bandwagon, wouldn't that be a moneymaker?"

She shook her head. "Organic doesn't simply mean the egg came from a happy farm chicken. There are strict guidelines to meet to get that stamp, and I don't have the time or energy for it. And by the time I go through the process of gathering, storing and delivering the eggs, the profit margin wouldn't merit the extra work."

"So you looked into it?"

She shrugged. "I've looked into pretty much everything. Even bees, since people love jars of local honey. The problem with that endeavor, however, is that it involves bees."

His laugh was rich and carried through O'Rourke's. A few people turned to look, but he didn't seem to care.

They talked for a while longer, covering a little bit of everything, until Gretchen noticed the server was going around the room with the coffeepot again.

"Do we want another refill?" She rarely said no to more coffee, but they'd both already had quite a bit.

"I don't know. What time is Ida supposed to be home today?"

"She said it wouldn't be until late, probably even after dark. They'll be at the craft show most of the day, and they'll want to have supper before they hit the road."

"So we could feasibly go back to bed for a couple of hours if we don't spend all day in town."

Gretchen grinned and put her folded-up napkin in her empty mug to signal that she was done. "I think I've had enough coffee."

Because they'd gotten distracted the night before and Ida was due home anytime, Alex volunteered to help Gretchen clean the kitchen. After spending the bulk of the afternoon in his bed, they'd thrown a quick meal together before helping each other shower.

But the clock was ticking on their alone time and Ida wasn't going to be impressed to come home to two meals' worth of dirty dishes sitting in the sink. She was laid-back about many things, but dishes in the sink was not one of them.

"You really don't have to help, you know," Gretchen said. "There aren't that many."

"Then we'll be done that much faster. I'll wash and you dry."

"You always wash."

"I hate drying and putting away. And you hate washing, so why are you complaining?"

"I wasn't complaining. Just an observation." She took the first mug he washed out of the drainer and ran the towel over it. "Speaking of observations, you've spent a lot of time digging into people's lives since you got here. Even mine, actually, since I *never* talk about my parents but ended up telling you all about them. You have this great ability to get people to open up to you, but you don't say much about yourself."

"People don't really ask. And if they did ask, it wouldn't require digging. I'm pretty much an open book." He thought about what she'd said for a second. "And I've told you things. I don't think anybody else in Stewart Mills knows I gained so much weight after football that I was extremely unhealthy and have to watch my diet. Not even Chase."

"I know you were married once. You never really talk about that."

His divorce wasn't something he was ashamed of, but it wasn't something he was really proud of, either. "Do most people just go around talking about their ex-spouses? Failed marriages don't usually make for great dinner conversation."

"Maybe not, but, like I said, you know more about me than I usually tell people. So you and your ex-wife didn't have kids?"

He looked at her, a little hurt she didn't give him more credit than that. "No kids. If I had children, they would *definitely* have come up in conversation. And I should point out you haven't told me about your romantic past, either, so it's not like I'm being secretive. It's just not something people randomly talk about."

"I've dated. I have yet to meet a man I want to keep who doesn't mind the idea of living on a farm. So we spend some time together and then, when it's run its course, we move on, and that's my relationship history in a nutshell. See? Not worth talking about."

It bothered him that she was so casual about it, though it took him a moment to realize why. Their relationship fit that pattern, too, so it was only a matter of time before he became somebody not worth talking about to Gretchen. It hurt him a little to think that someday she'd be as nonchalant about him as she was about the other men in her past.

"Did you meet your wife at college?" she asked.

"No. I met my ex-wife at a gallery showing of my work in Philadelphia. She's a lawyer and she stopped in with some coworkers because she liked a photo I'd taken in Hawaii and wanted to know which island it was."

"So you already traveled a lot when you started dating her? It seems like it would be different if you'd started your career *after* you got together, but she knew what she was signing up for."

He nodded. "She knew, but I guess she thought I would cut back when we got married. I never said that to her, but I think she built a new life for us in her head and didn't share it with me, so I never had the chance to agree or disagree."

"Did she ever travel with you? I mean, not when you went somewhere dangerous, but if you were doing photos for travel magazines or whatever."

He washed the last plate and pulled the plug before rinsing the soap away and setting it in the drainer. "She did once, when I was going to the Caribbean and she had some vacation time to burn. But she had her own career, and following me around the world wasn't going to help her climb the law firm's ladder."

Gretchen put the last dish in the cabinet and hung the towel through its loop. "How long did you plan to do the long-distance thing?"

He shrugged. "I don't know. We lived in Philly, which isn't hard to get flights in and out of, so I was probably home more often once we got married than I had been in the past. I probably would have cut back when it was time to start a family, but that wasn't something in the cards for her until she felt secure in her career."

"Well." She gave him a small smile. "I'm sorry it didn't work out."

"I guess if it *had* worked out, being here with you would be a whole lot more awkward."

"True. Hey, we finished just in time."

He heard the car a few seconds before its headlights splashed through the living room windows, and he hoped the momentary disappointment he felt didn't show on his face. As much as he liked Ida and Cocoa, he'd really enjoyed having some alone time with Gretchen.

By the time they got outside, Cocoa had already been set free and she ran to greet them. Once she'd received some affection and a high five from each of them, she set out to sniff every blade of grass in the yard to make sure nothing had changed.

Alex carried in Ida's bag while the women chatted, then made another trip for Cocoa's bag and the leftover food Ida had brought for her. There was also a large bag of yarn with Ida's name written on it, so he grabbed that, too.

"I had the most wonderful time," Ida said when her friends had gone and they were all inside. "So did Cocoa. She was so funny playing with those golden retrievers. I wish they lived closer so the dogs could have playdates."

Alex looked at Cocoa, who had immediately gone to her pillow in the corner and collapsed on it as though Ida had made her walk every square inch of the city. "She definitely burned off some energy."

"It's good to get out once in a while," Ida said. "But I think we're both glad to be home."

"I'm glad you had a good time, Gram. Was it crowded?"

"It was *very* crowded, but I met a lot of nice people. I gave out a lot of those business cards we printed up, with the picture of the sweater set on the back, and I got two orders before I even left."

"That's great, Ida. As the holidays get closer, you might actually have to turn people away."

"I hope not. I knit pretty fast, but I don't want to sacrifice quality. I'll just see how it goes."

She looked excited and hopeful, but he could also see how tired she was. She'd probably stayed up too late, talking with her friends, and then topped it off with a long walk around the convention center today. Gretchen looked tired, too, but for an entirely different reason.

Alex leaned back against the couch and let the two women talk. His mind returned to the conversation with Gretchen about his marriage to Laura, wondering what had prompted the question.

She'd seemed particularly interested in how he thought his profession had been a factor, but maybe that was his imagination. Her comments about her relationship history had made it clear she didn't have any problem with enjoying him for now, and then putting him out of her mind.

It stung a little, but it also eased his mind. He'd enjoyed having sex with Gretchen even more than he'd anticipated, and he already wanted to do it again. Even if being disposable bugged him on some level, knowing she didn't have a habit of romanticizing things actually made it easier, because he didn't have to worry about any hurt feelings when it was time for him to leave.

"It's going to be nice to sleep in my own bed tonight," Ida announced, pushing up out of her rocking chair. "I think I'm going to let Cocoa out one last time and then go upstairs."

"I'll carry your bag up and put it outside your door," Alex told her.

After he did that, he went back downstairs just in time to say good night to Ida and Cocoa. And then to Gretchen, who announced she was turning in a little early, too. He told them he'd lock up and watched them all go up the stairs, smiling at the way they talked right up until they parted ways at their bedrooms.

He went through the house, locking both doors and turning lights off, and then went upstairs to a bed that felt a lot more cold and lonely than it had just two nights before.

On Monday, Gretchen had to run into town to pick up a prescription for Gram at the pharmacy. The doctor had been impressed with her lower blood pressure, so he was making a few adjustments to her medications.

Since she was already in town, she decided to pop over to the high school and see Jen. She'd be in her office, as would most of the staff as they geared up for the start of the school year.

The secretary told Gretchen to go ahead back to Jen's office, where she found the door to the guidance office standing open. Jen had her head bent over a document and was rubbing her temple as she read.

"School hasn't even started yet and you have a headache?"

Jen looked up, then dropped her hands to the desk. "You have no idea. The kids start a week from tomorrow, but I swear there are new rules and new paperwork every year. I could literally move into this office and work twenty-four hours a day and still never be done."

Even though Jen was one of the very lucky members of the administration who had a window in the ancient brick school, it sounded like Gretchen's worst nightmare. "Hopefully the fall will be a little easier than the spring was since you can hold playing football over their heads again."

"Some of them. Others? It's all I can do to keep some of them coming to school on a regular basis, and I know they're going to drop out as soon as they find jobs. Sometimes I think it's time to move to a big city and get a job at some giant high school."

"I think you'd have even more stuff on your desk. It would just be a different kind of stuff. And it doesn't matter how many kids there are. You'll care about all of them."

"True." Jen sighed and leaned back in her chair. "Sit down. Tell me what you're up to."

"I had to pick up something for Gram, so I thought I'd pop in and say hi. See what's going on besides back-to-school craziness."

Jen shrugged. "This time of year, it's mostly just about work. What's happening out on the farm?"

"Work." She smiled. "A little bit of playing."

"Really? So this taking-in-a-boarder thing is really working out for you."

Gretchen laughed. "I'd like to think it wouldn't have worked out the same way with just any random stranger. But I'm enjoying having Alex around. For now."

"For now. That's what Kelly said, too."

The situations were entirely different, but Gretchen didn't bother pointing that out. Everybody could think whatever they wanted to. "Speaking of Kelly, was Chase home this weekend?"

"It took her an hour and a half to answer my text on Saturday, so I'm guessing he was." Jen picked up a pen and started doodling in the margins of a notepad. "Alex and Chase stay in touch now, don't they?"

"Yeah. Maybe not a lot, but I know they had lunch together a while back. And Alex mentioned a text from him about something."

"That's good. That they reconnected while they were here in town for Eagles Fest, I mean. Do you know if he stays in touch with any of the others?"

Like Sam Leavitt? "I don't really know."

"I was just curious." She was doodling so hard, Gretchen was surprised she didn't rip the paper.

"You know you can talk about him, Jen. To Kelly and me, I mean."

"I don't want to talk about him." She sighed and tossed the pen down. "When we . . . that night, it was an unplanned, heat-of-the-moment kind of thing, and when you're not planning to have sex, precautions aren't always taken."

When Jen paused, Gretchen assumed she was supposed to say something awesomely supportive and knowledgeable, but all she had was "Oh, no."

"I got very lucky," Jen continued. "I got a phone call from my doctor last week with the last follow-up. I tested negative for anything and everything that can be tested for."

Relief made Gretchen sag against the back of the chair. "Oh, I'm so glad."

"I guess if I was going to have stupid, reckless sex one time in my life, I picked the right time of the month and the right guy. Clean and never to be seen again."

"Yeah. Don't do that again, because that might be like winning the unprotected-sex lottery. You don't want to tempt fate too much."

"I know." Jen looked at her and smiled almost reluctantly. "It was so very freaking hot, though. That's the part that really pisses me off."

"Very-freaking-hot sex pisses you off?"

"Yes, it does. I've had good sex before. I'm not really shy about making sure it's good for me. But Sam . . . It's so unfair that he rolls into town, sets the sex bar incredibly high for the rest of my life, and then rolls back out again."

Gretchen sighed. "So now your qualifications are handsome, intelligent, financially secure *and* better in bed than Sam Leavitt?"

"Yeah. So the good news is that I'll never make you wear an ugly bridesmaid dress."

"You need to take those expectations down a notch. Or maybe you can come live at the farm and we can grow old together."

"You really don't think you and Alex will go anywhere?"

"Alex is going to go lots of places, but without me. That's just the way it is."

Jen gave her a sad look. "I wish it was different, because he seems like a really great guy."

"He *is* a really great guy. Just not the right guy for me." When Jen's phone buzzed indicating she had an incoming call, Gretchen jumped at the chance to get away from this conversation. "I'll let you get that. If you see Kelly, tell her I said hi."

Jen waved with one hand while she picked up the receiver with the other. Gretchen made her way through the maze of offices to the exit and breathed in the warm fresh air. Being cooped up in that school all day had been torture for her as a kid, and she didn't like being in the building any more as an adult.

After picking up Gram's medicine, she decided to run into the market for a few things. And more grapes. She didn't think she'd ever seen anybody go through as many grapes as he did, and now he had her and Gram hooked on them, too. If this pumpkin thing ever went south, maybe she'd turn the field into a vineyard and grow her own damn grapes.

12

Gretchen finished brushing the last of the three horses with a relieved sigh. She'd taken them each for a short ride, just for a change of scenery, and the switching of the saddle each time wasn't fun for her back.

"You won't be with me much longer, guys," she said as she secured the stall. Cinnamon snorted and tossed her head, so Gretchen moved down to her stall to give her a nose rub. "I know you like being with the kids. Soon, doll. I promise."

"Do they ever come ride them?" Alex asked from behind her, and Gretchen spun around.

"Don't sneak up on me like that."

"Sorry. I just assumed you heard me."

"No, I didn't. And they haven't been up very much this

summer. To be honest, I don't know why they don't just leave the horses down south. They used to come up a lot more often, but the older the kids get, the busier their lives seem to be. Did you need something?"

"Nope." He stepped closer to her, his intent suddenly clear in his eyes. "Just visiting."

"I was going to check the pumpkins next. Make sure the rain we had last night was enough for them."

"Have you ever had sex in the hayloft?"

Well, that certainly got her attention. "Is this some kind of farm girl fantasy of yours?"

He hooked a finger in the front of her jeans and tugged her forward. "Must be one of those weird proclivities your grandmother was worried about."

"Okay, but despite what it might look like in movies, hay is not actually very soft."

"So what you're saying is that I need to smuggle a blanket out of the house."

"A blanket would be nice, yes."

"I'll be right back."

Gretchen stared after him, unable to believe he was actually going in to get a blanket. It was almost the middle of the day, for goodness' sake. And how was he going to explain trying to smuggle out a blanket? He couldn't really shove it down his pants.

Sure she'd seen the last of Alex for a while, she finished up cleaning up and was just about to leave the barn when he stepped back inside and pulled the door closed behind him.

Under one arm was a folded-up quilt, and dangling from his other hand was a wicker basket.

"You have to be kidding me."

He grinned. "I can be enterprising when I need to be. I told Ida the light was perfect to get some shots of you out in the field and I wanted to walk, but then I very sadly realized it was too close to lunchtime."

"She made us a picnic lunch? To eat in the field?"

"Yup." He held up the basket.

"So now I have to hide in the hayloft to eat my lunch."

Shrugging, Alex started toward the wooden ladder. "We can do that, too."

Part of her could hardly believe his audacity. He'd fibbed to Gram and not only gotten a blanket, but a picnic lunch, too. But another part of her—namely parts of her directly involved in orgasms—didn't care how he'd pulled it off.

By the time she got up the ladder, Alex had set the picnic basket off to one side and was spreading the quilt over some hay bales. Then he sat down on it and bounced a little, as if testing a mattress. "What do you think?"

"I think it's perfect." She straddled his lap, bunching the front of his T-shirt in one hand. With the other hand, she tugged his hair, pulling his head back so she could press her mouth to his.

His hands gripped her hips, pushing her down against his denim-clad erection. When she dipped her tongue between his lips, he responded with a hunger that matched her own. His fingertips pressed into her flesh, and his hips lifted from the hay bale. Gretchen ground against him, the delicious friction making her throb.

Alex caught her lower lip between his teeth, biting down until she moaned. His hands rocked her hips gently, sliding her back and forth along the length of him. She'd never hated clothing as much as she did in that moment.

"We have too many clothes on," Gretchen whispered against his mouth.

"We can fix that."

A few minutes later, she was spread naked on the blanket-covered hay bales, under Alex. He was just as naked, except for the condom, and Gretchen shivered in anticipation.

She ran her fingertips across the smooth, hard planes of Alex's chest before bringing her legs up so she could use her heels to pull him closer. She wanted him inside her *now*.

He never broke eye contact with her as he lowered his hips and pressed the head of his erection against her. The muscles in his jaw worked as he slowly slid into her, tormenting them both. When she tried to lift her hips, he pulled back the same amount.

"Are you in a hurry?" he teased, but the husky rasp of his voice told her he was on the ragged edge of self-control. But still he didn't bury himself in her. Instead, he taunted her, pulling back a little more each time until her hands curled into fists and she wanted to scream.

He brushed his thumb over her nipple, causing a delicious ripple through her body. "I've had a few fantasies about you and this hayloft, but this is better."

"I like that real me is better than imaginary me."

He moved his hips in excruciatingly slow circles, deliberately trying to drive her crazy. "Real you is amazing. And my fantasies tend to be a little rushed in the shower, due to the hot water situation."

An image of him in the shower, taking himself in hand

while the water beat on his broad shoulders, had her raking her fingernails over his back.

Alex drove into her then, burying himself so deep within her, she almost came immediately. A small cry escaped her lips before she could bite it back, and she felt a shudder run down his spine. The muscles of his back worked as he moved in and out of her, slowly and with long, deep strokes.

Gretchen could never touch him enough to get her fill. She ran her hands over his back, his shoulders, over the flexing muscles of his upper arms. When she slid her hand down the side of his jaw, Alex turned his head and caught her finger in his mouth. He sucked hard, and she whimpered, raising her hips because she wanted more.

He reached down and took her left leg, pulling it over her right until she was turned away from him. With her foot on the floor and her other knee on the hay bales, he thrust deeper and harder, and Gretchen's muscles tensed. She panted, hovering on the brink.

"Come for me, Gretchen," he urged, his voice harsh with restraint.

She couldn't hold it back. Her muscles spasmed, clenching and releasing as he drove into her relentlessly, not letting up until she gasped his name, her fingernails digging into the blanket-covered hay.

When he came, he gripped her hips hard, pounding into her before leaning over to rest his forehead on her back. After a few moments so they could catch their breath, he pulled free of her and then tugged her sideways until they were both lying on the hay.

She turned so she could face him, and he kissed her. "I'm officially adding a farm girl and hayloft fetish to my list of possible weird proclivities."

Farm girl. Gretchen closed her eyes, inhaling deeply as he ran his thumb along the line of her jaw. "You make me want to be more."

"What?"

Dammit, she hadn't meant to say that out loud. "Forget it."

"Not a chance." The tip of his thumb skimmed over her lower lip and she shivered. "Look at me, Gretchen."

She did, looking into his dark eyes. "I just meant that you're probably used to . . . a more upscale woman. Fancy hotels, maybe. Nice sheets. All I have to offer is a hayloft."

"Honey, there is nowhere else I'd rather be right now than in this hayloft with you."

Right now. She caught the words, but couldn't tell if they meant anything or if she was reading too much into it. But she did know she didn't want this fun interlude to turn into something serious. "You know what's really nice about this hayloft?"

"Besides you being naked in it? What could be nicer?"

"There's a picnic basket with food in it."

He laughed and reached for his pants. "You do help a man work up an appetite."

She skimmed her hand over his back. "Mmm. But I'm also pretty good at helping you work *off* the calories, too."

"Very true." He tossed the pants back on the floor and crawled back over her. "I think she put cookies in there. Maybe another pre-lunch workout would make me feel less guilty about eating them."

Alex met Coach McDonnell for breakfast at O'Rourke's because it was one of the few times the man would sit still. Once the boys showed up for tryouts, the coach didn't rest until the football season ended.

But once a week, if he could, Coach would go to the restaurant for breakfast because his wife had taken strict control of his diet when his cholesterol levels concerned his doctor. Coach was a man who felt any life that didn't include the occasional hash omelet or a side of bacon with breakfast wasn't worth living, and Mrs. McDonnell seemed willing to pretend she didn't know.

"How's it going, son?" Coach asked once they'd been given big mugs of coffee and ordered their meals. "I haven't seen as much of you around the field."

"I can only use so many pictures of the kids running around in practice jerseys. I've spent some time trying to write but, to be honest, it's not easy."

"You wrote some damn fine essays in high school, but pictures were always your thing."

"It's more than that." Alex hadn't really articulated what he was feeling about the project, even in his own mind. But this was Coach, and if ever there was a man Alex could talk to, it was him. "I guess I'm having some reservations about the project and I've been trying to ignore them. Needless to say, that's a one-way ticket to writer's block."

"What kind of reservations?"

Alex raised his hands in a gesture of frustration. "I don't know. Like with Hunter Cass. He talked to me a while back. You know, his part in the story was probably the most compelling to me. But when he was telling me how things are better, it just felt so personal. I can't imagine putting a book out there that talks about some of the hardest times his family's been through."

"Isn't that your job? To make stories feel personal to the person reading them? To make people who look at your pictures feel the emotion behind them?"

"Yeah." He had a point. "But it feels like everybody's looking forward now, and maybe looking back doesn't do anybody any good."

Coach leaned back in the booth and gave him one of those direct looks Alex remembered from his youth. "Why'd you come back here, son?"

"I felt like the story was unfinished."

"Whose story?"

Alex opened his mouth to answer, hesitated, and then closed it again. "I don't know."

"You've been traveling for a lot of years, taking your photographs, and you kind of became a man with no home. Home is what keeps you grounded." Coach shrugged, rubbing the spot on his Eagles polo shirt between the top and second button like it was some kind of nervous habit. "Maybe you weren't done being a part of something again."

"I guess you could be right." He took a sip of coffee, wondering what the hell he was supposed to do with that realization. "The fundamental problem that leaves me with is the fact that my career kind of depends on me moving around the world at will. I can't just park myself in an office and wait for compelling human interest stories to happen outside my window."

"No, but you can keep it in your mind that you need to

recharge and reground yourself once in a while *before* you reach the burnout phase. What are you going to do with the story you've built so far?"

"I don't think I'm going to write a book. My subconscious seems to agree that's not the right way to go. I've run a few ideas by my agent and he thinks he can sell it as a web feature. Basically, a magazine would run an abridged story and extract in the paper edition, with the web address for the full feature. On the website would be a longer, more in-depth look at Stewart Mills. It would not only have photographs through the article, but it could have an accompanying photo gallery. I've done it once before and it's very effective."

"That sounds like a good compromise."

"It's long enough so I can tell the story I wanted to tell, but short enough so people don't expect the nitty-gritty personal details, you know? Really focus on where everybody's going and less on where they've been."

Coach looked up as the server brought their breakfasts, giving her a warm smile. "That looks amazing. Thank the cook for me."

"Sure thing, Coach." She turned to Alex. "You need anything else?"

"No, I'm all set. And it looks delicious." He eyed the plate when she'd walked away, taking in the mound of scrambled eggs and strips of bacon, to say nothing of the butter-soaked homemade toast. "They don't skimp on portions around here."

"No, they don't." Coach chuckled as he put cream and sugar in the coffee she'd refilled for them. "Mine are those fake eggs, though. Waitress accidentally let it slip a few weeks ago, and Cass confessed that she and Helen were in cahoots. I let her think they're getting away with it, though, because this sure isn't fake hash. I know how to pick my battles."

Alex laughed and dug into his eggs. "If I stay in this town much longer, I'm going to have to buy bigger pants."

"So how are things between you and Gretchen?"

Alex wasn't sure if that segue from staying in town much longer to his relationship with Gretchen was coincidental or deliberate on Coach's part. "We're, uh . . . enjoying each other's company."

"She's a pretty girl. And the Walkers have always been good people."

Alex nodded and shoved food in his mouth so he'd have an excuse not to reply. Though Coach was the go-to guy for advice and leaning on, he found himself strangely reluctant to talk about Gretchen with him.

"You know, after her grandfather passed away, nobody thought those two women had a chance of keeping that farm. They sure proved everybody wrong."

"It's not easy," Alex said. "They both work hard, but most of it falls on Gretchen."

"She's probably one of the most grounded women I've ever met, and she definitely has a strong sense of home and family." Coach pointed a forkful of hash at him. "Interesting mix, you being a guy with no home at all."

"First off, I do *have* a home. I have a very nice apartment in Rhode Island. And Gretchen and I aren't . . . mixing. Not the way you think."

"She doesn't strike me as the kind to do anything lightly."

"She's also not the kind who does emotional entanglements."

Coach shook his head, rubbing at that spot between his buttons again. "You can bullshit yourself if you want, but don't try to bullshit me."

"I'm not trying to . . ." Alex sighed. "She doesn't give me anything. Sometimes I can see right through her and other times, she's like a brick wall."

"The people with the thickest walls are usually the ones protecting the softest hearts." Alex snorted and gave him a *really?* look. "Okay, that was a corny one, even for me. You want football advice, I'm your guy. If you're trying to be a good man and live a good life, I've got that covered. But women? I need to read better greeting cards, I guess."

Alex laughed, but it was short-lived. "You feeling okay, Coach?"

"Yeah. Why?"

"You keep rubbing your chest. Just with your fingers, like on your breastbone, but you've done it a few times."

Coach shrugged. "I've been having some heartburn lately. Helen's been after me to give up coffee, but she's already got me eating egg-white omelets. A man can only sacrifice so much."

"Maybe Mrs. McDonnell should be after you to make sure it's not something more serious."

"Dammit, Jim, you're a photographer, not a doctor."

Alex laughed at the *Star Trek* reference, but it didn't change the fact that he was concerned. A doctor could do some tests. Maybe prescribe something stronger than antacid tablets to rule out heartburn.

"Stop looking at me like that, son." Coach gave him a stern look. "You all didn't work so hard to save the football team so I could kick the bucket before our first game. I'm not going anywhere."

Alex didn't even want to go there. He'd gone so long without Coach, and now that he was back in his life, if something happened to him . . . His mind shied away, not even willing to consider the possibility. "I'll hold you to that."

"I want to say one more thing about Gretchen, and then I'll stay out of it," Coach said. "You came back here because your story wasn't finished. You need to keep in mind life isn't always a choose-your-own-adventure kind of story. If you pick an adventure and don't like how it ends, you might not get to go back and choose again. Gretchen's a strong woman, and she can also be pretty unforgiving if she feels somebody's done her wrong. She's got a lot of her grandfather in her so, if you choose wrong, you might have to live with that."

Alex nodded to show he understood, but he didn't really have anything to say. His thoughts had become like a tangled ball of Ida's yarn, with two ends. One end was Gretchen and the other was his career.

And as he mentally pulled at one or the other, that messy knot in the middle just grew tighter and tighter.

Of all the chores Gretchen had ever had to do being raised on a farm, laundry was her least favorite. It was even worse than taking care of chickens, but if she didn't do it, she eventually ran out of clean clothes. As much as she might want to, she couldn't live in her cow pajamas.

Unfortunately, laundry was also Gram's least favorite thing to do, so they'd agreed a long time ago to each do their own and that way they both suffered. It was only fair.

Muttering under her breath about all of the outdoor things she'd rather be doing, Gretchen pulled a shirt out of the dryer and gave it a hard snap to shake the wrinkles out. Because she'd been outside, she'd missed the buzzer and this load had sat in a lump in the bottom of the dryer too long. Then she folded it and set it on her shirt pile on top of the dryer.

The next item she pulled out wasn't hers. For a second, she thought it was Gram's, but then she realized the light-weight zip hoodie belonged to Alex. Now that the mornings and late evenings were cooler, he sometimes threw it on and Gretchen remembered grabbing it off the back of the chair when she was putting this load in the washing machine. As she continued folding, she also found one of his socks, which she'd rescued from Cocoa's bed, and she put that with his sweatshirt.

As she folded a pair of her jeans, Gretchen thought about the signs of Alex scattered throughout the house. There weren't too many, because he was a neat guy who didn't have a lot of belongings with him, but there was the sweatshirt and the sock. His hiking boots, which he wore around the farm or in rainy weather, sitting by the back door. A spare phone charger in the basket on the kitchen counter, where Gretchen kept hers.

At first it had been so strange having him around. The first time she'd walked out into the upstairs hallway and smelled the lingering tang of shaving cream, it had stopped her in her tracks. But now he not only seemed at home there, Gretchen had gotten used to having him around, too.

She was going to have to watch that, she thought. While she'd given up on keeping a physical distance from him, it was even more important now that she keep her emotional distance. The more she got used to having him around the house and seeing him as practically a member of the family, the bigger the void was going to feel when he moved on.

The screen door slammed, followed by the thump of shoes hitting the floor. Speak of the devil, she thought. Gram usually wore slip-on shoes when she went out to the garden, and they were made of a light canvas that was almost silent. Alex was home earlier than usual.

He found her a couple of minutes later, and walked up behind her. "There you are."

"No matter how many notes I leave in my quickly emptying sock drawer, the laundry fairy refuses to stop at this house."

He chuckled, and then his breath blew hot across her neck a second before his lips touched the tender skin just below her ear. "I've heard she only works for cash."

Despite the keeping-her-distance pep talk she'd just given herself, Gretchen leaned back against his body. "Laundry mercenaries. I should have guessed."

He tucked a finger under the neck of her T-shirt and pulled it down so he could kiss the spot between her shoulder blades that made her shiver. "I ran into Cocoa outside, so I assume Ida's out in the garden?"

"Yes, she is. She's concerned about the soil, so she's graphing it all out so we can talk about rotation for next season."

Running his hand over her stomach to just under her breast, Alex nuzzled the back of her neck. "All I heard was *blah blah she's going to be a while blah blah.*"

Gretchen dropped her head to the side, offering him more access to her neck. So very tempting to maybe sneak upstairs for a few minutes. "She's already been out there for quite a while. I don't think she'll be much longer, especially since she probably heard your Jeep and knows you're home."

"Trust me, I don't need very long."

"I'm not having a quickie with you in the laundry room."

His sigh chilled the skin his mouth had just moistened with kisses. "I've heard the spin cycle can make things interesting."

When she heard the screen door close again, Gretchen stepped away from Alex as quickly as if she were a teenage girl caught with a boy in her room. Or what she imagined that would have felt like, anyway. There wasn't a boy in Stewart Mills willing to risk crossing her grandfather, even if she'd been inclined to sneak one upstairs.

"You realize we're adults, right?" Alex asked, the wry humor evident in his voice.

"Gram does *not* want to catch us making out in the laundry room. I don't care how old we are."

Cocoa found them first, giving an enthusiastic *woof* when she saw them, and Gram was right behind her. "You're still working on your laundry? I swear, I've been telling you practically your entire life that you should just do it and get it over with. You always drag it out so it takes the entire day."

Gretchen just barely managed to refrain from rolling her eyes while handing Alex his folded sweatshirt and the sock. "I found the sock tucked behind Cocoa's bed."

When he looked down at the dog, she raised her paw. "I'm supposed to give you a high five for stealing my sock?"

But Cocoa just let her tongue loll out of her mouth and

waited patiently until Alex gave in and slapped his hand to her paw. It didn't take long because, like everybody else in the house, he was at the lovable mutt's mercy.

"I'm going to go put these away," Alex said, and Gretchen caught the look he gave her over the top of Gram's head, full of sizzling promises he'd keep next time they were alone. "Thanks for washing them."

"He's such a great guy," Gram said when they were alone. "He fits right in here, too."

And that's why it was so important she not find them kissing in the laundry room. Gretchen was well aware she and Alex were both adults, and she understood where he was coming from, but Gram had been worrying about her finding a husband and having a family for a while now. Having an attractive man that they both liked *fit right in* wasn't as good as Gram thought it was.

As far as Gretchen could tell, the only way to keep her grandmother's hopes from being raised so high that she would be crushed when Alex left was to keep the kissing out of sight and her own feelings about the man locked down so tightly, even *she* wasn't sure what they were.

13

Alex's phone rang while he was in the process of rewriting a paragraph about the grants Jen Cooper had gotten for the Eagles fund-raiser, and he almost ignored it. Now that he'd made a decision not to go ahead with the full-length book, the words were starting to flow again, and he didn't need the interruption. But he couldn't stop himself from glancing at the caller ID, and when he saw that it was his agent, he sighed. Since he'd already let one call from him go unreturned, Alex answered the call.

"I was starting to wonder if you got eaten by a bear. Or trampled by a moose. Or maybe you fell through the hole in the outhouse and drowned in shit."

Alex wasn't really in the mood. "That stopped being funny the first time you said it, when you were trying to talk me out of coming here."

"Days after I sell your photos to an international news magazine is not the time to disappear off the planet."

"We've gone over this. I felt it was the right thing, and I still think it's the right thing for me. Feeling an emotional connection to my subjects is bringing back my passion for the art."

"That's great, Alex. Really. I'm glad to hear it, but I called to pass on an invitation to you. I would have forwarded the email, but some people in New Hampshire apparently still use their phones to make telephone calls with and there is no email."

Alex thought of Gretchen's ancient flip phone and smiled. Watching her painfully text by hitting each number key until she landed on the right letter was both amusing and excruciating. It tipped more toward amusing when she went past the right letter and had to cycle through again, since that made her vocabulary a little more colorful than usual.

"Anyway, somebody at the state university got wind that you're in New Hampshire. They're having a reception thing at a restaurant in Concord, which I'm told is the capital city and shouldn't be too hard for you to find. Some politicians, some folks from the university. Some museum people. They'll be showcasing up-and-coming local artists and raising money for the . . . something. I'll email you a link to the website for the people hosting it so you can read all that for yourself."

"So they're inviting me. That means what, exactly?"

"No speeches. The guy that called me is a huge fan of yours and basically they want you to show up so they can say you'll be there. Huge inspiration to young artists and the awards you've won and blah blah blah. You know the drill."

"How long do I have to think about it?"

"The reception is Friday night, so not long. An answer right now would be good."

"This Friday?"

"Which you'd already know if you'd returned my last call. But before you say anything else, I think this would be good for you. It's going to get some local press coverage, and it's always a good idea to make nice with university people, because you never know when you might want to teach some photography classes in your spare time."

"I'm not going to teach."

"I'm glad, because I don't get a percentage of that. But also, I think being around aspiring artists will be good for you. You said you're trying to recapture your passion or whatever. Being around people who aren't jaded or tired or worried about burning out could be good for you."

And it would be nice to get out of Stewart Mills for a night. He'd get a hotel room in Concord and spend the night, so he wouldn't have to make the two-hour drive back afterward. And he had one suit with him. It would need pressing since it had been rolled up tightly to fit in his bag, but he never traveled without at least one suit.

"And you're welcome to bring a plus-one, of course," his agent continued. "The seating arrangement for dinner includes a guest for you."

"I'll go. And I'll see if Gretchen wants to go with me. I think she will."

There was a short pause. "Gretchen. Isn't that the lady who owns the farm where you're staying? With the chickens and the pumpkins or whatever."

"Yeah. She might enjoy getting away for a night."

"Does she know which fork to use at the dinner table?"

Alex frowned, not liking the flare-up of anger he could feel inside. Thanks to Coach, he didn't lose his temper anymore and hadn't in years. So he took a deep breath and reminded himself his agent was a big-city guy who probably couldn't help himself.

"Yeah, she knows which fork to use. It's whichever fucking fork she wants to." Okay, maybe he should have taken two deep breaths.

"Oh." Another pause. "Okay. I didn't realize it was like that."

It wasn't like that. But it wasn't totally *not* like that, either. Alex didn't know exactly how or what it was, so he let it go. "Send me the info and let them know I'll be there."

"Sure thing. And I'd love to get together with you and have lunch or drinks. Talk about where you want to go from here. Are you going to be in the city soon?"

Alex knew the correct answer was yes, he'd be in the city soon. Though taking a break was nice, his career wasn't going to simmer on the back burner forever. But being in the city meant leaving Stewart Mills, and he wasn't sure he was ready to do that. "I'll get back to you on that and we'll schedule something."

Once the call was over, he shut down the computer and decided he'd go find Gretchen. The more notice she had, the more likely it was she'd go with him, and they were down to two days already.

He found her in the garage, where she was sitting on the floor, taking apart a lawn mower engine. "Hey. How many lawn mowers do you own?"

She looked up at him and smiled. "This one belongs to the neighbors. It's not running right, so they asked me to take a look at it. What's up?"

"I got a call from my agent a few minutes ago."

He saw the subtle shift in her expression, like a mask slipping into place. "Is he sending you somewhere to take pictures?"

"No. He can't actually do that, by the way. He can tell me there's an opportunity or that somebody wants to hire me for something, but he can't actually tell me what to do. He was letting me know I was invited to an art reception at a restaurant in Concord on Friday night."

"That sounds like fun." She pushed herself to her feet and brushed off the back of her jeans. "Bit of a long drive."

"Yeah, I'll get a hotel room for Friday night and come back Saturday. I was hoping you'd go with me."

She blinked and then frowned. "To an art reception? I don't even know what that is."

"A bunch of people hanging around, talking about art. Actually, I'm not sure *reception* is the right word, because there's a dinner. I think. He was a little fuzzy on the details, so he'll email me later."

"Is it a dressy kind of thing?"

"A little bit. I mean, it's not black tie, but the women will probably be in dresses. You do own a dress, right?"

"Of course I own a dress. People do die in Stewart Mills, you know, and when they do, we have funerals for them."

"Of course." He couldn't tell if she was screwing with him or not. "Which is perfect, because the art crowd loves black."

"I don't really think it's my thing," she said. "But thanks for inviting me."

"I was hoping going out for a night and enjoying a hotel room with me would be your thing." He gave what he hoped was a charming, slightly naughty smile.

"I can't just leave the farm like that."

Disappointment surged through him, but he wasn't ready to give up just yet. He'd let her think about it while she worked and bring it up again later. "Well, just think about it. I'll let you get back to work."

"Okay. And Alex? Leave my grandmother out of it."

"What do you mean?"

"Don't fill her head full of me going to some fancy art thing if only I would leave the farm."

He grinned. "Do you really think I would do that?"

"If you do, I'll evict you."

He laughed and left the garage, but he wasn't done with the conversation yet.

Several hours later, without any prompting from him, Ida provided the perfect opening for him over dinner. "So, Alex, do you have any plans for this weekend? The weather's supposed to be nice."

"Actually, on Friday I'm going to Concord for an event. I'll stay in a hotel, so it's an overnight."

"Oh, really? That sounds like fun. Is it the sort of thing you should bring a date to?"

When Gretchen glared at him, assuming he was in cahoots with her grandmother, Alex held up his hands in an *I'm innocent* gesture. He had nothing to do with it, even if he was cheering Ida on in his mind.

"The invitation included a plus-one, yes."

Ida didn't even ask if he was considering anybody. She just looked directly at Gretchen, her eyebrow raised in a questioning way.

"You know I can't leave the farm," Gretchen said in a flat voice.

When Alex saw the look Ida leveled at her granddaughter, he was surprised Gretchen didn't go up in flames. "I may not know how to change the oil in the truck or diagnose a broken tractor, missy, but I can gather eggs and feed horses."

"I know you can. But what if something happens? I mean you fell going to the bathroom in the middle of the night and—"

"Don't you start," Ida interrupted. "I didn't collapse. I tripped over my damn slipper. Remember the time you were working on the barn and fell off the roof? Did I wrap you in Bubble Wrap and prop you up in a rocking chair?"

Alex tried to smother his chuckle with his napkin, but it didn't work. Gretchen scowled at him, which only made him laugh harder.

"I didn't just fall off the roof. I got dive-bombed by a bird."

"Yes, I saw," Ida said. "And when you screamed and waved your arms around, you fell off the roof."

"I didn't scream. I might have yelped a little, but I never scream."

"My point is, I am perfectly capable of taking care of the farm for one night. Don't forget who your grandfather relied on for decades before you were an adult."

"I don't know anything about art."

Ida shrugged. "So. You know *everything* about Alex's current project, so you can talk about that. And you're perfectly capable of making polite conversation about art that's right in front of your face, which I know since I raised you to be an intelligent woman."

"Fine," Gretchen snapped, glaring at Alex. "Fine, I'll go. Just stop talking about it."

It wasn't the most gracious acceptance of an invitation he'd ever received, but he didn't care. She could be as prickly as she wanted to and he wouldn't let her off the hook. He'd been living in her world for a month now. She could spend one night in his.

All Gretchen had to do was send one simple message— Alex fancy event Friday dress help—and the texts started flying. Mostly the texts flew between Kelly and Jen, since they had cell phones with actual screens and keyboards, but Gretchen did her best to keep up when it came to reading the messages.

So it was that she found herself at Jen's house the following afternoon. While Jen wasn't as slim as Gretchen, she was closer in height than Kelly was, so they'd decided Gretchen had a better chance of fitting into her clothes. She did what she was told and showed up when they said to.

"This is going to be so fun," Kelly said, rummaging through Jen's closet. "Your foot's only like a half a shoe size bigger than Jen's, right?"

"I think so."

"Some of those might fit her, then," Jen told Kelly. "Every manufacturer sizes differently, so some of them are a little loose."

Kelly stepped out of the closet with a pair of black pumps. "These are simple, but sexy. And they're not open-toe. I'm going to take a wild guess and say you haven't had a pedicure in a while."

"I clipped my toenails just yesterday, thank you very much." Gretchen eyed the high-heeled shoes dangling from Kelly's fingertips and shook her head. "I don't think I can even stand up in those, never mind walk."

"Just try them." Kelly set the heels on the floor in front of Gretchen. "Women wear heels all the time. It's not rocket science."

"When's the last time *you* wore heels?"

Kelly gave her an *are you crazy?* look. "I'm a police officer. You never know when I might have to run."

"I wear them all the time," Jen said. "But I think Gretchen's right. She's not going to be able to walk in those."

"She should try. I think Alex is the first man she's ever dated who was tall enough so she could wear high heels."

Hoping she wouldn't fall and break any bones, Gretchen slid her left foot into a shoe. As expected, they were a little tight, but not too bad. Then, holding on to Kelly's shoulder, she got her right foot in. Instantly taller, she waited until she felt steady and then let go of her friend.

Jen smiled. "Stomach in, shoulders back, and pretend your head is attached to a bunch of helium balloons. Okay, now walk."

Gretchen took a deep breath and made her way across the room. She was a little wobbly and stumbled twice, but with some concentration and her hands out for balance, she made it to the opposite wall without falling down.

"That was . . ." Kelly paused. "Not graceful."

"So not sexy," Jen said at the same time.

"It's also not comfortable. I told you I couldn't do this. I'm going to tell Alex I'm having second thoughts about leaving Gram and the farm, and he should just go without me."

"No!" both women shouted at the same time.

"I think he'd rather go alone than take a woman in barn boots." She braced her hands against the wall and pulled her feet out of the pretty shoes.

"There's a pretty wide range of footwear between heels and barn boots," Jen said. "And that gives me an idea."

Kelly nodded. "Boots."

"It's perfect."

Gretchen was fast approaching the end of her ability to tolerate this conversation. "What's perfect?"

"Hold on." Jen disappeared back into her closet and emerged a minute later with a pair of boots.

They were far from barn boots, though. Black leather, with no heels, they looked soft and expensive. "Try these, Gretchen. You're tall enough so nobody will think twice about you not wearing heels, and since it's going to be an artsy crowd, you can make whatever style statement you want."

"Style statement?" Gretchen laughed and took the boots before sitting on the edge of Jen's bed to put them on.

Kelly tilted her head. "A long pencil skirt, a blouse and jewelry. Statement pieces."

"Was there a memo about statements I missed?" Gretchen asked, tugging on the boots. They weren't as tight on her as the heels had been, and she had no trouble drawing the zippers up over her calves. "Style statements. Statement pieces. I have no idea what you're talking about."

"*Statement pieces* is a more expensive-sounding way to say *big costume jewelry*."

"Oh!" Jen actually clapped her hands together. "I bet Gram has some cool jewelry. Then it's retro and that's even better."

"I don't have any childhood memories of Gram running around the farm decked out in sparkly gems," Gretchen pointed out.

"That small field behind the old mill had a building on it before we were born," Kelly said. "It was a luncheonette when it burned, but before that it was some kind of social club. On Friday nights, the good people of Stewart Mills had quite the parties there, from what I hear. The women loved to dress up and they all had their hair done on Friday afternoons."

A memory floated to the surface of Gretchen's mind. "I remember seeing an old picture of my grandparents. They were laughing with friends, and they were all dressed up. Gram had a drink in her hand. I don't know why, but I assumed they were at a wedding or something."

Gretchen wasn't sure just how much of the town's history Alex wanted to include in his project, but she made a mental note to mention the social club to him. He may have already read about it while digging around the library's archives, but just in case he hadn't, she'd bring it up.

She stood and retraced her steps across the bedroom, almost sighing in relief. The boots had a flexible sole and the leather was so soft, it was almost as though she were barefoot.

"Those are *so* you," Jen said. "I'm curvier than you, so to get them to fit my calves, they're a little bit big in the foot and I almost never wear them. They look amazing on you, though."

"They feel amazing."

Twenty minutes later, Gretchen stood in front of the full-length mirror and had to admit Jen and Kelly were damn close to being miracle workers. She didn't quite look like her usual day-to-day self, but she didn't look like a little girl playing dress up, either. Or like an actress playing a role.

The long black skirt was straight, almost hugging her legs, and suited the sleek boots. And Jen had found her a blouse in a blue that matched her eyes. It was in a soft fabric that didn't feel constrictive, and the neckline tastefully accented just a hint of cleavage.

"I was wrong," Kelly said, and Gretchen frowned at her friend's reflection in the mirror. She thought she looked pretty freaking fantastic. "About the jewelry. No statement pieces."

"I agree," Jen said. "That hair is the statement and the whole look is so classic as is."

Gretchen felt the nerves kicking in again. They'd pulled the ponytail holder out of her hair, so it was loose, but messy. "I'll tell you right now I'm not doing curling irons or hot rollers or blow dryers or whatever it is you're thinking about. And no gunk."

They both laughed, and Kelly smoothed the dark strands. "No gunk. If you wash it and comb it out, it'll be perfect. It's straight and long and frames your face beautifully."

"No gunk on her face, either," Jen added. "I have a cream that's like a light foundation. It just evens out the skin tone a little. Some mascara and lip gloss. Not really makeup, but just a little polish."

Gretchen nodded, liking the sound of that. And a bit of the dread that had sat like a lead ball in the pit of her stomach disappeared, leaving nothing but a little anxiety about poking her eye out with a mascara wand. Every time she'd thought about going away for a night with Alex, the anticipation had been undermined by images of herself tripping in fancy shoes or looking like a clown in badly applied Cherry Hot Pants lipstick.

"Alex is going to play hell trying to concentrate on the event," Kelly said. "He'll probably forget everything he was going to say with you looking like this."

Gretchen smiled at her reflection, trying to imagine the look on his face when he saw her. There was no doubt he found her attractive, but part of her was really looking forward to showing him she could dress up for a night on the town, too. Sure, it took the help of her two best friends and a borrowed wardrobe, but she could do it.

"Now comes the fun part," Jen said. "What are you wearing to bed?"

"My cow pajama pants." She thought they'd laugh, but instead she was flanked in the mirror by two horrified faces. "He likes my cow pajama pants."

"Was he laughing when he said it?" Jen asked. "Or maybe drunk?"

"No, he was serious. He said it's like a little secret nobody else knows, except Gram, of course. Everybody sees serious, hardworking me, but he knows at the end of the day, I have silly cows on my butt."

Jen chuckled, but Kelly got a soft, goofy look on her face. "Oh, Gretchen. You have to keep him."

Keep him. She'd entertained the thought for a moment or two before, but every time she did, she ended up tossing and turning half the night. "It's not going to happen. He's made it clear he's not a farm boy."

"I love you," Kelly said. "You know I love you, so I'm going to be the one to say it. You can't give up a chance at love and happiness for a pumpkin patch and chickens."

Gretchen not only felt her body tense, but she saw it in the mirror, too. Her back straightened and her chin lifted. But she took a deep breath and forced herself to think before she spoke. "The farm's a lot more than a pumpkin patch. It's my home. And it's Gram's home."

"I know, but I think you've made *home* into something more than it needs to be. You could make a home anywhere, and take Gram with you."

"Says the girl born and raised on Eagles Lane." She tried to say the words lightly, but they came out with an edge. "Maybe I have made the farm into more than what it is. Do you think I don't know it's an old farmhouse that needs some work, some outbuildings that need even more work, an ancient tractor and some land?"

"Your grandfather wouldn't want you to be tied to it," Kelly said softly and, because she was still looking in the mirror, she saw the sharp shake of Jen's head. Gretchen watched the whole exchange.

Then she sighed and started unbuttoning the pretty blouse as she turned her back on her reflection. "It's not about Gramps. I love the farm. It's my home and not because it was the first place I even knew what that word meant."

"There's no reason he can't travel from the farm, is there? He has an apartment in . . . Rhode Island, is it? Why not here instead?"

Gretchen placed the blouse back on its hanger and unzipped the skirt. "He's hardly ever at his apartment, so how often would he be here? And it's very different. He chose

Providence because he can get to Boston or New York City easily, and hop a flight to Baltimore or Washington or Philly. It's not easy to get here, even from Boston."

"Chase is in New Jersey right now, but we make it work. Phone calls and video chats and emails."

"Yeah, but it's temporary. There's an end point. Video chats are okay when it'll be, what? Six months at the most?"

"If that."

"Exactly. Would you be happy with Chase if he was going to be working in New Jersey *for years*?"

"I don't know," Kelly said in a low voice. "I really don't know."

"Hey," Jen said. "You have a hot guy who wants to take you down to the city, show you a good time, and then have hotel sex with you. Let's focus on that for now."

"Is hotel sex different than regular sex?"

Kelly smiled and took the skirt from her. "Oh, yeah."

"Worth putting a mascara wand near my eyeball kind of different?"

Both women nodded, and Gretchen shoved aside the lingering negativity of her conversation with Kelly so she could focus on the possibilities of hotel sex. If she was going to wear the kind of clothes that needed ironing and risk blinding herself with a goopy brush, she was seriously going to reap the benefits.

14

On Friday, Alex woke with a sense of anticipation he couldn't quite explain. He'd been to so many different kinds of art functions that attending this one shouldn't have been any more exciting than a trip to the grocery store.

Nonetheless, the first thought he had upon opening his eyes was, *The reception's today!* He went straight from his bed to the shower, since he never had to worry about the hot water heater that way. Ida either took her shower before he was even awake or waited until after breakfast, and Gretchen usually preferred taking hers in the evening.

Once he was dressed, he went downstairs and, as soon as he walked into the kitchen, realized why he was looking forward to tonight's event. It was because the gorgeous woman in the blue jeans and red flannel shirt thrown over a tee was going with him.

"Good morning," she said, setting a coffee cup on the table for him. "Were you warm enough last night? I know it was a little on the cool side, and you might not be as used to it as we are."

"I slept like a baby." He wanted to grab her and kiss her until she forgot what she was doing, but Ida being in the room stopped him. Tonight, though, they'd be staying in a very nice hotel, and tomorrow he would kiss her good morning to his heart's content. "I pulled up the quilt that was folded at the foot of my bed and was plenty warm enough."

"What time are you two leaving today?" Ida asked, setting a plate piled high with pancakes in the center of the table.

"By two, I hope." Alex served each of the women a pancake and then slapped one on his own plate. "It starts at five, so factoring in a rest stop along the way, three hours should do it."

"And you're not checking into the hotel until after?"

"I have a reservation, so the room will be ready when the event's over. But you have Gretchen's cell phone number and mine, so you can reach either of us if you need to."

"I'm sure I'll be fine. Dana might come over and play cards for a while this evening, and I'll have you know who for company."

They tried to avoid saying Cocoa's name while they were eating because she would hear it, and she wasn't allowed into the kitchen. Whining often ensued.

While Gretchen launched into a list of people Ida should contact for different situations ranging from one of the horses getting loose to the well pump quitting, Alex pondered the fact that Ida hadn't even blinked when he said the room would be ready, not the *rooms*, plural. It was kind of ridiculous, at their age, for him and Gretchen to be pretending they weren't involved because of her grandmother, especially since she'd practically thrown them at each other.

Sex was one thing. Alex had never had sex with a woman in his mother's home, and he could understand Gretchen feeling the same way about her grandmother's home. The problem was it was *also* Gretchen's home and, as a grown woman, she needed to be able to have some privacy. It was definitely a sticky situation with no clear-cut answer.

But he wasn't sure why they were going out of their way to not even touch in front of Ida. A kiss good morning. Holding hands on the couch. He knew without even testing the theory that Gretchen wasn't a public-displays-of-affection kind of girl. But this kitchen was far from public.

After breakfast, they went their separate ways and Alex didn't see Gretchen again until about an hour before they were supposed to hit the road. She came in from doing whatever it was she'd been doing outside, and the expression she wore when she walked into the living room and saw him made him laugh.

"You look like you're going to get a root canal, not heading out for a night out in the city."

She shrugged, then gave him a chagrined smile. "I'm not dreading it quite as much as I would a root canal."

Pulling her close, he gave her a quick kiss. "If you really don't want to go, it's okay, you know. I want you to be there with me, but not if it's going to make you miserable."

"I just . . ." Her expression closed off, and he gave her a questioning look. "I don't want to embarrass you."

It hadn't occurred to him she might feel that way, because it was the furthest thing from his mind. "Embarrass me how?"

"I don't think I'm going to fit in very well with the art crowd."

"You'll fit in very well with me." That he was very sure of, and he made sure the conviction was in his voice. "We could go right now and I'd be proud as hell to have you on my arm tonight."

She laughed and brushed some loose hair back from the sweat still glistening on her forehead from whatever she'd been doing. "Thanks, but I guess I'll take a shower first."

Since Alex had taken his shower already, all he had to do was get dressed. While she got ready, he put on most of his suit, though he carried the coat downstairs on the hanger. He'd wait until they arrived to put it on since it was warm and he didn't want to get sweaty.

He was watching CNN with Ida and Cocoa—trying not to be sorry he and his camera weren't in the Middle East at that moment—when he heard the bathroom door upstairs close and then a creak in the floorboards halfway down the hall. After tossing the remote control on the table, he stood to wait for her.

He felt like a teenage boy watching his prom date come down the stairs, and she took his breath away. "Wow."

"Oh, Gretchen," Ida whispered.

Alex guessed Kelly or Jen or maybe both had had a hand in her outfit, and he thought maybe he should send them a thank-you card. The long, slim black skirt and calf-hugging black boots emphasized her height, and the classically cut blue blouse matched her eyes. She wore no jewelry, but with her hair brushed out and gleaming past her shoulders, she didn't need any. Her makeup was simple—maybe even just mascara and lip gloss—which suited her.

"You look stunning," he told her, and he meant it.

She gave him a warm smile as she reached the bottom of the stairs. He met her there and took her overnight bag. "Thank you. The skirt's even a little stretchy, so it's very comfortable. And I haven't told Jen yet, but I'm not giving these boots back."

"You look beautiful," Ida said, putting aside her knitting so she could stand up. "Now give me a kiss and get going. You don't want to be late."

Even though she was talking to Gretchen, Alex gave Ida a quick peck on the cheek and Cocoa a high five before grabbing his suit coat. He hung it in the backseat of the Jeep and slid her bag in next to his, closing the door just in time to open the front passenger door for Gretchen.

She slid into the seat and then laughed when he leaned inside. "What are you doing?"

"I'm helping you with your seat belt." He pulled the seat belt out and across her body, and then touched his mouth to hers, not caring if Ida was watching from the house.

He felt Gretchen startle, but she relaxed after a second and let him kiss her. Then he clicked her seat belt securely and closed her door. Whistling a happy tune, he walked around the Jeep and got in. The second he started the engine, Gretchen hit the seek button on his radio, looking for the station she liked.

He laughed and put the Jeep in gear. It was going to be a good night.

They spent most of the drive talking, though sometimes Gretchen would get caught up singing along to the radio, so quietly he almost couldn't hear her, while watching the scenery go by. In between songs that caught her attention, she talked about the pumpkins and her grandmother's pumpkin pie filling, and the imminent departure of the horses, among other things.

He loved listening to her talk about the farm. The affection she felt not only for her grandmother and the dog but also for the land itself made her voice warm, and he would happily listen to her for hours.

When they arrived at the restaurant, he told her to wait and got his suit coat out of the back. He slipped it on and then walked around to her door. He opened it and then offered her his hand.

He wondered for a moment if she'd scoff at the gesture, or even laugh out loud. She was such a strong, capable woman used to doing things for herself, so it would probably seem silly to her.

But she put her hand in his and gave him a slow, sexy smile as she swung her legs over and slid out of the Jeep. "You're quite the gentleman tonight."

He lifted her hand and kissed her knuckles. "For now."

"Just so you know . . . " she began, and it took him a fraction of a second to acknowledge to himself that if she said she wasn't wearing any underwear, they were getting back in the Jeep and going straight to the hotel. ". . . I didn't pack my cow pajamas."

It wasn't quite a lack of underwear, but just the way her voice dropped as she said the words was enough to make him a little uncomfortable in the dress pants. "I've grown rather fond of those pajama pants."

"I think you'll be pretty fond of the nightgown I bought, too." She took a few steps across the parking lot, and then she turned and looked back at him with a mock-innocent expression. "Don't you want to go inside?"

No, he didn't. He wasn't even sure he wanted to take the time to drive to the hotel. It was tempting to drop the seats in the Jeep and climb right into the back with her. But they were both too tall and he'd miss out on the nightgown.

"Yeah," he said, swinging her door shut with a bang and hitting the lock button on the key fob. "But we're not staying long.

Gretchen was pretty sure her mouth had frozen into the shape of a polite smile at least an hour ago.

Luckily, everybody at the reception seemed to love the sound of their own voices, so nobody appeared to mind that she did a lot more smiling and nodding than she did talking. But she had to admit she was having a better time than she'd anticipated.

She didn't know what anybody was talking about half the time, but she could tell they not only knew who Alex was but also had a lot of respect for his work. While she'd seen him sit for what seemed like hours, analyzing photos he'd taken around Stewart Mills, the men and women around them tonight actually understood and appreciated the art of what he did.

They ate, filling their plates from an assortment of the restaurant's finest dishes, served buffet-style. Then they mingled some more, and Gretchen was thankful she hadn't tried to manage shoes with heels since the only time they sat down was during dinner. Now she sipped a glass of ice water and listened to the conversation Alex was having with a man named Ed, who seemed to have something to do with a famous regional magazine she'd never heard of.

"So, Murphy, when are you going to stop wasting time here in New Hampshire and get back out into the thick of things?"

The words cut Gretchen to the bone, though she struggled to make sure her reaction didn't show on her face.

That was the question, wasn't it? When would Alex get tired of wasting his time in the middle of nowhere with her and go back to traveling around the world, taking photographs that brought in money and awards, and the adoration of people like these? It was a thought that circled through her mind more and more often as the days passed, but hearing it said out loud—and in such a blunt way—shook her more than she cared to admit.

Alex only squeezed her hand, as if he knew the question would bother her, and smiled at the man. "I'm getting some great photographs in Stewart Mills, actually. Having an emotional connection to the subject brings a depth to the work—layers, if you will—that you can't fake."

That seemed to satisfy the man, who turned the conversation to some kind of grant he was applying for. Gretchen feigned interest, making sure the bland smile stayed plastered on her face, but her attention was mostly on the way her fingers were interlaced with Alex's.

His thumb brushed up and down the length of her index finger in what was probably a subconscious gesture. It was comfortable and easy, and it gave her something to focus on besides the people milling around them. Every once in a while, he'd give her hand a squeeze and she'd glance at him. He'd give her a questioning look and she'd smile to show she was fine.

About a half hour after the *wasting his time* question, he leaned close enough to whisper in her ear. "Let's get out of here."

He didn't need to ask her twice. It took probably ten or fifteen minutes to get through the room and say their good-byes, and then she was outside, breathing in the fresh air. It was starting to cool off as the sun started going down, but she welcomed the light chill after the stuffiness of the restaurant.

"How bad was it?" Alex asked once they were out of the parking lot and driving through the city.

"I had a good time."

He snorted and glanced over at her. "You can be honest."

"I am being honest. It's not something I'd want to do all the time, but some of the people were very nice. The food was good."

"Really?"

"Okay, it wasn't as good as what Gram makes, but I didn't have to wash the dishes." He laughed and reached over to grasp her hand. Lacing his fingers through hers, he rested his forearm on the center console. "It was neat, seeing you in your element. It was obvious everybody there really respects you."

"Yeah, some of them do. The others . . . well, within the week I'll be getting emails asking me for something. An introduction to my agent or teaching a free workshop or a good word with some committee or another."

"Does that happen a lot?"

He shrugged. "Sometimes, especially after an event like this. But in my field, your career pretty much lives or dies in the shot, and most people recognize that. There's only so much I can do to help a person out."

Gretchen wanted to ask him what he'd thought of the guy who said he was wasting his time in Stewart Mills, but he flipped his blinker on and turned into the hotel parking lot. Of course he opened her door for her, but she drew the line at him carrying both bags.

She felt conspicuous, standing next to him in the lobby with the handle of her overnight bag clutched in her hands. It was a nice enough bag—a black quilted material that was fairly timeless despite belonging to Gram—but she wondered what the desk clerk would think of their small, separate bags. If they were really a couple, they probably would have packed together in one small suitcase.

But she supposed it didn't really matter what the desk clerk thought. And they weren't really a couple . . . she didn't think. At this point, she wasn't sure *what* they were, and she didn't want to ruin the evening by dwelling too much on it, so by the time Alex led her to the elevator bank, she'd returned her focus entirely to the here and now.

And the here and now was Alex unlocking the door to their room and pushing it open to reveal a whole lot of expensive-looking room and a giant bed. "Oh, my."

He flipped the light switch on before letting the heavy door swing closed behind him. She noticed he caught it at the last second so it closed with a click instead of a bang, and remembered he spent a lot of time in hotels. Then he flipped the safety bar and took her bag from her.

She explored the room, with its well-cushioned armchairs and fancy lamps. There was even a desk, and a television that was definitely newer than the one at the farm. The bathroom was huge, with an assortment of fancy miniature bottles on a silver tray next to the sink.

"If you don't use those, you can bring them home to Ida. I bet she'd get a kick out of them," Alex said from the doorway.

"Isn't that stealing?"

"If you use a little bit of each, they'd have to throw the rest away, anyway."

When he grinned, she scowled at him. "Are you laughing at me?"

"Only on the inside."

"I've never stayed in a hotel before." She picked up one of the little bottles and unscrewed the cap so she could smell it. Then she put the cap back on. A little flowery for her taste, but Gram would like it. "I think I lived in a few motels when I was a kid. With my parents, you know? But they were . . . not like this."

She braced herself for sympathy or some kind of disapproving sound, but he just arched an eyebrow at her. "If this is your first time in a hotel, you're not going to believe the pillows."

Gretchen set the bottle back on the tray and made a bee-line for the bed. "How different can a pillow be? They're pillows."

"Trust me."

She pulled back the white comforter to get the pillows, but the fabric in her hand distracted her. "These sheets are amazing. What do you think they're made out of?"

He shrugged. "I don't know. Sheet material of some sort."

"Feel how soft they are." She grabbed his arm and pulled him forward. "Feel them."

He ran his hand over the luxurious fabric, and then smiled. "You're right. They're very soft."

"They're almost worth stabbing myself in the eye with a mascara wand for." When he looked alarmed, she smiled. "I didn't, but it was a very real risk. Trust me."

"I'm glad you didn't stab yourself in the eye. And you looked stunning tonight." He leaned over to kiss her softly on the mouth.

"Thank you. I had a good time."

"Did you really?"

That was a loaded question. As a whole, it wasn't her kind of party. But she'd enjoyed watching Alex do his work thing for a little while. "I already told you I did."

"Yes, I know. You didn't have to wash the dishes. But is it the kind of thing you'd want to do again?"

She wasn't sure exactly what he was asking, but there was a seriousness in his eyes that made her feel inexplicably anxious, so she tried to avoid answering. "Only if they're serving that chocolate truffle."

He smiled and stood up straight again. "You haven't tried the pillows yet."

"I was just thinking about how good that nightgown's going to feel with these sheets."

That seriousness in his gaze gave way to heat in an instant, and he pulled her to her feet. "Let me get your bag for you."

15

Gretchen wasn't surprised to find Alex was already naked and in bed when she came out of the bathroom. As she walked across the hotel room, enjoying the feel of the plush carpet under her bare feet, he watched her, seemingly without blinking.

When she was almost to the bed, he folded back the covers and stood up. He definitely liked the nightgown, she thought, and had to bite back a giggle she didn't think he'd appreciate very much.

"Damn, Gretchen." He put his hands at her waist and then slid them up her satin-covered sides. She wasn't sure if it was satin, actually. But the white material was soft and shimmery, and it hugged her body. It was a simple design with a slit up one thigh and a deep V-neck, with thin straps over her shoulders.

"Do you like it?" She looked down at it, loving the contrast between the delicate fabric and his big, tanned hands. "I bought it once on a whim. A splurge, I guess. But I've never worn it."

"Then I'm not only hard as a rock, but honored, too."

"That's hard to miss, actually." He wasn't lying.

He bent his head and kissed the spot where the V-neck ended between her breasts. Then he closed his mouth over her breast and sucked one taut nipple through the thin nightgown.

"So I hear hotel sex is supposed to be different from regular sex," she said.

He straightened, arching an eyebrow at her. "Who did you hear about hotel sex from?"

"Girls talk." She laughed at his expression. "But not always in great detail, so I ended up looking forward to hotel sex without knowing what's supposed to be so special about it."

"I had no idea hotel sex is supposed to be special." He grinned. "No pressure or anything."

"It's probably just the sheets."

"Maybe." Alex slid his hand through the slit so his hand was on her thigh. Then he slid it upward until his thumb brushed her clit and she sucked in a breath. "And you have two choices in a hotel. You can be loud and scream my name, and everybody around us will know what we're doing. Or you can try to make love very quietly."

Gretchen felt a flush of heat across her cheeks that had nothing to do with his hand between her legs. "I don't want everybody to know."

"Then I guess you'll have to be quiet." He slid one finger into her as he grabbed her ass with his other hand and pulled her hard against his body. She gasped and grabbed his upper arms to steady herself. "If you get carried away and moan too loud or yell my name, everybody near our room will know I'm fucking you."

Heat rushed through her body and she parted her legs a little more. His finger slid deep inside her as his thumb pressed against her clit with delicious pressure. She'd been thinking about this moment since he first asked her to go away for the night with him, so it wasn't going to take much to send her over the edge.

"You know what's nice about this particular hotel room?" he asked, pulling his hand from between her legs. "Besides the sheets."

"I really like the sheets."

"We'll get there. But I like the mirrors." He took her hand and led her to the small dressing area between the bedroom and the bathroom. Both of the closet doors were mirrored, and a huge mirror hung over the vanity across from them.

He slipped one strap down over her shoulder and pulled the neckline to one side, baring her breast to his gaze and to his mouth. He licked the nipple, teasing until it was almost painful, before closing his mouth around it. Then he did the same for the other, but through the silky white cloth.

"Turn around," he said. "Brace your hands on the vanity."

She did what he said, which put her right in front of the big mirror. Her skin was flushed and because his mouth had dampened the fabric, her nipple was clearly outlined. Her other breast was still bared for the mirror and she reached up to fix the strap.

Alex caught her hand before she could slide it back over

her shoulder. "Don't. You look like a Grecian statue right now."

She might have laughed, except Alex let go of her hand to pick up a condom she hadn't noticed on the edge of the vanity. A few seconds later, she felt the whisper of her nightgown on her thighs as he pulled it up over her hips.

He put his hand on her back, and reached between their bodies with the other to guide himself into her. She sighed with pleasure as she pushed back against his thrust. The angle wasn't like anything she'd felt before, and she closed her eyes to savor the sensation.

Alex's hand skimmed over her breast and then up her neck. "Don't close your eyes. I want you to watch in the mirror."

She opened them, looking at their bodies move in the reflective glass. He used his thumb to tilt her chin away from him, giving him access to the side of her neck. His tongue blazed a hot trail up her skin before he bit gently at her earlobe.

All the while, he moved his hips in an easy rhythm, driving fully into her with every thrust. She watched in the mirror as her lips parted and her breath quickened. Alex touched his fingertip to her lower lip and she sucked it deep into her mouth, swirling her tongue around the knuckle.

His jaw tightened and he thrust into her hard, startling a groan from her.

"Shhh." His mouth was against her ear, and the reminder they could be heard made her shudder. "Watch the mirror."

When her gaze locked with his reflection's, he reached down and stroked her clit with his fingertips. It was too much and Gretchen's grip on the slick marble tightened as she jerked her hips backward against Alex.

When the orgasm passed, she opened her eyes again to see a flushed version of herself, eyelids heavy and mouth parted as she tried to catch her breath.

"So fucking beautiful," Alex said, his voice low and rough. He withdrew from her and then ran his hand up the back of her neck. "Do you like the mirror?"

"Yes," she whispered, though she wasn't sure if it was the mirror or the effect the mirror seemed to have on him that she liked.

"Good. Let's go try out those sheets now." He took her hand and led her to the bed, and he shook his head when she mentioned taking the nightgown off. "I *really* like that fabric."

With Alex using her arm to steer her, she ended up crossways on the huge bed and she slid her hands across the soft sheets. "I'm sideways, you know."

"I know." He grabbed her ankles and pulled her forward until her ass was lined up with the edge of the mattress, her nightgown gliding across the sheets.

Her hands curled into fists as he pushed into her, withdrew slightly, then pressed a little deeper. It was excruciating and she finally put her hands on his hips, trying to pull him closer. He resisted.

"You're not rushing me tonight."

Alex stood between her thighs and then lifted her hips so he could enter her again. She rested her heels against his shoulders and gasped when he thrust hard. Open to him as she was, she had no control and his strokes were deep.

"You're being quiet, remember?" he asked, and she could hear the amusement in his voice.

He thrust even harder, maybe hoping to get her to yell,

but she grabbed one of the many pillows and held the corner of it against her mouth. She didn't care if it was cheating.

He made her come again, stifling her cries with the pillow, and it was at least a minute before she caught her breath enough to realize Alex wasn't done with her yet. After lowering her legs to the floor, he tucked his hands under her arms and lifted her. After shifting her so she was totally on the bed again, he stretched out over her.

"How are you doing?" he asked, grinning down at her.

She ran her fingertip over his Adam's apple. "I'm doing pretty good. How are you doing?"

"I'm about to be doing exceptionally well."

He pushed up her nightgown again and settled himself between her thighs. This time there were no hard thrusts, though. With small, teasing strokes, he slowly filled her completely, and then he stopped. He looked down at her with that hot intensity he got when he was inside her, and she wrapped her arms around his neck to pull him down for a kiss. As he began to move, she moaned against his lips.

With stroke after stroke, the tension in her body built, and she bit down on her knuckle, trying to be quiet as she came again. Then his thrusts quickened and he fisted his hand in her hair. Alex groaned against her neck, thrusting again and again through the orgasm.

They lay there for a few moments, breathing heavily. Then Alex went into the bathroom for a moment. On his way back, he shut off the bedside lamp and then stood by the side of the bed. "Are you going to put your head on the pillows?"

Gretchen made a negative sound rather than summon the energy to talk or to move. She was pretty content being crosswise on the bed, but it did seem like a shame to waste all those fabulous pillows.

With a reluctant sigh, she sat up and repositioned herself the right way. Once her head was on the cloud of pillows and Alex had flipped the covers over her, it seemed worth the effort.

"I like hotel sex," she muttered, snuggling against his side.

He lifted his arm so she could rest her head on his chest and then kissed her hair. "If you think the mirrors and the sheets are nice, wait until we take a shower in the morning."

Gretchen wanted to think about that a little bit—imagine them in that big marble shower together, all slick and soapy—but as soon as she closed her eyes, she drifted off to sleep.

Alex opened his eyes and, after a glance at the clock, closed them again. He could sleep in today. No getting up early because Ida had breakfast on and Gretchen was letting the screen door slam on her way to do her morning chores. No Cocoa tap-tap-tapping her nails on the floor outside his door as she paced, waiting for him to come out.

He could sleep a little more, then kiss Gretchen good morning. Then kiss her some more.

Maybe they'd take a very long, very hot shower together just because they could. He definitely planned to make love to her again before they headed back to Stewart Mills. Somewhere in there, he'd order up some room service.

But first he was going to will himself back to sleep, just because he could.

"I thought you'd never wake up."

He chuckled and rolled onto his side so he could pull her close and nuzzle her hair. "No chickens here. Go back to sleep."

"You can take the girl off the farm, but you can't take the farm out of the girl. Or something like that."

"Five more minutes, farm girl."

"Okay. You sleep five more minutes while I get dressed and go find someplace that has coffee."

Scowling, Alex finally surrendered to the inevitable and opened his eyes. "Or you can pick up the phone and ask them to send up coffee. And don't tell me it's stupid to pay somebody to do something I can do myself."

"My principles are a little more flexible when it comes to coffee." She sat up, looking at the phone. "I've never used room service. Is their number written down somewhere?"

"I'll make a deal with you," he said, pulling her back down onto the pillows. "You let me kiss you for a little while, and then I'll order you an entire carafe of coffee."

She actually looked skeptical, which might have offended him if he were awake enough to care. "Do you mean kissing or do you mean sex? Because I have a no-sex-before-coffee rule."

"You do?"

"Yes, I do. It's kind of a new rule, though, so I don't know if I've mentioned it before."

"I just want to kiss you good morning." He pushed her hair back, loving the way sleepiness softened the lines of her face.

"I haven't brushed my teeth yet."

"Neither have I. Do you have a rule about that, too?"

She smiled, shaking her head. "I don't if you don't."

He didn't, and the next five minutes were some of the best he could remember. Cocooned in the cloud of luxury that was the hotel bedding, he kissed Gretchen until he thought he might be satisfied. Then he stretched to reach the telephone and ordered a pot of coffee before kissing her some more.

"Are we going out for breakfast?" she asked while they waited for the coffee. "I like breakfast almost as much as I like coffee. And I'm starving, too."

"We can order breakfast after our shower."

She scowled and burrowed farther under the covers while he pulled on just enough clothing to not scandalize the hotel staff. "It would have been more efficient to just eat it fast before our shower, or shower fast and then eat. Now they have to make two trips."

He cinched the drawstring on the sweatpants he'd thrown in his bag, and then leaned across the bed to shut her up with another kiss. "We will not be showering fast. We're going to have a nice, long, very hot shower, and then we can decide if we want room service or if we want to check out and find a place on the way home."

Once Gretchen had put two cups of coffee in her system, she stretched and declared she was ready to start the day. "So we're taking this shower together?"

Damn straight, they were, he thought. He'd chosen this particular hotel not only because of the excellent coffee and nice luxurious touches but also because of their shower. He stripped down and gave her a *come on* look before heading into the bathroom.

Steam was already beginning to roll through the bathroom when Gretchen stripped the nightgown off and stepped into the enclosure with him. She'd taken the time to tightly braid her hair and wind it up in a knot. He imagined that much hair could be a pain to deal with when wet and away from home.

"Wow," she breathed. The water was hot and rained down on them from dual showerheads. "I can't believe the water pressure. Does that mean we'll run out of hot water sooner?"

He picked up the bottle of body wash the hotel provided and squeezed a generous dollop into his palm. Then he rubbed his hands together before reaching for her. "We won't run out of hot water."

The sound of pleasure she made when he started spreading the liquid soap over her body shot straight through Alex and he was instantly hard. She tried to stay out of the water streams long enough for him to get her nice and slick, and he found himself watching the intense pleasure flitting across her face.

It was a simple thing, really. It was a shower. A modern shower hooked up to a state-of-the-art heating system. But to a woman who'd grown up in a house where showers had to be scheduled to ensure hot water for everybody, and whom he'd heard complain more than once about barely having enough to wash the shampoo out of her mass of hair, it was a pleasure she was obviously going to enjoy to the hilt.

When he ran his hands over her slick breasts, she groaned and leaned forward to rest her forehead against his chest. "This is amazing."

"Better than the sheets?"

"Oh." She looked up at him. "That's a tough one."

With the water flowing over her bare skin and her brow

knit in concentration over the question, she looked adorable, and he couldn't keep the grin off his face.

"What? What's so funny?"

"Nothing's funny. I'm just having a good time."

"Good." She took the bottle of body wash off the shelf and poured some into her palm. "I bet you can have a better time, though."

He groaned when she put her slippery hands on his chest and started working her way south. "I wouldn't bet against you."

Gretchen had her hand on the door handle, ready to get out and say hello to an overexcited Cocoa, when she realized she had no idea how to act now.

Gram was neither stupid nor blind. She knew Alex and Gretchen were a little more than landlord and tenant, and had been for a while. But they'd both been pretending she *didn't* know because it was just easier that way. Maybe Gram was planning her granddaughter's wedding in her head, but she hadn't said anything out loud, which meant everybody could continue on as if nothing was happening.

But now there was no doubt what they'd been up to. She was pretty sure Alex had even mentioned having only the one hotel room before they left. It would be stupid to keep up the pretense that they weren't stealing kisses every chance they got, but Gretchen wasn't sure how she felt about Gram actually *seeing* that they had a relationship. Somehow that made it all seem more real.

And it wasn't all about Gram getting ideas in her head

about a wedding and grandchildren in the near future. Gretchen didn't want Gram to know how she felt about Alex, because when he inevitably left, Gram would fuss over her. If Gretchen were the only one who knew she'd let herself get attached to Alex, maybe nobody would know she was hurting.

"You okay?"

Gretchen shook off her thoughts and looked at Alex, who'd turned off the ignition but seemed to be waiting for her to get out. "Yeah. I just got lost in thought for a second."

He nodded, looking as though he wanted to ask her what she'd been thinking about, but he didn't. "Cocoa's going to totally come undone if you don't say hi to her."

Gretchen forced a laugh and opened the door. She barely managed to get out with a dog instantly tangled in her legs, but as soon as her feet hit the ground, she crouched down to give Cocoa a hug. "Did you miss me, silly girl?"

Cocoa was so happy to see her, it took three tries to be still enough to get a high five, and then she went around the Jeep to greet Alex. Gretchen grabbed her bag out of the back and left them to their reunion.

Gram met her in the middle of the living room. She was still drying her hands on the dish towel, so Gretchen knew she'd been in the kitchen. "Hi, Gram. Everything go okay?"

"Of course." She kissed Gretchen's cheek. "Did you have a good time?"

"Yeah. I didn't know what anybody was talking about half the time, but there was a really good chocolate truffle dessert. It wasn't the kind of place where you asked for the recipe, which is too bad, because you would have liked it." Gretchen set her bag on the bottom step to carry upstairs later. "And it was interesting listening to Alex talk about his work to people who knew what the technical stuff meant."

"Was the hotel nice?"

The more Gretchen tried to concentrate on keeping her expression neutral, the more her lips twitched. And she knew the heat in her cheeks would give her away, anyway. Finally she gave up and let the smile happen. "The hotel was very nice. I had room service."

"Good." Gram returned the smile. "A girl should get to stay in a nice hotel and be pampered once in a while."

Gretchen followed her into the kitchen, not sure if they were talking in euphemisms, or if Gram actually thought staying in a hotel was good for a woman. Either way, the conversation was over since Alex walked through the front door with Cocoa just as they went into the kitchen. She heard the thump of his feet on the stairs as he presumably carried his bag up, but she wasn't going to take the chance of him overhearing her talking about their sex life with her grandmother.

"Did the animals give you any trouble?" she asked, changing the subject.

"Not at all. Dana and I even took Cocoa out for a walk to see the pumpkins. I know it's not time yet, but I'm worried about you harvesting them all yourself. There are so many now."

"I know my limits, Gram, and we don't have more than I can handle. I can't do any more than what we have, but I've got this crop under control."

"Still, so many." Gram put on a kettle to heat water for her tea. "Maybe Alex can help you."

And so it began, in however subtle a way. "Alex is a

photographer, not a pumpkin farmer. And he probably won't be here much longer."

"Has he said anything?"

"No, but he can't stay here forever. And since he's not doing an entire book, probably already has enough to do his story." She peeked in the cookie jar, then took out a single cookie. If she started shoving comfort food in her mouth during this conversation, she might make herself sick. "Everybody at the reception seemed surprised he's been here as long as he has and talked about opportunities he's missed."

"Maybe he doesn't care. He's made a lot of money from his pictures, or so I've heard."

She was grasping at straws, and Gretchen didn't know how to make the situation clear without being harsh. "Photojournalism isn't just a job he's way too young to retire from. It's his passion. He needed a break, but he's going to go back to it and probably soon."

Watching the way her grandmother's mouth pinched, Gretchen realized it would be better if Alex left them sooner rather than later, because her fears hadn't been invalid. Gram was getting too attached to the man and, relationship with Gretchen or not, she was going to be heartbroken when he left. They'd become good friends, Gram and Alex, and his absence would leave a void.

For her, too, Gretchen thought. She'd miss Alex's friendship.

He walked into the kitchen just as the kettle whistled, and Gram gave him a bright smile. "Do you want some tea?"

"No, thank you. I'm just going to grab some water."

"I didn't plan anything big for supper. I wasn't sure exactly what time you two would be back."

"How about you call in a pizza order and I'll go into town for it," Alex offered, pouring himself a glass of water. "We can pick a movie and eat in front of the television."

Gretchen rolled her eyes. Gram would never agree to that. Meals were eaten at the kitchen table. Even when she was younger and her lunch was a peanut butter and jelly sandwich on thick slices of homemade wheat bread, she'd have to sit at the table and wolf it down before she could go back to helping her grandfather.

"That sounds wonderful," Gram said. "And they'll give you a few paper plates if you ask, so we won't even have to wash dishes."

"Perfect." Alex glanced at Gretchen, and then back at Gram. "Did Gretchen tell you she stole the toiletries from the hotel?"

"You said I should!"

He laughed at her outrage, which made Gram laugh, too. "You should have seen her, Ida. She rolled them in her shirt and tucked them in her bag, and the whole time she looked like she was robbing a bank for the first time."

"I did not," she muttered, but Gram probably didn't hear her over the sound of her laughter.

When Alex winked at her, Gretchen couldn't help but laugh along with them. First, purloined hotel toiletries and then pizza on paper plates in the living room. He made her and Gram laugh, and it was good for them.

God, it was going to be hard when he left.

16

On Tuesday, Alex left the house early so he was at Stewart Mills High for the first day of school. He knew they'd hung a banner for the Eagles football team in the main hallway, and the principal had given him permission to take a few photos of the kids arriving.

Standing off to one side of the hallway, he managed to catch some of the players not only arriving but also jumping up to slap the bottom of the sign. The mood was good, and he got some great shots.

"It's a good thing Edna Beecher can't see you right now," a voice said from beside him, and he lowered the camera to smile at Jen Cooper.

"Heard about that, did you?" He would have been worried about it, except for the fact that he trusted Jen almost as much as he trusted Kelly.

"Kelly and I both live in a world of trying to protect the privacy of people in a town with no secrets. Sometimes we vent to each other, and she was pretty outraged on your behalf."

"I was pretty outraged on my behalf, too."

"I understand that, but trust me when I tell you a total stranger could show up in town in the dead of night in a black trench coat and reeking of cheap booze and have more credibility than Edna."

That made him laugh. "You paint quite the picture."

She shrugged. "It's a gift."

"Speaking of gifts, Gretchen looked amazing this past weekend."

"What's the gift part?" She tilted her head. "She's not giving those boots back, is she?"

"Hey, that's between you and her." He lifted the camera in time to catch Coach McDonnell pass PJ, the Eagles cornerback, in the hall and give him a high five. "The gift part is just how great she looked, I guess, while still being comfortable. She was relaxed and had a good time, I think."

"I know she did." When he gave her a questioning look, she shrugged. "It was her first night out in as long as we can remember. Of course she gave her best friends the details."

"Oh. Uh, how many details?"

Jen's smile was as enigmatic as the Mona Lisa's. "I heard the chocolate truffle was incredible."

"It was." And he needed to extricate himself from this conversation. "I guess I've got the shots I need."

She sighed. "And I should get to my office. The first day of school is always alcohol-worthy."

"I should have a rough draft of the story soon," he said. "I'd like to email it to you so you can take a look at it in its entirety, if you don't mind."

"Of course I don't. And tell Gretchen she can keep the boots. Not only do they not fit me right, but now that I've seen how they look on her, I'll never wear them again."

He laughed and waved as she walked down the hall. Since he had what he needed, and it looked as if Coach had gone into one of the main offices, Alex decided to call it a day. It was drizzling, with a slight chill in the air, so rather than roam around town, he drove back to the farm.

He waved to Ida, who was in her garden with a basket looped over her arm. Cocoa wandered over to him and he gave her a high five and an ear scratch. Gretchen was nowhere to be seen, so he assumed she was either in the garage or the barn, or maybe out with the pumpkins.

When he started for the back door, Cocoa followed him, and he looked over at Ida. She just laughed and waved them on, so Alex held the door open for the Lab and then kicked off his shoes.

"Guess it's you and me, girl."

They settled on the couch and Alex opened his laptop on the coffee table. After downloading the photos he'd taken that morning, he pulled each one up individually. The one of Hunter slapping the banner and Coach greeting PJ, he put in a folder for further consideration. The others he put in a separate folder to offer the yearbook committee, but they wouldn't work for his story.

Sitting on the couch with his feet on the table and the computer on his lap wasn't ideal as ergonomics went, but he enjoyed the feel of Cocoa curled against his leg. She wasn't really supposed to be on the sofa, but he wasn't the only one in the house who skirted that rule. Every time somebody watched television, she stretched out with her head in their lap, which probably explained why the dog hadn't hesitated to jump up next to him.

Pulling up another folder, he clicked on the picture of Gretchen he'd taken just before he kissed her for the first time. Then he clicked a button, and a sequence of photographs played out on the screen.

Gretchen playing with Cocoa in the yard. Stroking a horse's neck before leading it back into the barn. In one of his favorites, even though she'd been annoyed when she heard the shutter sound, she was sitting cross-legged on the floor in front of her grandmother's rocking chair, holding a hank of yarn while Ida wound it into a ball.

While he'd already given Gretchen a printed copy of the shot in the pumpkin patch with the truck for Ida's Christmas present, he planned to have a photo book made of all the shots he'd taken on the Walker farm. Most were of Gretchen, but he'd also taken quite a few of Ida and Cocoa, as well as the property itself. They were personal and not for his story, but he wanted the women to have them.

He clicked out of the slide show and then, with a deep sigh, closed the laptop. He was going to have a hard time leaving this all behind. Leaving *them* behind. But he couldn't stay. After working so hard for his entire adult life to build the career he had, how could he stay here and spend the rest of his life turning pumpkins so they didn't get flat on one side?

And he had no idea how Gretchen would react if he

even hinted at staying. She held her emotional cards so close to her chest, he could never be sure how she really felt about him. Or if she even had feelings for him at all.

That was probably for the best. Since he was nearing the end of the work he'd come here to do and would probably move on soon, the last thing he wanted was for Gretchen to fall for him. He didn't want to be another person in her life who'd let her down.

Cocoa poked at his arm with her nose, making a low whimpering sound. She'd probably picked up on the turmoil of his thoughts, so he took a deep breath and stroked her head. She rested her head on his knee, partially covering the edge of the laptop, and stared up at him with sad eyes.

"Aw, don't look at me like that. I'm not a guy who stays in one place, Cocoa. But it's not about you. I promise. I'm just a wandering kind of guy, and bringing the world to people through photographs is part of who I am." She sat up to give him a high five, and then snuggled against his side again to resume her nap. "I'll miss you, though."

"Are you breaking up with my grandmother's dog?"

Startled, Alex looked at Gretchen in the kitchen doorway. She was leaning against the jamb, her arms folded as if she'd been there a little while. "Just trying to keep some distance between us so she doesn't break my heart when I have to leave."

Her smile was on the tight side, and he realized Gretchen might assume he was actually trying to send *her* a message. And maybe he was. Hell if he knew. Maybe subconsciously he was working out what he'd say to Gretchen if leaving the farm turned out to be even harder than he thought. A preemptive pep talk for himself.

"She's not supposed to be on the couch," was all she said.

"I could tell by the way you two were snuggling while watching TV the other evening."

This time when she smiled, it looked less forced. "Busted. It's hard to say no to her."

He ran his hand over the dog's sleek brown fur, and she sighed deeply. "Yeah, it is."

"She'll miss you, too, when you're gone." She looked at them for a few seconds, her face like stone, and then she turned and went back into the kitchen. A moment later, he heard the screen door slam.

He'd stayed too long. Somehow renting a room from an old schoolmate had turned into making himself a part of the family, and extricating himself wasn't going to be easy on any of them.

And with each passing day, it was only going to get harder.

Gretchen watched the big dually pickup inch its way down her driveway, trying not to jostle the horse trailer it was towing. She'd miss the horses, but when she'd talked to Beverly on the phone to finalize pickup plans, it had sounded like they'd be back in the spring. This wasn't the year they'd move south for good, which meant she had one more year of that income.

That was how life went. Just keep making it from tax bill to tax bill and try to enjoy a little bit of life along the way.

The timing worked well for her, too. Most people didn't go south for the winter until deeper into fall, but Beverly's daughter's birthday was in September and she preferred spending it with her friends down there. Since the kids were homeschooled, they were free to do whatever they wanted.

That meant Cinnamon and the other horses departed before it was time to start harvesting the pumpkins, which was pretty exhausting work. With Gram taking care of the household garden and doing the pumpkin seeds and canning, Gretchen took care of the chickens, the wood supply, and cutting pumpkin stalks until she could barely straighten her back.

It wasn't ideal, but it was doable. And there was a possibility she'd have help a few hours a week, though it wasn't definite yet. Jen and Kelly had been working on a program to help kids who were getting in trouble, but nothing serious enough to give them a police record that might hold them back later in life.

Similar to community service, it would pair a teenager with a community member for a certain number of volunteer hours. Ideally, the adult would serve as somebody to talk to, almost as a mentor. They could try to share life experiences with the kids and help them get back on track before they went too far off the rails.

Unfortunately, they were finding themselves mired in red-tape headaches. There would have to be background checks done on every adult involved, just as they would if they were school volunteers. And there could be insurance complications for businesses that brought in a minor to do any work. Jen and Kelly were trying to use the Walker farm as a test run, because Gretchen always needed help and there was a variety of work to do. But there was also farm machinery and splitting mauls and all manner of things that could be dangerous in the hands of an inexperienced or troubled teenager.

Once she could tell by the sound of the engine that the truck had managed to make the turn from her driveway to the road and was accelerating, Gretchen headed back to the barn to start the process of giving it a thorough cleaning.

The hard work would serve two purposes. One, it would wear her body out so she'd sleep without too much tossing and turning. And two, it would keep her out of the house and away from the cause of the tossing and turning.

It wasn't the ache of sexual desire making her restless now, though she certainly didn't want him any less than she had in the beginning of his stay. It had been two days since she'd heard him practicing his good-bye speech on the dog, and now every time she saw him, she wondered if today was the day he'd tell her he'd be moving on.

She thought maybe she'd fallen in love with him, and she wasn't even sure when it had happened. Maybe it had been a slow, comfortable process, just the way he'd settled into being practically a part of the family.

Maybe she was wrong, though. She wasn't sure exactly what love was supposed to feel like. Not family love because, thanks to her grandparents, she knew what that felt like. But in the movies and books, falling in love with a man seemed like a huge moment of awareness, accompanied by a lightning bolt and a musical crescendo.

While she certainly felt the sizzling jolt of heat when he touched her, she knew sexual chemistry wasn't love. But she suspected feeling like the world had just lit up whenever she saw him and counting the minutes until that would happen again when they were apart might be. There was a sense of completeness when she was with him that was quiet and didn't come with big music, but was very real nonetheless.

Pulling the wheelbarrow over to the first stall, Gretchen grabbed the big bow rake and started cleaning up the straw. She yelped when strong arms slid around her waist from behind.

"Don't do that," she said, slapping Alex's forearm. "You scared me. What if I'd hit you with the rake?"

He kissed the back of her neck. "Why do you think I wrapped my arms around you instead of just slapping you on the ass like I wanted to?"

"I'm not usually so easy to sneak up on."

"No, which is why I had to do it. Cocoa must have worn herself out watching the horses being loaded, because she chose napping in her bed over coming outside with me, and you were so lost in thought, you didn't even hear me trip on that stupid floorboard coming in."

She needed to fix that. One of the floorboards was starting to warp, and she should pull it up and flip it before it got too out of shape to reuse. It was just one of the many things on her list of things to do when she wasn't busy. Or when she wasn't being distracted by the man currently pulling down on the collar of her shirt so he could kiss more of her neck.

"What were you thinking about?" he whispered when she didn't say anything else.

She was thinking about loving him, which she wasn't about to admit out loud. Not yet, anyway. Not when she could still replay his discussion with Cocoa word for word in her mind. "I was wondering if we have enough wood split for the winter yet."

Alex laughed, his breath tickling the nape of her neck. "Of course you were."

"What *should* I have been thinking about?"

"Texting me and asking me to sneak out here and make out with you in the hayloft."

Even though she knew she should be putting some distance between them, Gretchen couldn't hold back the flood of warmth his words triggered. And his hand sliding up under her T-shirt to cup her breast didn't help that any.

"I could probably take a break for a few minutes," she said, leaning the rake against the wheelbarrow.

"A few minutes? I can make that work."

A couple of days later, Alex looked out over the field of pumpkins, then gave Gretchen a skeptical look. "I still don't see how you're going to harvest all of these."

"One stalk at a time," she said in that practical way of hers. "It's not like they're all ready on the same day, anyway."

Hand in hand, they walked between rows of pumpkins. Every so often he'd have to let her go so she could bend down and check a pumpkin or roll one in danger of developing a flat spot, but then she'd straighten and her fingers would thread through his again.

Cocoa had abandoned Ida to join them, and she would run ahead before stopping to sniff thoroughly at anything that caught her attention. Then she'd run ahead again.

It was a beautiful day, and with Gretchen at his side and the dog playing in the sunshine, Alex couldn't think of a single place he'd rather be. For right now, in this moment, he was content.

He leaned over and kissed her, stopping her in midsentence about the proper way to cut a pumpkin stem. She kissed him back, and then gave him a questioning look when he broke it off. "What was that for?"

"Does there have to be a reason?"

"No." After a moment, she smiled and then resumed their stroll through the field. "I guess not. It's starting to get late. Are you ready to head back?"

"No, but we should, anyway. Ida will be starting supper soon, I imagine."

They'd hoofed it out to the field, so they had a long walk back to the house ahead of them. Cocoa was slowing down a little, probably ready for a drink, so the three of them went side by side.

"Did you hear back from Kelly's dad or Jen or about your rough draft?" she asked as they walked.

"Not yet. I just sent it to them." He'd finally decided it was time to let a fresh set of eyes or two see the story, plus he wanted their approval for the content. "And there's no rush, since there's no deadline or anything. The beginning of the school year and football season probably wasn't the best time to hit them up."

She laughed, their hands joined and swinging between them. "Not the best timing, I guess."

"I wish you'd let me put you in the story."

"I love the picture you took for me to give to Gram. I really do. But I'm not comfortable with the rest of it."

"I know." He squeezed her hand. "That's why I didn't push harder."

"Gram loved the picture of her knitting with Cocoa curled up at her feet, though. And the bit you did about her sweater sets and her pumpkin pie filling. I know her friends will make her feel like a celebrity when everybody finally gets to read it."

"I'll make sure, no matter where or how it's published, that she gets a copy worth showing off."

He wondered if she would let go of his hand when they neared the tree line that separated the fields from the backyard of the house, but she didn't. While she still wasn't one for open displays of affection in front of her grandmother—and probably never would be—she was loosening up.

When they reached the yard, she stopped. "I left some parts soaking in carburetor cleaner. Tell Gram I'll be in in a few minutes, okay?"

She stood on her tiptoes to give him a quick kiss, and then let go of his hand. He watched her walk away, utterly enjoying the view, and then gestured for Cocoa and continued to the house.

Once he'd refilled the dog's bowl with fresh cold water and relayed the message to Ida, he went upstairs to wash up and grab his phone. He'd plugged it in to charge earlier, and he was surprised by how often he left it lying around the house now. Not so long ago, it would never have been out of his reach.

After he washed his hands and used a washcloth to clean his face and neck, Alex unplugged his phone and noticed the icons indicating he'd missed a call and whoever it was had left a message.

The missed call was from his agent, and the voice mail was a terse demand to call him back, so Alex hit the call button. "Hey, I got your message."

"I've got good news for you, Alex."

Good news generally equaled money in his agent's eyes, which meant work. Work that would mean leaving Stewart Mills. Leaving Gretchen. "What's going on?"

"I'm going to assume they don't get CNN wherever you are?"

"Of course they do. I've just had better things to do than monitor it twenty-four seven. What's up?"

What was up was a labor dispute growing in Central America that had the potential to change the economic and political landscape of the country involved. "I've already heard from three major news outlets asking if you're there yet, so you'll be the man if you get there five minutes ago."

He wasn't ready. It was too soon to leave Stewart Mills. Saying good-bye to Gretchen would . . . He wasn't ready.

"Look, Alex. This could be big. You're familiar with that area and you already know some of the key players. You know how to get access to places and people others can't. I can get you on an eleven a.m. flight out of Boston tomorrow and your photographs will be the ones going out with the breaking news updates when this thing blows up."

Almost against his will, Alex felt the thrill of the hunt rising in him. The hunt for the perfect image to tell a story—an image the world would remember a pivotal moment in history by.

"Alex, you know you've got to come back at some point. But sure, go ahead and take a few weeks and maybe a cruise line will be looking for somebody to take pictures of happy families going down midship water slides. Or you leave now and remind everybody why the entire world pauses to look when an Alex Murphy shot comes on the screen."

"Book the flight," Alex heard himself say, and his stomach tightened. "Email me the details and I'll be there."

When he ended the call, he just sat there staring at the phone in his hand. It was the right thing to do. He needed to get back to work and this was just the kind of situation he thrived on. Documenting history. It wasn't the kind of story any random teenager with a smartphone could tell, the money would be good, and it was the kind of challenge that had always appealed to him.

All he had to do was say good-bye to Gretchen. Turning the phone over and over again in his hand, he tried to picture himself doing that, and it wasn't easy. He couldn't draft the right words in his mind. Nor would it be easy leaving Ida and Cocoa behind, but it was Gretchen's face that stayed front and center in his mind.

He could come back, he thought. There was no reason he couldn't keep paying rent and, when the story was over, come back to the farm. Sure, the distance from Boston or even Manchester made travel inconvenient, and the Internet wasn't as fast or reliable as he was used to. And the place in Providence, which *was* convenient and had kick-ass amenities, wasn't cheap to maintain for no reason.

But the apartment in Rhode Island was missing one thing he wasn't sure he wanted to make do without anymore, and that was Gretchen.

17

Something was wrong with Alex tonight, and Gretchen sensed it as soon as they gathered in the kitchen for supper. He smiled at them both and laughed when Gram told him a funny story about Cocoa, but he was tense. It showed around his eyes when he looked at her, which was something he seemed to be avoiding.

Gretchen had just taken her last mouthful of pot roast when Gram said she'd gotten a DVD copy of a movie they all wanted to see from the library, and Alex actually flinched. She stared at her plate, slowly and mindlessly chewing the food.

He was leaving.

She'd known from the first time he walked into her house that this moment would come. She'd known it when he'd kissed her out in the pumpkin patch. And she'd known it when she'd stripped him naked for the first time.

"I got a call from my agent today," Alex said quietly. "There's a story brewing in Central America and I'm catching a flight out of Boston tomorrow morning."

After swallowing, she took a sip of her drink without looking up. For somebody who'd known all along Alex would leave, Gretchen was surprised to find herself so unprepared now that the time had come. It hurt, like a hard kick to the gut, and she was too busy trying to breathe normally to come up with words to say.

"Oh." Even Gram was struck speechless for a moment, but she rallied faster than Gretchen. "What kind of story?"

Alex started talking, but all Gretchen heard was a blur of words running through her mind. It didn't matter what kind of story it was. He was leaving and then it would be just her and Gram and Cocoa again.

But it wouldn't be like it was before. Now she would miss him. She would miss having somebody to curl up with on the couch and somebody to kiss good morning. Somebody to rub her shoulders when she was tense. She'd miss holding hands with him when they went for walks.

She stood, her chair scraping across the hardwood floor, and carried her plate to the sink. "I've got stuff to do."

When she opened the back door, Cocoa came running, even though she wasn't supposed to be in the kitchen during dinner. After shoving her feet into her shoes, Gretchen motioned for the dog and they went outside.

After breathing in a few gulps of fresh air to shove back the sensation of wanting to cry, Gretchen walked to the garage and flipped on the lights. Sitting on the stool in front of the workbench, she dumped a coffee can of assorted nuts and bolts and ran her hand over them. Cocoa walked around, sniffing at a few things, before going back out the door to explore the yard.

The sound of Alex's voice a moment later wasn't exactly welcome. She wanted to hide in the garage and figure out how to make herself believe she didn't care if Alex left or not.

"Hey," he said from the doorway. "Need some help?"

Once she was sure she could face him without tears, she swiveled on the stool to look at him. "Not really. I'm just looking for the extra cotter pins for the snowblower."

"Of course you don't need help."

"What's that supposed to mean?"

He sighed. "You don't need anybody, do you?"

Anger sparked inside her. Was he actually disappointed that she wasn't crying and wrapping her arms around him, begging him not to go?

That wasn't going to happen. Her parents had walked away from her and she'd been fine with her grandparents. Gramps had passed away, and she and Gram had been fine with just each other. Alex could walk away and Gretchen would just keep on being fine.

Maybe she wouldn't be as happy as she thought she'd been before, but she'd be okay.

"Cocoa, come on in here with me," she heard Gram call, followed a few seconds later by the screen door banging.

Alex stepped into the garage and closed the door behind him. "I'd be an idiot to pass up this opportunity, Gretchen."

"And you're not an idiot, so you won't pass it up," she said, keeping her voice as casual as possible. "You were about done with Stewart Mills, anyway."

He winced. "Don't say it like that."

"Shouldn't you be packing?" The words sounded cold, even to her, but she didn't wince. She needed the distance between them.

"I don't want to leave like this." He sighed and scrubbed a hand through his hair. "Gretchen, I can come back."

She let herself believe that for a moment. She could almost hear Cocoa's joyous barking at the sound of his Jeep coming up the driveway and feel Alex embrace her as she threw her arms around his neck.

But she wasn't stupid. She knew how far off the beaten path Stewart Mills was. She saw how just the drive ate into the time Chase and Kelly had together, and they were doing it on a temporary basis. Long-term, it would be exhausting and inconvenient for Alex's travel requirements, and over time he'd start complaining. Best-case scenario, he'd try unsuccessfully to get Gretchen to move farther south in New England. Worst case, he'd find reasons to be home less and less often, until he finally stopped coming home altogether.

And if it hurt like this every time he left, she wanted no part of that.

"We had a good time together," she said in a quiet, calm voice. "We'll miss having you around, of course. But we'll probably have rented your room to somebody else by the time you're done wherever it is you're going."

She watched her meaning sink in, and saw the instant he realized she was telling him not to bother coming back.

The sadness dulled his eyes and he gave a quick, sharp shake of his head.

"If that's how you want it," he said quietly.

"Sometimes things just are a certain way, whether we want it to be or not." Gretchen took a deep breath, determined not to break down until he'd gone back inside the house. "I'll probably be out here for quite a while. I've let some stuff slide that I need to take care of."

He stared at her for what felt like forever, and she wondered if he would push the issue. Push *her* and get her to admit to feelings that wouldn't change anything. But he didn't. "Okay. I'm going to go start packing, then. I'm leaving early in the morning."

"How early?"

"I'll see you before I go. But I won't have time to eat breakfast with you. I'll grab something on the road once I'm closer to Mass."

She nodded, because she suddenly didn't have any words to offer. After one last, sad glance, Alex left the garage, closing the door softly behind him just as the first tear rolled down her cheek.

Tomorrow morning she was going to see Alex just like she did every day. But tomorrow he was going to say good-bye and walk out the door. And he wasn't coming back.

Alex turned onto Eagles Lane and drove slowly up the street to the McDonnells' house. He parked in the driveway and was getting out when Coach stepped out onto the porch.

"You look wrung out, son, and the day's barely begun."

Alex climbed the stairs and took the mug of coffee Coach handed him before taking his place in one of the rockers. "It was tough, saying good-bye."

That was an understatement. It had been wrenching, and he'd done the leaving as quickly as he could, like ripping off a bandage. Ida had hugged him tightly, tears glistening in her eyes. She'd made him promise to keep in touch, sniffling the entire time.

Even with her emotions shuttered behind that mask of indifference Gretchen clung to, he'd seen her sorrow. She'd kissed him and wished him luck before walking out the back door without looking back. Cocoa had watched him drive away, sitting at the top of the driveway until he couldn't see her anymore.

Tough didn't even begin to describe it. He took a huge gulp of coffee, hoping to scald away the lump in his throat.

"I hope it's not another decade and a half before we see you again," Coach said after a few minutes of companionable silence.

It was on the tip of his tongue to assure Coach that wasn't going to happen, but he couldn't bring himself to say the words. "I hope not."

"But no promises?"

Leave it to Coach McDonnell to back him into the corner. "I think it might be hard for a while. To come back, I mean."

"But not so hard it would be easier to stay?"

"I can't . . . I don't . . ." Alex rocked back in the chair, staring out at the trees that lined Eagles Lane, and blew out a long breath. "I can't pass up this opportunity. And she just . . . I don't know how to explain it, Coach, but

Gretchen already closed the door on me. She said good-bye and she meant it."

"She's a tough nut, that one." Coach nodded. "She came to Stewart Mills pretty broken, and the man who taught her about family and love . . . well, I admired the hell out of him, but he wasn't one for sharing emotions."

"I told her I'd come back, but she made it clear she didn't see a point."

"If ever there was a person who believed actions speak louder than words, it's Gretchen Walker."

"I have to go," Alex said, his voice sounding choked to his own ears. "I have a career and even if this was a story I could ignore, I've committed to it."

Coach rocked back in his chair. "Of course you have to go. She's gotta have a little bend in her, too. What time did you say your flight was?"

"Eleven. I would have been on the five thirty flight, but I'm getting too old for overnight drives."

"I'm glad you got the later flight so you could stop by."

"Me, too." He'd called the night before and Coach had insisted he and Mrs. McDonnell would be awake and wanting to see him at six in the morning. "I'm also glad I came back, even though . . . well, you know."

When Coach chuckled, Alex glanced over to find the man grinning at him. "I had a conversation pretty similar to this with Chase Sanders not too long ago. He made it almost halfway back to New Jersey before he pulled his head out of his ass and turned around."

"I don't think the pilot or my fellow passengers will go along with that."

"Probably not, but that's not my point. You keep in mind that once the leaving is done, if you realize you've made a mistake, don't wallow in it. Come back and try to make it right."

"Shutters," Alex muttered, almost to himself. "It's literally like when she sees emotional upset coming, she closes the shutters so the storm can't touch her."

"But you've seen what's inside, son. Maybe it's worth prying them open." Coach paused, rocking in silence for a few seconds. "I know you've gotta do this thing in Central America. Maybe it'll give you both some time to think."

In other words, maybe Gretchen would miss him as much as he knew he would miss her.

Alex drained the rest of his coffee and then stood. "I should say good-bye to Mrs. McDonnell. Is she in the kitchen?"

"Of course." He stood, too, and they went in together.

Coach's wife kissed his cheek. "I read your paper, and saw the pictures that go with it. It's a wonderful story, Alex. You really did Stewart Mills proud."

"Thank you. You know I have you and Coach to thank for that. Not just for encouraging my love of photography, but for loving me when I was pretty hard to love. And teaching me how to love myself."

"You've never been hard to love." She hugged him. "Keep in touch, Alex."

He squeezed her. "I will."

Once he was in the Jeep and headed back down Eagles Lane, Alex took a few deep breaths and tried to focus on the task ahead of him rather than the people he was leaving behind.

He was almost out of town when he saw the blue lights flashing in his rearview mirror. Cursing under his breath, he put on his blinker and pulled to the side of the road. Those damn stop signs.

As luck would have it, Kelly McDonnell got out of the cruiser and walked to his window. He hit the button to lower it as she approached, and gave her a friendly smile, which she returned.

"Going somewhere in a hurry?" she asked.

"Just how many new stop signs are there in this town?"

"We'll never tell. How do you think we pay for gas and coffee?"

He laughed and shook his head. "I should remember them by now, but I don't think I've come this way but a couple of times since I got here."

"It's early, too." She rested her hand against the Jeep to lean on. "I saw your bags in the back. Leaving town?"

"Noticed those, did you?"

She shrugged. "It's kind of my job."

"Yeah, well *my* job beckons. I've got an eleven o'clock flight out of Boston and it's not a fun drive from here, so it was an early morning."

Kelly nodded, looking like she wanted to say more. Then she sighed. "So . . . after the job?"

"I'll probably go back to Providence and take care of some business stuff I've neglected. Go into New York and have some meetings."

"Okay." He could see that she got his meaning. "I know you and Chase have been keeping in touch, so don't be a stranger."

She stood straight, but before she could walk away, he

called her name. "Maybe you could give Gretchen a call later? Or stop by and see her? You know how she is. I can't tell if she's . . . Maybe you could just give her a call?"

"I'll stop by when I get a chance. Maybe Jen and I will drag her off the farm for a girls' night out."

He nodded, unable to say more, and then returned her wave. After pulling back onto the road, he turned up the radio and—once he was out of the jurisdiction of the Stewart Mills Police Department—put more weight on the gas pedal.

"Men suck," Kelly shouted vehemently. But then she paused, listing slowly to the left as she looked at the shiny engagement ring on that hand. "Wait. Most men suck. Not all of them. Just some. Okay, fine. Alex Murphy sucks."

Even though hearing his name hurt, Gretchen laughed as she put out her hand to brace her friend, who'd left the neighborhood of sobriety about two glasses of wine ago. Gretchen and Jen weren't feeling a lot of pain, either, but they were still managing to sit upright. Or so Gretchen assumed. Jen looked pretty straight.

When Kelly had shown up with a plan to wash Gretchen's heartbreak away with as much wine as they could drink without throwing up, Gram had put her foot down. It had been a long time since she'd had all three girls under her roof for a sleepover, but if they were going to drink, they'd do it where she could keep an eye on them.

Before they'd uncorked the first bottle, Gram had stuffed them with her macaroni salad to ensure they weren't drinking on an empty stomach, and then gone upstairs with her knitting and a book. But Gretchen knew if there was an exceptionally loud thump, a call for help, or she heard one of the big doors open and close, Gram would be down the stairs in a split second. She had hearing like a bat.

"He could have at least stayed until you harvested all those damn pumpkins," Jen said. "Oh, that reminds me. I have a note on my desk reminding me to call you and beg for a bunch of free pumpkins. Like the little ugly ones nobody wants."

Gretchen sipped her wine, pleasantly surprised when she realized it tasted better than it had when they first started drinking. She wasn't much for wine, but the more she drank, the more she liked it. "Why do you want a bunch of ugly pumpkins? Is that the homecoming theme this year? Support the Eagles—get your ugly pumpkin here!"

They all giggled for a few minutes before Jen shook her head. "We need ugly pumpkin babies for health class."

They both stared at her, trying to make sense of that, but Kelly spoke first. "We didn't have ugly pumpkin babies. Maybe that's why we don't have men— Oh wait. I have one. Never mind."

"I would call a cab to send you home, but Stewart Mills doesn't have cabs," Gretchen said. She knew her friend wasn't being snarky and was simply having trouble remembering her current relationship status thanks to her intoxication, but Gretchen didn't want to hear about Chase. "You're not going to inject my pumpkins with STDs or anything, are you? They might just be pumpkins, but I raised them and I don't want you to give them syphilis."

Jen looked at her like she'd lost her mind. "What kind of monster do you think I am that I'd give ugly pumpkin babies a sexually transmitted disease on purpose? I'm so offended right now."

Gretchen sighed and refilled their glasses, giving Kelly decidedly less. "I'm sorry."

"Thank you. Now, we can't afford those fake robot babies and we've had many requests from parents to stop teaching the children how hard it is to be a parent by making them take care of eggs."

"I dropped mine," Kelly said, and Gretchen choked back a laugh when her friend's eyes filled up with tears. "I named her Charlotte and made her a little flannel dress. Then I dropped her and my dad made a joke about scrambled eggs and I cried."

"So anyway," Jen continued. "Last year, one of the girls lost her infant egg. She tried to tell us the egg ran away because they were boring and didn't have good Internet, but a substantial amount of time later, they discovered the egg baby had slipped between the seats of their minivan. When it broke, Mom threw up and she ended up paying two hundred dollars to have the minivan professionally cleaned. So we're thinking we can have the kids paint faces on the pumpkins and care for them. They're still fragile, but not *as* fragile."

"Do they get extra credit because their babies are ugly?" Kelly asked. "That seems kind of mean."

Jen slid Kelly's wineglass a little farther from her hand. "I want ugly ones so they'll be free, dumb-ass."

"Mean *and* cheap," Kelly muttered, flopping back against the couch.

"You can have some little pumpkin babies," Gretchen promised. "It sounds like a fun project."

"Right? The little faces will be so cute. It's too bad Alex won't be around to take pic—" Jen stopped talking and covered her mouth. "Sorry."

Gretchen started to laugh, intending to wave a careless hand and assure her friend it was no big deal. But, without being sure how it happened, she ended up with her head in Jen's lap, sobbing.

She was vaguely aware of Jen leaning over to set both of their wineglasses on the table and Kelly asking Cocoa where Gram kept the extra boxes of tissues, but mostly she just felt the pain wash over her until she couldn't hold it in anymore.

Jen stroked her hair, not trying to stop the tears with empty platitudes and stupid inspirational sayings she'd seen on the Internet. At some point, Kelly shoved a wad of tissues into her hand and then sat on the floor, resting her head on Gretchen's side.

She wasn't sure how long she cried, but eventually the tears slowed to a trickle and she mopped at her face with the tissues. "I'm sorry."

"Hey, if you can't drain your sinuses on your friend's favorite sweatpants, what's the point of having friends?"

Gretchen managed a rough laugh, pushing herself back to a sitting position. "I love him. Alex. I love Alex."

"It would be weird if you loved some other guy," Kelly whispered.

"We are really bad at being drunk," Jen said. "We're supposed to be making you feel better. You don't look like you feel better."

Gretchen swiped at her nose again with the wad of tissues, and then dropped it on the table so she could pick up her wineglass. She probably shouldn't have any more, but her mouth was dry. "I do feel better. I needed to cry. And you guys being here reminds me that my life isn't over. I don't have Alex, but I still have everybody else I love. Plus, I'm going to help enrich the lives of the next generation of Stewart Mills with my little ugly pumpkin rejects. I'm making a difference in the world."

They all drank to that, and then drank again. Kelly set her glass down and then flopped backward, which put her in Cocoa's bed. The Lab immediately licked her face and scooted over to make room for her new best friend.

"You know Gram's going to be so loud in the morning," Jen said.

"Oh, yeah." Gretchen nodded. "And she's going to make something really gross and slimy for breakfast to teach us a lesson."

"I hope she doesn't make scrambled eggs," Kelly said. "Poor Charlotte."

When she started sniffling, Jen laughed and looked at the inch of wine still in her glass. "We really are the worst drunk people ever."

"But you're the best friends ever," Gretchen said, and then she took another sip of the wine.

It was enough, she tried to tell herself. Her farm. Gram. Cocoa. Kelly and Jen. Eventually she'd stop thinking about Alex. She hoped.

18

It was two weeks before Gretchen made the decision to move back into her own room, and it was harder than she'd anticipated.

She and Gram had both agreed, with barely any discussion at all, that they didn't want to rent the room to anybody else. Gretchen knew Gram missed Alex almost as much as she did, and neither of them could imagine a stranger—or even somebody they knew—taking his place in the house. And Cocoa was still whining for him, pacing back and forth in the hallway or the driveway, waiting for Alex to show up and give her a high five.

Rather than continue sharing a bathroom, Gretchen knew it made sense for her to take her room back and return to the way it had been for so many years. But the first couple of times she crossed the threshold, memories of Alex had immediately driven her away.

But she'd been raised on common sense, not foolish emotion, so she sucked it up and took this rainy Saturday to move her stuff back where it belonged.

Gram had cleaned the room thoroughly. Gretchen knew she'd been in there several times, scrubbing and spraying. The bedding had been laundered and put in the linen closet, and the mattress cleaned. By the time Gretchen had her own favorite bedding back on the bed, put her clothes away and once again littered the bathroom with her toiletries, any lingering trace of Alex's scent was gone.

She didn't need to be able to smell his soap or shampoo to be overwhelmed by thoughts of him, though. No matter what, it would be many nights before she could sleep in this room and not remember being there with him.

But for now, she decided, she was going to make the most of the rest of the day. With the weather the way it was, she was mostly stuck indoors, so she'd organize the pantry for Gram. With autumn just around the corner, it was time to pull everything out of the big pantry. Gram could take stock of what they had and check expiration dates while Gretchen gave the oversized closet a thorough cleaning. Then they'd put back what they didn't throw out, making sure it was packaged in a way that wouldn't attract small, furry winter guests.

Gretchen was walking through the living room on her way to the pantry when she heard Alex's name come out of the television speaker. The knitting needles in Gram's hands stilled as they both turned to the screen.

The photograph filling the screen was breathtaking and

heartbreaking. A man in some kind of military or police uniform had a gun in one hand and was holding the arm of a little girl in the other. He was trying to drag her away from the body on the ground—a man he'd presumably just shot, based on the uniformed man's stone-cold expression.

The little girl was crying, her face a snapshot of emotional agony, and Gretchen could see the whiteness of her knuckles where her little hands were clinging to the dead man's shirt. She was actually lifting him slightly off the ground in her effort to resist being taken away.

The dead man was her father, according to the woman somberly reading the story for the camera. He'd broken out of the picket line when he spotted his daughter—whom he hadn't seen for days and who had broken free of his wife's hold—running toward him. Tensions were so high, he was shot before anybody fully understood what was happening.

Photographs started scrolling by that captured the violence following that tragic moment—each with Alex's photo credit in small print in the bottom corner—and Gretchen found herself unable to look away.

She knew he had a gift. The photo framed and wrapped and ready to be given to Gram for Christmas was proof of that. As were all of the other photos he'd taken around the farm and Stewart Mills. But this was different. These photographs were *important*.

They'd taken words that were simply background noise about a situation that people didn't understand in a place they'd never heard of and made them stop and watch. Now, because of a picture that froze a tragedy in time, people knew this violence was happening in the world.

Maybe it helped, Gretchen thought as the news went on

to the next story and she continued to the kitchen. It was easier to understand why Alex had to go off and take pictures when those pictures kept a government from covering up the murder of hundreds of low-income workers who just wanted fair wages so they could feed their families.

It didn't make her miss him any less, though. No amount of work could exhaust her so completely that she didn't think of him the second her head hit the pillow. The constant ache wasn't eased by physical labor or showers that used up all the hot water.

She'd known the pain of missing him would be sharp, but she also thought it would fade quickly as she geared up for pumpkin harvest time. She'd been wrong. Two weeks later, it was still hard to breathe when she thought about Alex. And she thought about him almost constantly.

At least a dozen times a day, she asked herself if she'd made the right choice. Maybe she should have asked him to come back. Now that he was gone, Gretchen fully understood that, while having him away was hard, knowing he wasn't coming back at all was much worse than waiting for him to appear.

"What on earth are you doing in there?" Gram said from behind her.

"It's raining, so I'm going to empty the pantry."

"Maybe you should take a break, honey. We can watch a movie. A Bourne movie, if you want to."

The worry for her was clear as day in Gram's eyes, but Gretchen shook her head. If she sat still, she was going to think. And if she thought, it would be about Alex. "I want to get this done. It's harder to fit into the to-do list now that the pumpkins take up the fall season."

Gretchen started carrying items from the pantry to the kitchen table, stacking them neatly so they'd have enough room for everything. Gram got a garbage bag for anything that had expired, and started sorting. If it didn't go in the garbage bag, it went onto the kitchen counter to be put away after the shelves had been washed down. If they were running low on something, Gram added it to a separate shopping list so they could watch for coupons and sales to stock back up.

It was mindless work, but at least it was something to do. Rather than let her mind wander to Alex, she tried to come up with her favorite of Gram's recipes for each of the items she pulled off the pantry shelves. It was silly, but it worked. More or less.

"I think it might be time to sell the farm."

Grams words didn't make sense to Gretchen at first but then, as the simple sentence fell into place in her mind, the warmth seeped out of her until all she felt was cold shock.

She walked to the table and set down the five boxes of spaghetti noodles she'd gathered. "I don't understand."

"It's time, honey. Honestly, it's probably long past time, but I wasn't strong enough to admit it." Gram pulled out a chair and sat down, her hands fiddling with a box of black pepper. "I probably should have sold it right after your grandfather passed, but you were so . . . It gave you comfort walking in his footsteps and I couldn't take that away from you."

"It still does give me comfort."

"You need to make your own path. This was his path, not yours."

Gretchen was beginning to understand Gram was very

serious about this, and panic welled up in her chest. "I've worked so hard, Gram. I've given *everything* to this farm. How could you do this to me?"

"I know you've given everything for this farm. And for what? For the future generations of Walkers? There aren't going to be any precisely *because* you've sacrificed everything."

"I'm only thirty, Gram. I think it's a little early to cast me as the childless spinster."

"Your age has nothing to do with it. This farm—this piece of dirt with a stupid old house sitting on it—is the reason you let Alex go."

"What was I supposed to do, Gram? Beg him to stay? He has a career. He travels and makes money and wins awards. You just saw the work he does. It's amazing and important. Was I supposed to ask him to stay and pick pumpkins with me for the rest of his life?"

"You could have gone with him."

Gretchen couldn't even wrap her head around that. "No, I couldn't."

"Yes, you could. If not for this farm and feeling like you have to take care of me, you could have gone with him."

"And then what, Gram? He's in some place in Central America I can't even find on a map. I'd be sitting all by myself in an apartment in Rhode Island. How is that better than my life here?"

"Because he'd come home to you."

"This is the only home I've ever known. This was the first place I felt safe. And loved. And . . . this is my *home*."

"That wasn't the farm, Gretchen. That was *us*. It was your grandfather and me who made you feel safe and made you feel loved. We're your home, not the land. You still have your grandfather in your heart, and you have me. The house I'm in doesn't matter."

"Forget what I'm doing with my life." Gretchen decided to try logic since emotion wasn't getting her anywhere. "How about practical things, like where are you going to live?"

"I've been looking at the senior housing in the city. It might be nice to have restaurants and stores nearby, within walking distance."

"Okay, where am *I* supposed to live?"

"You need to make a new home with the man you love. Maybe that's in Providence, or maybe you find a house in between. Maybe still in New Hampshire, but closer to the airport."

She didn't want to talk about Alex. Not now and probably not anytime soon. "You can't have Cocoa in senior housing."

The dog had stretched out near the fridge to watch them, and she lifted her head when she heard her name. Maybe feeling the tension in the room, she whined slightly and thumped her tail on the floor.

It worked. Gram's mouth softened and her eyes shimmered with tears. Gretchen didn't like seeing it, but Gram had to come around.

"Maybe she could go with you," Gram said quietly. "And visit me."

"An apartment in the city isn't going to make her happy. And it's not going to make *me* happy."

Gram set the pepper on the table and squeezed her hands together. "I feel like I'm holding you back. Me and this stupid old house and a bunch of dirt."

Gretchen walked over to stand behind her. Bending, she wrapped her arms around her grandmother's shoulders and kissed the top of her head. "Never—not for one single second—have I ever felt like that."

"I won't sell the farm without your blessing, Gretchen. I love you far too much to do that to you." Gram reached up and squeezed her hand. "But I want you to think about what it is you want in life. Not what your grandfather wanted. Not what you think I want. I want you to really think about what *you* want."

"Gram, I know you mean well, but even if you sell the farm now and I have nowhere else to be, Alex and I are done. He's not coming back, and I'm not going to leave everything I love here to go be alone in the city."

"I'm sorry, honey." Gram heaved a big sigh. "I guess he wasn't the right man for you, after all."

"No, he was," Gretchen said, without really meaning to say it out loud. "Almost. There was just no way for us both to be happy. But I have you and Cocoa, and he's off doing what he loves. It's enough."

*I*t isn't enough anymore.

With a layover in Houston, Alex had found a restaurant and made himself comfortable. An hour later, he wasn't quite as comfortable, and the flash of self-awareness about not being satisfied with his life anymore wasn't the most welcome thought he'd ever had.

He shifted on the hard chair, running the thumb of his free hand under the waistband of his pants where it was cutting into him. Then he sighed and set down his fork.

One of the things he'd learned about himself, back during the long and tough road to being physically fit, was that he ate his emotions. And he'd sure been eating the hell out of them since leaving Stewart Mills. Salt. Sugar. Fats. It didn't matter what it was. If something was good for his taste buds but bad for his waistline, he'd eaten it in the last two weeks.

He knew what he was doing and what he had to do to stop the backward slide. Identify the feelings that were causing him to comfort himself through food. Write them down. Then either work through the feelings or brainstorm ways to go through the process of dealing with the underlying causes of those emotions. The key was in finding some kind of resolution that would enable him to feel in control, even if it wasn't a problem with an immediate fix. Professionals had helped him find the tools to handle problems without junk food.

But Alex didn't need a pen and paper for this one.

His career was important to him. It always would be. But it couldn't be *everything* anymore. Not now that he'd taken long walks, holding the hand of a woman he loved and watching a dog play in the grass.

What he wanted right this minute, now that the assignment was over, was to head back to Stewart Mills. Cocoa would meet him in the driveway and he'd give the dog a high five before wrapping his arms around Gretchen and kissing her until they were both dizzy.

But he couldn't do that, so he'd stuffed his face with a loaded cheeseburger and fries before chasing it with a slab of cheesecake. And alcohol. As if Scotch could wash the pain away.

Nothing washed the pain away. Not booze and not empty

calories. Not even the occasional punishing workouts he'd forced himself to do when the guilt got to him. The hurt was bone-deep and there was no external cure for it.

Maybe part of his emotional vulnerability stemmed from the events he'd left behind. He'd seen some gut-wrenching things through his camera lens and he never left any assignment unchanged in some way. It was especially hard when children were involved. He didn't need to look through his professional archives to picture the face of every child he'd photographed. They stayed with him forever.

But that wasn't the whole of it, though, and he knew it. He'd known it before Stewart Mills disappeared from his rearview mirror. He left a part of himself in New Hampshire, and the last two weeks had proven to him it was a part he couldn't reconcile to living without.

It was time to come up with a resolution. Alex might be an artist, but behind the photographer's eye was a very practical brain, so while his heart and soul might want to run back to Stewart Mills and ask Gretchen to marry him, his mind was riding the emergency brake pretty hard.

As he'd told the guys during Eagles Fest, with his lifestyle, it was easier to not have a wife than to keep one happy.

Alex rotated his wrist, swirling the amber liquid in the bottom of the glass. Gretchen wasn't like Laura. Gretchen was strong and independent, and she wouldn't come undone if the man in her life had to travel for an assignment. She'd do what needed to be done and leave a light on for him.

But to make that work, he'd have to compromise and not take advantage of that. In exchange for her being able to handle him leaving, he'd have to cut back on the actual leaving, and that would impact his career.

How much was he willing to sacrifice? He was too good and had been too driven for too long to settle for advising the Eagles yearbook committee and taking freelance photos for the local weekly.

But nothing said that was *all* he could do. He'd enjoyed digging into the history of Stewart Mills. The northern part of New Hampshire was rich with stories to tell through the camera lens. And when a major assignment offered itself, he'd talk to Gretchen and decide together if he should take it or not.

No more war zones. No more revolutions in small, violence-wracked countries. He'd suffered his share of injuries over the years, and he'd have to pass on those. Maybe he'd be nominated for fewer awards and make a little less money.

But he wanted a family. And when he had Gretchen and their beautiful children—of course they'd be beautiful because they'd look like their mother—and maybe another dog to keep Cocoa company, he was going to make damn sure he came home to them in one piece.

Suddenly his mind was filled with images of walking through the pumpkin field, hand in hand with Gretchen. Ahead of them, running and laughing, were a couple of kids with their dogs.

Alex pushed back the plate that still had a few bites of cheesecake on it and downed the rest of the Scotch in one gulp before pulling out his wallet to pay. He didn't have to change his flight, since he'd been flying into Boston anyway, but he had to cancel and reschedule some things.

Everything else could wait. Right now, it was time to go throw open some shutters.

Gretchen was setting a log on the chopping block when Cocoa lifted her head. She'd been napping in the shade, but now she stood, her body practically quivering as she looked toward the driveway. Then she barked and took off running.

She heard it herself, then. A vehicle was coming up the driveway that sounded an awful lot like Alex's Jeep. Unable to make her feet move, she stood there and waited. If it was a stranger, Gram would already have gone to the front door to see what Cocoa was carrying on about. If it was Alex . . . But he wasn't coming back.

Cocoa's bark changed to an excited yip and Gretchen could see the dog in her mind, spinning in joyful circles as somebody she loved and missed came home to her. Cocoa wouldn't hold his absence against him. She would just pick up loving the man where they'd left off.

Gretchen felt frozen as she waited. Her hands were cold, despite the heavy gloves, and she felt the goose bumps that made no sense in the warm sun. Breathing seemed to require a conscious effort on her part. *Breathe in. Now breathe out.*

When Alex finally walked around the corner of the house, the dog almost tangling in his feet in her desire to be near him, Gretchen just waited. The cold seemed to have spread to her face, because it felt like stone.

When he was close enough, she spoke first, as if she could build a wall of words that would keep her heart out of it this time. "We didn't think you were coming back. But since you left, we made the decision not to rent that room out anymore."

He blew out a breath and ran his hand over his hair. "God, you make it so hard. You're not going to give me anything, are you?"

"I'm not sure what it is you want." She was surprised her voice sounded so emotionless, because it felt as though every emotion in the human spectrum was a swirling hurricane on the inside.

"Maybe you could put down the big ax and we could talk."

She leaned the splitting maul against the chopping block and then slowly pulled the gloves off. After tossing them onto the block, she rubbed her hands together for a few seconds before shoving them in the pockets of her jeans.

Then she looked at him, wanting to say something unemotional or at least casual. Instead, she felt the sting of tears, and her bottom lip quivered. "What do you want to talk about?"

"Why didn't you want me to come back?"

She looked at him for what felt like forever, waiting for the walls to come up. His clothes were rumpled, as was his hair. Judging by the scruff, he hadn't shaved in a while, and exhaustion showed around his eyes. But he'd still come here. No matter what his other travel arrangements, the only way to get from the airport to Stewart Mills without a private helicopter was a lot of driving.

Coming here wasn't something he'd done lightly, so blowing him off to protect her own feelings wasn't something she could do.

"I wanted you to come back," she said quietly. "But it hurt

so much that you were leaving and I couldn't imagine what it would feel like to have you leave over and over again."

"But if this was my home, I'd also come back over and over again."

"For how long? Look at you. You're exhausted from driving up here. How many times would you do that before you were sick of it and decided it was easier to be back in Providence?" She took a deep breath, trying to steady herself. "Then the arguments would start. And you'd start pushing for me to move to Rhode Island and—"

"No." He shook his head. "You would hate Providence."

It touched her that he knew that. Unequivocally and without her needing to explain it, he knew she would be miserable in a city. "I would. And you would hate it here and . . . it just seemed easier to do it now."

"It's not. Easier, I mean. So I came back even though you told me not to. And I came back even though it's a pain-in-the-ass drive from the airport. I know this is where you belong and that, even if you didn't love this farm, you'd never leave Ida and Cocoa."

The dog was overjoyed to hear her name in Alex's voice, so she turned a happy circle and then leaned against his leg until he reached down to stroke her head.

"This is all a part of who you are," he continued. "And I love who you are. I love *you*. But I'm not going to spend the rest of my life trying to guess how you feel about me."

Her stomach tightened, and she felt the tears rising again. *I love you, but . . .* "I don't know what that means, Alex. You said I don't give you anything, and I don't know how to take that."

"I want you to tell me how you feel about me." He said it plainly, without drama, and then simply waited.

Gretchen's wall crumbled and she couldn't rebuild it faster than the bricks tumbled down. She felt her lip quivering and the tears dripping from her chin, and she threw up her hands. There were no defenses anymore. Not against Alex. "I love you. I love you and for the rest of my life, I want *you* to be my home."

He crossed the space between them in the blink of an eye and then she was in his arms. Her shoulders shook as the tears really broke loose, but he held her close while she cried into his shirt.

Cocoa bumped against her leg, making whining sounds because she didn't understand what was going on. Gretchen knew when one of Alex's arms dropped away from her, it was to comfort the dog, and that made her love him even more.

"Don't ever hide your feelings from me," he said against her hair. "I don't care if you're angry or sad or happy or scared. I can take it all."

"What about your job?" she asked, pulling back and mopping at her face with both hands.

"I'll still do my job. I'll just be more picky about which assignments I take. No overtly dangerous ones, because I hope to have a wife and kids waiting for me at home." He smiled and it felt as though her heart literally fluttered in her chest. "And a grandmother-in-law and Cocoa. And maybe another dog, too, because then Cocoa would have somebody to high-five all day."

Cocoa panted and offered up her paw. Gretchen, still sniffling, smiled when Alex slapped it. Then he turned back to her. "We'll talk about assignments and decide together if they're worth taking, factoring in the travel and what might be going on here. And every single time I go on a job, I will come back to you. Because I love you, Gretchen Walker, and you're my home, too."

She threw her arms around his neck, and he lifted her off her feet. "I love you so much, Alex Murphy. And I believe in us."

"So you'll marry me, then?"

She didn't hesitate or try to buy time to think. She laughed and then kissed all over his face. "Yes. Yes, I want to marry you."

He kissed her until she could barely breathe and then set her back on her feet. "I guess we should go tell Ida she'll be cooking for three from now on."

"I can see her over your shoulder and I think she already knows, since she has her face plastered against the window and she might be crying."

When Alex looked over his shoulder and then made a *come on* gesture, Gretchen laughed. Gram was out the door and across the yard faster than Gretchen had ever seen her move before, and they shared a tearful hug. Alex got dragged into it when he told Gram they were getting married, and they both kissed his face.

"Since you're going to be Gretchen's husband," Gram said, "you should probably know that I don't mind if you kiss her once in a while. Even in front of me."

Alex laughed and did just that, and Gretchen didn't pull away. She would be kissing this man for the rest of her life, and the big farmhouse was going to be filled with love. Not just the quiet, steady kind of love her grandfather had shown her, but the open and loud and sometimes messy love she wanted her children to feel.

Cocoa nuzzled her hand, looking for attention, and Gretchen crouched down to ruffle her neck. "He came back to us, Cocoa."

The dog licked her face and then offered her paw. Gretchen gave her a high five and then stood. With her fingers intertwined with Alex's, they walked back toward the house with Gram and Cocoa beside them.

Please turn the page for a sneak peek at

Homecoming

*The next book in the Boys of Fall series
by Shannon Stacey*

Available soon from Jove Books

Sitting in a hospital waiting room with a pack of scared and sweaty teenage boys while wearing a little black dress and high heels wasn't Jen Cooper's idea of a fun Friday night.

Nothing could have dragged her out of there, though. Not even the promise of flip-flops and her favorite yoga pants. The police officer leaning against the wall and staring at the ceiling was her best friend, Kelly McDonnell. It had been Kelly who was the first to arrive when the 911 call came in from football practice. Kelly's dad—Coach McDonnell—had collapsed on the high school's field and they were afraid he was having a heart attack.

When Kelly called her from the emergency room, Jen had been in her car, on her way to a second date with the first guy in a long time who actually had potential to make her forget the man who didn't, but she hadn't even hesitated before canceling. Kelly needed her.

"Miss Cooper, do you think it'll be much longer?"

Jen looked at the young man who'd asked the question in such a low voice, it was almost a whisper. PJ, the team's cornerback, bore the same solemn expression as the rest of the football players in the room. Coach was more than the guy who taught them to play football. He was a mentor and a role model and, when need be, a father figure.

"I don't know, PJ. If it's too much longer, we'll start working on how to get you all home."

"We're not leaving," Hunter Cass said. The running back gave her a look that practically dared her to try asserting authority over them.

As the school's guidance counselor, her authority didn't technically extend to hospital waiting rooms. This was her hometown, though, and as far as Jen was concerned, her sense of responsibility for these kids didn't end when the dismissal bell rang, and it never had.

"Nobody's making you leave right now," she said. "But if we don't hear something soon, you guys will need food and rest. And your parents will want you home before it's too late."

She could tell he wanted to argue with her but, after a glance at Kelly, Hunter shut his mouth and leaned his back against the wall again. Jen almost wished he had pushed back because she wouldn't feel so damn helpless. Keeping teenagers in line and on track was her job, and she was good at it. But she had no idea what to do for Kelly or her mom.

Coach McDonnell's wife, Helen, sat quietly on the couch opposite Jen's. She was leaning forward, with her elbows resting on her knees, and was staring at her clasped hands. She hadn't really said anything after thanking the boys for being there, and Jen's heart was breaking for her.

It was at least another fifteen minutes before a nurse walked into the waiting room. "Officer McDonnell? Helen? You can come with me."

Jen tried to read the nurse's facial expression before the three women stepped out. She couldn't remember the woman's name off the top of her head, but they'd met a few times. The hospital wasn't very big, but it served a large area—including Jen's hometown of Stewart Mills, New Hampshire—so it was inevitable they'd crossed paths. And based on those few interactions, Jen could see the nurse had been relaxed and didn't appear to be dreading talking to Coach's wife and daughter.

The boys, though, managed to ratchet the tension up to an almost palpable level. Jen hoped she was right in her assessment of the situation, because if the news wasn't good, she had no idea what she was going to do with an entire football team of emotionally devastated boys. Especially after the roller coaster this year had been. The low of the budget cuts that canceled the football program, which had kept many of the boys on track in the economically depressed town. The success of Eagles Fest, the community-wide effort to raise the money to keep the boys on the field. Losing Coach now would be a low they wouldn't recover from for a long time.

When the door opened and Kelly walked in, Jen knew she wasn't the only one holding her breath. Her friend had been crying, but whether they were tears of sorrow or relief, she couldn't tell.

"He's going to be okay." Kelly paused for a moment to let the boys react to the good news. "He had a heart attack, but he's awake now and hooked up to a bunch of monitors."

"Can we see him?" one of the boys asked.

"Not for a while. They've moved him to ICU, which is family only. We don't know yet how long he'll be in there or if they'll put him in a regular room. Cody, you're a captain, so you're going to be my liaison. You and I can keep in touch, and you can keep the rest of the team up to date. I don't need all of you calling my mother or my dad's cell, okay? Or me."

Cody Dodge, tight end for the Eagles, nodded, as did the rest of the boys. Jen smiled and stood up, stretching her back. "I'll make sure everybody has a way home."

Kelly nodded. "You mind sticking around after? I'm going to go see Dad, but then I'll need to get the cruiser back and change, and I don't want my mom here alone."

"Tell her I'll be right here if she needs anything."

It took almost half an hour to empty the waiting room of football players, and then Jen pulled out her phone and relaxed against the couch. She checked her email and caught up on Facebook, managing to kill the time until Kelly walked in and plopped down next to her.

Jen dropped her phone in her lap and reached over to squeeze her best friend's hand. "How is he?"

"Pale. Weak." Kelly exhaled a long, shuddering sigh. "Frail. He looks frail."

"His body might be having a frail moment, but he's strong. He'll be okay."

"Yeah." Kelly turned sideways on the cushion to face her.

"He wants Sam to come back to Stewart Mills and coach the boys."

"What? No. No, he can't. Nope." Jen shook her head, just in case Kelly wasn't clear that this ridiculous idea was getting a big old *oh, hell no* from her. Sam Leavitt was supposed to go home to Texas and never come back.

"It's his only request and it's pretty important to him."

Kelly couldn't possibly be considering this, Jen thought as her mind spun. "You don't call a guy who lives in Texas and ask him to run up to New Hampshire to temporarily coach high school football for a few weeks. There are assistant coaches."

"Did you see any assistant coaches here tonight?" Kelly waved a hand around the waiting room. "Dad was running practice alone tonight. Charlie quit because he got offered a better job down south. Dan's wife is having a baby any minute and, since it's their first, he's running home every ten minutes."

"Joel?"

"Joel's the gym teacher, so he works them out and puts them through their paces, but he's not a football coach."

Jen couldn't believe this was happening. "Decker played for the Eagles. He could coach. I know Chase has to work in New Jersey, but what about Alex? Now that he's moved in with Gretchen, he's in Stewart Mills enough."

There had to be another option. Kelly's fiancé, Chase Sanders, and Alex Murphy, who'd fallen for their friend Gretchen, had both come back to town after fourteen years away to support Eagles Fest. Their team had been the first in Stewart Mills to win the championship, and the highlight of the fund-raiser had been the exhibition game between the current team and the alumni team. There were other options. Almost *any* option was better.

"He wants Sam," Kelly said quietly. "You know how he is. There's more to it than what he's saying, but I think he believes Sam still has unfinished business here and it's important to him that Sam come home and coach."

Unfinished business. That was seriously bad news. The three men—Chase, Alex and Sam—had returned to town, along with a couple of the other guys. Chase had fallen in love with Kelly. Alex had fallen in love with Gretchen.

And Sam had set the bar for sweaty, toe-curling sex with Jen on the hood of her car.

As far as she was concerned, that business needed to stay finished. He wasn't the kind of guy for falling in love.

Sam Leavitt looked at the cell phone vibrating its way across the glass-topped patio table and sighed. He was pretty comfortable, with his ass in his favorite camp chair and his feet up on a cooler of cola on ice.

The name on the caller ID screen caught his attention though, and he reached for it. He'd exchanged a few text messages with Kelly McDonnell since Eagles Fest had ended and he returned to Texas, but she hadn't called.

He hit the button to answer the call. "Hey, Kelly."

"Hi, Sam. Are you busy right now?"

He looked over the exceptionally flat horizon, watching the hot breeze play with the sand. It was cooler in the shade of his trailer, under the awning, but the only thing he'd done for the last hour was stay out of the sun after a long day of working in it. "Nope. What's up?"

"Let me open with the fact he's going to be fine."

Coach. Despite the reassurance meant by her words, fear sucker-punched him in the gut. "What happened?"

"My dad had a heart attack last night. But he's okay. I promise."

Sam dropped his feet off the cooler so he could lean forward and rest his elbows on his knees. "Was it bad?"

"They've seen worse, but he's going to be benched for a while."

At least he'd be okay. Coach was strong and nothing could keep him down for long. "I'm glad you called to let me know. Even if, the last time you called, it was to sucker me into going back there to play football against a bunch of high school kids."

"Yeah . . . about that." Kelly hesitated and Sam braced himself for more bad news. "Dad wants you to come back to Stewart Mills again—to step in for him and coach the team."

He wasn't sure what he'd been expecting, but that wasn't it. "I don't get it. There are other coaches. Other guys."

"He wants you."

Sam rubbed the bridge of his nose. "Why?"

There was a long moment of silence, and then she sighed. "To be perfectly honest, Sam, I don't know. What I do know is that it's important to him. And you know how he is. He probably thinks you needed a little more time in Stewart Mills. But whatever his reasons, they're personal."

There was a time—essentially the last decade and a half— when thinking of his hometown had brought up painful memories of a shitty childhood, an alcoholic mother who couldn't protect him from it, and what was an adolescence headed toward self-destruction until Coach McDonnell got hold of him. Coach had taught him to be a part of a team—a brotherhood, even—and how to be a man.

Since the trip back for Eagles Fest, though, thinking of his hometown evoked the sweet memory of Jen Cooper's legs wrapped around his waist, her back arching off the hood of her car as her fingernails dug into his forearms. His mind had been evoking *that* particular memory a lot lately.

"Sam?"

Kelly's voice dragged him back to the present, which hadn't included a woman's company since he left New Hampshire. "I'm still here."

"What are the chances of you being *here*?"

He thought about what he had here in Texas. A decent job as an oil field electrician. A good truck. A mobile home that suited his needs well enough and didn't demand much upkeep. And he had some friends he'd hit the local bar with once in a while, even though he stuck to soda.

Then he weighed that against what Stewart Mills held for him. There was the only man who'd ever given a shit about him and who needed his help. And a mother struggling to stay sober, who wanted to make amends Sam wasn't ready for yet. And there were the good friends he'd gone too long without, but he hadn't known just how long until he saw them again.

And there was the woman who'd shifted the earth under his feet with just a touch.

"I know it's a lot," Kelly said. "The season can go into

November if they make the play-offs, and the doctor hasn't given us a time frame for Coach's recovery yet."

"They'll make the play-offs," he said. He'd seen them play and they were damn good.

She laughed softly on the other end of the line. "Maybe that's why he wants you."

Maybe. But Sam suspected the old man simply wasn't done with him yet and had seen an opportunity to bring him home. "I'll be there. I have to wrap up a couple of things, and I'm going to drive this time instead of flying out. It'll probably be a week."

"Thank you, Sam. It'll mean everything to my dad."

"He means everything to me," Sam responded, and he was surprised to find himself a little choked up. "He's really okay?"

"He really is. Weak, like I said, but the damage wasn't too bad. He won't be sneaking any more hash omelets at O'Rourke's, though, if my mom has anything to say about it."

"I think Mrs. McDonnell will have a *lot* to say about it."

When the call was over, Sam propped his feet up on the cooler and leaned his head back against the chair.

He'd been in Texas a long time—longer than any of the many other places he'd lived in over the years—but he had to admit it had never really felt like home. He'd stuck it out in New Hampshire until he got the high school diploma that meant so much to Coach and Mrs. McDonnell, and then he'd hit the road with no destination in mind but anywhere else. He'd worked a lot of odd jobs, landing in Texas, before going back to school so he could make more money.

But in fourteen years, he'd never really settled down. He'd never bought a house, instead making do with short-term rentals. He hadn't found a woman he wanted to spend the rest of his life with or started a family. He didn't even have a dog. Maybe, deep down inside, he'd always known he'd go back to New Hampshire someday.

When he talked to his employer, an extended leave somehow became quitting his job. And filling a couple of duffel bags turned into packing his belongings into boxes, which he then tied into big garbage bags because his truck didn't have a cap on it.

Nine days later, Sam drove into Stewart Mills and paused at the main intersection. He let his truck idle at the stop sign a little longer than was necessary to avoid getting a ticket, since there was a crop of new signs and it was easy to forget them. Then he started toward Coach's house because, dammit, he needed a hug from the man.

When he left after high school, he never thought he'd ever return to this town. But now he was back in his hometown for the second time this year, and this time he had everything he owned in the truck.

FROM *NEW YORK TIMES* BESTSELLING AUTHOR

SHANNON STACEY

Homecoming

Sam Leavitt has two goals when he returns home to Stewart Mills to fill in for Coach McDonnell: to keep the school from finding a permanent replacement while Coach gets back on his feet, and to reconnect with his mother. As substitute coach for the high school football team, Sam must work hard to keep the boys on track, and that means spending time with the sexy guidance counselor he shared a hot night with months ago.

Jen Cooper knows what she's looking for, and it's not Sam—he wasn't even supposed to come back. She wants a cultured, romantic soul, not some rough-around-the-edges guy with calloused hands and a hard, muscular body. But seeing him every day forces Jen to question what she really wants out of life. And as Sam begins to deal with his past, Jen discovers there's more to him than she imagined...

COMING SPRING 2016

shannonstacey.com
penguin.com

M1708T0715